Also by Matthew Duffus

Dunbar's Folly and Other Stories (Unsolicited Press, 2020)

Swapping Purples for Yellows

Share Your Thoughts

Want to help make *Swapping Purples for Yellows* a bestselling novel? Consider leaving an honest review on Goodreads, your personal author website or blog, and anywhere else readers go for recommendations. It's our priority at SFK Press to publish books for readers to enjoy, and our authors appreciate and value your feedback.

Our Southern Fried Guarantee

If you wouldn't enthusiastically recommend one of our books with a 4- or 5-star rating to a friend, then the next story is on us. We believe that much in the stories we're telling. Simply email us at pr@sfkmultimedia.com.

Matthew Duffus

Swapping Purples for Yellows

SFK
PRESS

For Cheryl

One

He'd done it again. He hadn't meant to—he never meant to—but when Rob Sutherland woke up the Friday morning of Homecoming Weekend, he was on the couch. He couldn't tell what hurt worse: his head, thanks to his wife, or his back and shoulders from being compressed on their grad-school-leftover of a couch. This had been happening with increasing regularity. He'd been waiting for his wife to reappear after their latest argument, only to find himself drifting off, and then he was in full-on sleep mode. The door to her study was finally open. He could hear the sound of her *ujjayi* breathing. She was doing yoga. He knew that *ujjayi* meant victorious, and he hated how apt that word must seem to her after the previous night. Though he would have declared it a stalemate, she always viewed herself as the decisive winner.

He collected his wallet, keys, and satchel as quietly as he could and slipped out the kitchen door and into the carport. Unable to face Molly after their fight, nor his older daughter, Katie, who'd surely eavesdropped on most of their argument, he would only miss seeing Robin, who still slept the peaceful slumber of preadolescence. She would be the lone member of the family to awaken refreshed and ready to take on the day. As for him, he'd shower on campus, and he hoped that he had a fresh change of clothes in the faculty locker room.

It was cool outside, still dark, and as he started the car, he thought about the other reason the day was important. It wasn't just the start of homecoming weekend, when the past came back to haunt the present in the flesh. It was also Halloween, when Robin would join the other young ghouls in haunting their shabby, and otherwise sedate, neighborhood. She looked forward to the holiday the way she used to prepare for Christmas, beginning a list for Santa as early as August. Now, she had Katie sketch mockups of various outfits for weeks before settling on the most appropriate one, which she refused to unveil until the night of the festivities. He figured the finishing touches had been what had kept Katie up the night before—though only seventeen, she was already a better seamstress than her grandmother—but even the hum of her electric machine wouldn't have covered her parents' dramatics downstairs.

At school, he waited for the gym to open at seven, showered, and cobbled together a semi-clean outfit from the leftovers among his intramural basketball gear. By eight, when the campus began its long, labored awakening, he was on his second cup of coffee and fourth aspirin. His head felt fine, as long as he didn't turn it to the right or breathe in through his nose, and though he had a stack of essays that required his feedback, he found himself staring out the window instead.

Kreider Hall, home of the English department, sat on the outskirts of campus, adjacent to the town cemetery. Most of the time, when he looked out the window, he took pleasure in the way the sun glinted off the rows of uneven tombstones across the street. It seemed fitting that three-hundred years of history should lie so close to a college campus, that he could leave his office and find himself surrounded by veterans of every war this country had ever fought. He hadn't taken such a stroll in years, not since Robin was learning to walk, but just the possibility usually buoyed him. Not that morning. When his eyes alighted on the twelve-foot-tall obelisk at the center of one family plot, he was reminded of Shelley, a poet he didn't even like. *Look on my works, ye Mighty, and despair.* Like Ozymandias, that family had died out long ago, leaving a ridiculous monument in a small-town graveyard as its legacy.

He heard a knock at the door, followed by the voice of his friend, Professor Herman Delacroix. "So you're a closet Romantic after all."

"I'm sorry?" He spun away from the window too quickly, making himself dizzy.

"You were talking to yourself. 'Round the decay of that colossal wreck, boundless and bare the lone and level sand' something, something, something." In typical Delacroix fashion, he had on a three-piece suit, even on a Friday, and he smoothed the pinstriped vest as he eased himself into the chair opposite Rob. He tapped the desk with the school paper, rolled into a baton, a question clear from his wrinkled forehead.

"Too busy grading."

Delacroix cocked his head in the direction of the window. As with all of his movements, this one was precise, almost fussy. "Someone less perspicacious might suggest the amount of time you spend brooding over that cemetery bears some connection to your increasingly gloomy disposition."

"Contemplating, not brooding."

"Then *contemplate* this for a moment."

Rob took *The Daily Crier* from him and looked at the front page. Headlines announcing the crowning of the Homecoming Court and the afternoon pep rally filled his vision. A banner at the top of the page welcomed alums back to campus in a gigantic font.

"Beneath the fold," Herman said.

"'Famous Alum to Announce Major Gift Saturday,'" he read aloud.

"Contrary to conventional wisdom, my money's on a video game arcade. Rows of EvRo games pinging and bathing the campus in an electric glow so bright it'll be visible from space."

"You're showing your age. Even my daughters have games on their phones."

"My mistake." Herman frowned at the essay before Rob, turned it around on the desk so that he could read the opening. "Future freshmen won't know what they're missing."

"Excuse me?"

"When you rise to the ranks of the well-endowed, professorially speaking."

"That's a rumor, Herman."

"Robert Sutherland, Evan Wykoff Endowed Chair of English Literature," his friend mused, still flipping through an essay on the lack of commuter parking.

Rob had considered bringing it up the previous night, after Molly dropped her bomb in his lap, but if it were truly happening, wouldn't he have heard something by now? Wykoff's gift was presumed to be large enough that the president was handling it himself, and though Rob passed him at least once a week in the faculty dining hall, Dr. Vessey had yet to tip his hand.

"I hope it comes with a nicer office," Herman said. "This place is a dump."

"This whole building is a dump. If Evan wants to make a meaningful contribution, he should donate a new one."

"A bit grand, don't you think?"

"That's what people probably thought before the Kreiders plunked down their grocery store money to build this place."

A year earlier, Evan Wykoff (CC '04) had given the keynote address at TED. Wykoff's business with his friend Ross Howard, EvRo Productions, had vaulted onto the video game design map five years earlier, cornered the market on quasi-educational, historical reenactment-style games, and had already begun creating their own TV and movie tie-ins. In his TED Talk, Wykoff had decided to focus on the setbacks that had ultimately led to his success, particularly on one that had occurred all the way back in college. He mentioned Rob by name, describing a course he'd taken with him and its disappointing result. "In a way," he said, "I have Dr. Sutherland to thank for where I am now. Without that C, I might have gotten into Yale's graduate program, like I'd planned, and ended up becoming yet another tenure-obsessed English professor." Instead, so the story went among Rob's colleagues, the C in History of the Novel forced Evan to settle for a fallback school which he left without even an MA once he and Ross designed their first—and most popular—game, *The Service*.

While Evan had been a good student, he was unexceptional compared to the scores of other would-be Shakespeareans graduating every year. Nevertheless, the mythology around Evan had grown, as had Rob's role as the villain, when the young man dropped out of his fallback school to found EvRo Productions. As *The Service*, which he'd helped design instead of focusing on his MA program, became more popular and garnered more awards, Rob's colleagues began referring to him as "*our* Evan Wykoff," the possessive demarcating the line between those who had supported him and those, like Rob, who had failed to see the greatness residing just beneath the surface. The TED speech changed all of that. As Herman, who'd only been at the school for eight years and was both above the fray and endlessly amused by it, had told him, he'd suddenly taken the lead in the Evan Wykoff BPE—Best Prof Ever—contest. To Rob, such a victory, if one could even call it that, was no more welcome than the pop-up ads that appeared when he surfed the web. Congratulations! You're the Winner of the Evan Wykoff Sweepstakes! Click Here to Claim Your Prize!

"You're doing it again," Herman said. "Brooding."

Rob's eyes refocused on the newsprint before him. Without meaning to, he'd crumpled the paper in his hands. "Whatever happened to the life of the mind?"

"We don't get paid for that anymore." Herman took the newspaper between thumb and forefinger and deposited it in the trash can.

"You mean we still get paid?" The faculty hadn't had a raise since the economic downturn, six years earlier, though the college had added two new vice presidents and countless administrative positions in that time.

"That's the rumor."

Just that fall, the administration had instituted limits on departmental photocopying budgets, frozen acquisitions at the library, and begun a new energy-conservation program that seemed, as far as Rob could tell, to consist solely of emails reminding the faculty to turn off their lights and to recycle.

"You're more irritable than usual," Rob said.

"I have to sit at the departmental table before the game."

"Homecoming and a campus-visit day all at once?" he said. "No way I'm making it through this without vast quantities of alcohol."

"You love Homecoming. All your adoring fans returning with stories of your classroom heroics."

"I'm talking a once-in-a-lifetime bender. I want to make terrible choices, embarrass myself in front of large groups of people. Whatever it takes to get to Monday as quickly as possible."

"What about Molly and the girls?"

"I've embarrassed myself in front of them so many times, they hardly notice." Though he knew he'd tell Herman about the previous night, he'd need a glass of courage, so he withstood the urge to spill. "We're full professors. That ought to come with some perks, right?"

But thinking of perks only reminded him, as most things did that morning, of the previous night. He'd been grading online discussion-board posts when the provost had emailed to convene an emergency meeting of the Core Curriculum Committee, for which he represented the English department.

"That figures," he'd said, drumming his fingers against his laptop, as though composing a furious response were a possibility. He waited for Molly to look up from her book, to ask *what figures*, to grunt in acknowledgement of his existence.

"I have a CCC meeting next Thursday. Nothing like pontificating, grandstanding, and turf-protecting to keep the Homecoming spirit alive."

"Uh-huh." Molly turned the page, made a notation with her pencil.

"We'll each spend ten minutes explaining why we shouldn't be the department that gets the axe, complete with thinly veiled finger-pointing at other, more vulnerable programs, and then, at the stroke of five, pack up and flee the scene."

"A bit dramatic," she said, without looking up. *What's so damn fascinating*, he wondered.

All he wanted was five minutes' worth of her attention. Robin was in bed, Katie was quiet in her room, if not asleep. It was Thursday night, when most couples he knew took time to relish the coming weekend, to coordinate schedules and make plans. But his wife studied *Philosophical Troubles* as avidly as some people read supermarket tabloids. He stared at the computer screen.

"Sometimes I envy you," he said, trying a different strategy. "No committees, no departmental service, no mandatory meetings."

"Want to trade paychecks and offices?"

He ignored her tone, took satisfaction in the few seconds her eyes strayed from the page to glare at him. At least he'd gotten a reaction. "Hell, you don't really have a department to report to."

"Tell that to Jim Woodruff."

Woodruff, the chair of Social Sciences, had inherited Molly. Once the Board of Trustees had forced Dr. Ignatius into retirement and denied tenure to Dr. Trillo, Molly, an adjunct, had become the last person standing, which was just as the college wanted it. Who needed Aristotle or Wittgenstein when all the students wanted was logic, so they'd excel on standardized tests? That had occurred during the last round of staff contractions, but the administration often threatened another when they sensed pushback on other cost-cutting measures.

Rob stretched his long legs, taking up most of the coffee table between him and his wife, and shifted the laptop onto the couch next to him. The cushion sagged beneath the weight of the seven-year-old machine—his daughters begged him to get a new one every time this one froze or failed to open an attachment. He could feel the machine's residual warmth through his slacks.

"You'll have to take Robin to therapy," he said. He rolled his eyes, hoping to garner sympathy or at least convey derision, but Molly had gone back to her book.

"I can't," she said, finally placing a finger between the pages and closing the book.

"We can't cancel. Her anxiety's been through the roof."

"Then Katie will have to drive her. I might have my own meeting."

"Adjuncts of the world unite and take over?"

"Funny." She put down the book and crossed her arms. "I may be receiving a job offer."

"You applied for that tutoring job after all?" They'd spent August debating whether or not she should try for the position as head of the college's remedial education program, finally deciding against it. She'd been passed over so many times that she'd grown jaded, no matter how ideal the position seemed.

"It's a teaching position."

"I haven't heard anything about them reopening the Philosophy department."

"Confluence College is still safe from the pernicious influence of Plato and Kant," she said. "It's at Rocky Mount."

He nodded. "Good school." A little larger than Confluence, with better students and a beautiful campus, but on the other side of the state. "Quite a commute, isn't it?"

"It's a visiting professorship, with the possibility of something more permanent."

"You don't have a PhD." He winced as soon as the words escaped his mouth. They'd long argued over whose fault it was that she'd failed to finish: him, for getting her pregnant and taking a job a hundred miles from her program, or her, for giving up too quickly when the distance became an issue.

"It's the damnedest thing," she said. Rob could tell from her tone that they were entering dangerous territory. "The chair at Rocky Mount believes I have something to offer students, degree or not."

"What about the girls?"

"I'd be back on weekends to make sure you don't let this place go completely."

"How am I supposed to do my job and look after them?"

"They're teenagers. They hardly need looking after."

"That's your answer? Let them run wild?" He knew he was exaggerating, that this was a weak line of defense. At seventeen, Katie spent most of her time in her room, sewing and poring over fashion websites, while Robin was just as busy practicing the piano and composing avant-garde jazz pieces. If his wife weren't so single-minded, he'd wonder where the girls came by their obsessions. "Nice of you to tell me about this."

"I thought that's what I just did."

"You're right. Why mention it when you saw the ad or when you composed your cover letter or had your interview? I assume you did go through all of that. They aren't just choosing someone at random, are they?"

"Thanks for being so condescending."

"You know about these visiting appointments, right? Yet another of academia's brilliant creations. 'We'll call them assistant professorships so we get better applicants, but we'll treat them like adjuncts. And they'll be out before we risk having to pay them real money.'"

"Go on," she said, leaning forward. "I so love having my profession explained to me like I'm a child."

"You honestly think a school like Rocky Mount is going to give a potential tenure line to someone without a terminal degree? They probably got twenty applications from the Ivies alone."

"You're a dick."

"And you're supposed to be a logician. What kind of *logic* does this situation make? You've got a family and a job, but you're willing to chuck it all, move five hours away, and take an equally shitty position just to spite me?"

"Not everything is about you."

"It is any time you need someone to blame for your situation."

She stood up and pointed her book in his direction. "Maybe if you'd published something in the last five years, Rocky Mount would be interested in you. I'll compare CVs with you any time, even without the fucking degree."

He stood up as well, not because he wanted to escalate the confrontation but because he'd heard a noise upstairs. Katie was a night owl, like her father, and eavesdropping had become one of her favorite ways of passing the time.

"Go ahead," he hissed, spraying spit with the words. "I won't even lord it over you when you fall on your face."

He'd gone too far. He knew it as soon as the words came out of his mouth. He should have been supportive, or at least remained neutral, but she'd blindsided him with the announcement, the same way she blindsided him when she threw her book, which caught him in the side of the head, hard enough that he actually saw stars.

The book nailed him flush, right behind the ear.

He caught himself making a fist, then forced himself to open his palm and check his head for damage. The blow had broken the skin, and it stung when he probed the wound. His fingers came away streaked with blood. He held out the hand for her to see, feeling foolish immediately. The muscles in her forearm were taut, her jaw set in preparation for whatever defiance she would need to offer. But what could he do? He couldn't possibly hit her. And it was after eleven, far too late to launch into a trial over what had just happened.

"I didn't realize *Philosophical Troubles* was meant to be taken so literally," he said. "I would have settled for a lecture on the categorical imperative."

She dropped back into her chair. "Don't bother. I've heard all your jokes." She refused to make eye contact.

"You hit me, but I'm supposed to feel bad?" He couldn't stop himself, even as he realized they'd arrived somewhere unknown and strange, potentially dangerous. He'd always been the one to back down. He should have been nervous, and maybe he was, he couldn't be sure, not while his head throbbed and his brain raced to catch up with what was happening. He stood over her, squaring his shoulders to display his full six-and-a-half-foot frame.

"What, you're going to hit me?" she said. She stuck out her jaw, offering him a target.

"This is pointless," he said. "You don't care what I think. If I did hit you, you'd just tell me how I did it wrong." There was that noise again, the creak of a floorboard. He turned toward the stairs and listened. Though it was quiet, he still called out, "If you aren't in bed before I get up there, you're going to be sorry."

He turned back in time to hear the door to his wife's study close. It was off the living room, and she'd made it inside so quietly, so swiftly, that he hadn't known she'd even stood up. No matter. He decided to wait her out on the couch. At least that would give Katie a chance to absorb what she'd heard. But he fell asleep twenty minutes later, the door still closed and locked. If he hadn't been so tired, if his head hadn't hurt so much, he would have wondered if his wife actually felt guilty.

They'd fought for years, but no more than most couples he knew. That was wrong. Though he'd tried to convince himself it was true, their disagreements had reached a frequency and ferocity that he knew was beyond the normal range. Ever since Katie had reached high school, the disparity in their positions at Confluence had become unbearable to Molly, and though he tried to be sympathetic, he was tired of being cast as the villain.

What had happened that night was too much, even by their standards, and the possibility that Katie had heard filled him with horror. What could he say to her? How could he face her? A smarter man, he knew, would wonder the same about dealing with his wife, but as she had always made clear, she was the brains of their operation.

Two

A tote bag full of interlibrary loan books threatened to pull Scott's right arm out of its socket as he walked down the steps from the library. The weight of the books, not to mention the creaking of the bag's seams, made him wish Breen-Higginbottom was still open. But instead of simply walking across Old Quad from B-H to Kreider Hall, he had to follow the brick pathway from the far end of New Quad, past the engineering and business buildings, around Weaver Student Services, across Cooper Street, and into Old Quad. By then, he'd switched the bag from hand to hand, finally opting to carry it before him on both arms. Though Dr. Delacroix's office was on the top floor, he'd have to take the stairs, the service elevator being off-limits to him. He didn't mind, not entirely, seeing how he spent most of his time answering phones, proctoring exams, or listening to the department's other work-study student summarize the latest episode of whatever TV show she was currently obsessed with. Picking up Dr. Delacroix's weekly cache of books was as close as he came to doing anything intellectual.

Scott had once overheard Dr. Sutherland remark that the college was so obsessed with columns that if you stood still long enough, a pair of Doric pillars would sprout up around you. Personally, Scott liked that no matter the style of the architecture, the buildings shared this one trait; plus they came in handy at times like this, when they anchored the Welcome Back banners that flapped in the breeze outside every building. Except the old library. It had closed after Scott's freshman year, when the Ledbetter Library and Technology Center had opened. B-H had been in disrepair for years. The roof leaked, rusty water ran from the faucets, and power surges set the lights dimming at random intervals. At least it had style.

While his friends had complained about the lack of light, natural and otherwise, Scott had enjoyed the faux-Gothic architecture and marveled at all the hidden nooks. In his down time, he'd wandered through the stacks, picking volumes off the shelves just to see how long it had been since they'd been checked-out. Many of the older books had never been outfitted with electronic barcodes, so he could slide the actual library card out of the pocket inside the cover, something he hadn't done since elementary school. He found books from every Library of Congress subject heading that hadn't left the building in fifteen, twenty years. Nevertheless, B-H represented all that he'd wanted college to be—the promise of constant discovery, becoming part of a shared history—which was why Confluence's founders had chosen to build it first, before the administrative building, the dorms, or even the classrooms.

The new library looked like any number of such buildings he'd seen on campus tours, made of shiny metal and polished glass. Seemingly endless rows of computers began a few steps inside the front door, with special labs for graphic design and engineering secured behind locked doors and ID card scanners. With the exception of the Reference Room, one had to climb the circular staircase to the second floor to find actual books. Even then it seemed as though the books were hidden from view. The periodicals section predominated, racks of *Sports Illustrated*, *People*, and *Vogue* crowding out *The New England Journal of Medicine*, *Callaloo*, and *The American Scholar*. Scott couldn't figure out how the librarians had managed to cram all the books from B-H into what amounted to less than two floors at Ledbetter. Then, over the previous summer, he'd been looking for books online and come across a cheap library edition of Robert Stepto's *From Behind the Veil*. When he clicked on "location of seller," the words "Elgin, NC" appeared on the screen. He didn't have the heart to mention this to Dr. Delacroix, so he'd done his own digging and discovered that the college had been forced to reduce its collection in order to fit into the new space.

By the time Kreider came into sight, Scott realized he'd wasted the entire walk daydreaming when he should have been preparing. Today was the day he wanted to ask Dr. Delacroix to write him a letter of recommendation for graduate school. He wanted to be a full-time devotee to the pursuit of knowledge B-H stood for, not a mere four-year pilgrim who looked back on his undergraduate days with nostalgia and regret. Dr. Delacroix, of all people, would understand that. And a strong letter from someone of his stature would be the clincher. If only the man didn't scare him so damn much.

Delacroix was the only professor at CC who could be considered a giant in his field—African-American Literature—which, when added to his standard inarticulateness around his professors, made it almost impossible for him to force out a complete sentence in the man's presence.

He wasn't alone in this. Even the laziest and least intimidated of his classmates called Dr. Delacroix *sir* or *professor* at all times and came to every class prepared, no matter how heavy the reading load—Dr. Delacroix loved to pile on the work. Only once, in private, had he heard a student jokingly refer to the man as *Herman*. Even among a group of fellow students, the worried looks that came over everyone at that moment made it clear such a slip would never occur again.

Twenty minutes until History of the Novel. Maybe it would be best to wait, to try Dr. Delacroix after lunch, or on Monday. But Kreider was a ghost town on Friday afternoons, the professors' offices uniformly dark and locked. Monday would be no better. Delacroix was notorious for hating the beginning of the week even more than the students did. It had to be today.

He shifted the tote bag from one hand to the other again and knocked, too hard, on the door. The bag's straps had cut off the blood flow to his hands. A faint voice came from the other side of the door, so he opened it, confident that—if nothing else—his professor would appreciate getting his books promptly.

"I feel guilty having you run my errands," Delacroix said. Even at his desk he wore his suit jacket and kept his tie knotted at his throat. "But I feel even worse when I see you sitting in the office with nothing to do." The slightest smile, evident only at the corners of his professor's mouth, made it difficult for Scott to tell how sincere the last comment had been.

Free of his load, Scott sat down in the chair closest to the desk. No matter how hard he tried, he could never keep his eyes from roaming around the room, at the three walls' worth of books. Unlike the other faculty, who had shoddy, mismatched bookcases in their offices, Delacroix's books resided on matching cherry shelves that he dusted twice a month. Posters advertising the debut of four August Wilson plays and an Amiri Baraka broadside of "A Poem for Speculative Hipsters," signed especially for the professor, filled the remaining one. It didn't even bother Scott that Delacroix kept copies of his own books prominently displayed on his desk. If he'd written four books, he'd want people to know, too.

"I was assigned to a big-shot professor my first year of grad school. Thought I'd be digging through archives, lending my thoughts to his articles-in-progress. Instead, I photocopied his syllabi and kept his grade book up to date." Delacroix looked at him out of the corner of his eye, as though waiting for a reaction. He had a gray goatee that didn't seem to move when he talked and black hair that had gone salt-and-peppery at the temples, as though he was graying from the chin up. His default expression was a bemused frown that he shared equally with all of his students. "In the end," he said. "I think he was teaching me a lesson. Pricey fellowship notwithstanding, everybody starts at the bottom."

"So what's my lesson?" Scott would have been more pleased with himself if his voice hadn't quavered with the final word.

"Old professors with bad backs need help," he said with a smile. Even though Scott always saw the professor and Dr. Sutherland laughing about something or other, Delacroix rarely did so around students. Scott couldn't think of a better opening.

"I've been thinking about graduate school."

"Yes?"

Scott had already hired a tutor to help him review math and had reread *The Canterbury Tales* and most of Shakespeare's major works. But how best to put this into words? "I want to become a professor," he said, thankful something inside him had resisted the urge to add, *like you.*

"Close the door," Dr. Delacroix said, remaining silent for a full minute after Scott had done so. The smile was gone, replaced by a more severe frown than usual. While he stared past Scott at the closed door, his fingers spun a fountain pen around on the blotter. "Are you independently wealthy?"

He almost laughed. Would he be working two jobs if he was rich? "Not by a long shot."

"Plan on marrying into wealth?"

"I wouldn't mind it." Ten minutes until Dr. Sutherland's class. Where was this going?

"You're an excellent student, but unless you've got serious money coming in from some other source, I can't recommend graduate school."

Where to begin? The first part thrilled him, the kind of affirmation he'd never gotten, even from his parents, who excelled at fault-finding. But the last part, the *can't*, was awful enough to cancel out any praise.

"I'm sure you didn't expect to hear that, but saying you want to be a professor is like saying you want to be an elevator operator. Assuming there was a golden age for professors, which is itself debatable, it's well in the past. This profession is only viable now thanks to the underpaid labor of grad students and adjuncts."

"But I've already taken the GRE." He wanted Dr. Delacroix to ask about his scores—90th percentile—but the professor didn't seem to care.

"So you're out a few-hundred bucks. Beats wasting *thousands*, not to mention most of your twenties. I went from BA to PhD-in-hand in five years. But that was thirty years ago. Now, unless you get into an Ivy, the average time is closer to a decade. Not because you're learning more than I did, but because they need your cheap labor. Most of my friends teach fewer classes per year than their grad students do. And in some cases, the students are better teachers, because they work at it. But the teaching slows down their progress and distracts them from scholarly pursuits, so they hardly ever get tenure-track jobs after."

Scott felt dizzy, sick to his stomach. He wanted to run out of the room. He wanted to sink deeper into his chair. He wanted to disappear.

"Maybe I shouldn't tell you this. You might resent me for it. Too bad. You know why I'm here? I spent seventeen years watching how the sausage gets made at flagship university—the brass ring of academia—and I didn't want to be a part of it anymore. People had gone from applying for fifty jobs to eighty to well over one-fifty, and for the ones that didn't win the academic lottery, we conveniently had instructorships available. Between the adjuncts and the grad students, the tenure-track faculty never had to teach anyone who wasn't an upper-level English major. So, while I—we—taught seniors and grad students, the instructors, these folks who were *our* students and mentees not that long ago, got ground up in all that teaching and grading. I knew I had to get out. I looked for a department with zero adjuncts and no graduate program, and of the few that I found, only Confluence was hiring. I took a huge pay cut to come to this backwater, but at least my conscience is clear. Now I teach like a motherfucker—pardon me—but I love it. Sure, it takes me longer to write a book, but it's worth it."

"That's what I want to do." Scott said this so softly he wasn't sure the words actually came out.

Dr. Delacroix sighed. He picked up the Maltese Falcon replica on the corner of his desk and tossed it from palm to palm like a football. "Let's look at the numbers. Ten years to get your degree. Even with an assistantship, you'll be in debt unless you take a side job, off the books, of course, because your program will tell you that outside work is forbidden. Welcome to the ascetic life. If you do take a second job, it'll take you longer to finish, or you'll produce sub-par work. So, for the sake of your future career, we'll assume you focus on the degree and accept the debt. Then, on average, five years from finishing your degree until you get a job, if you survive the instructorship morass. Even if you don't accrue more debt during those years, which is unlikely seeing how poorly instructorships pay, you're thirty-seven when you start a job that will keep you in debt for at least another decade. Plan on starting a family at any point?" He paused for another sigh after he saw the look on Scott's face. "Don't even think about marrying a fellow academic. You'll be lucky to get jobs in the same time zone."

Two minutes until History of the Novel. Never his favorite class, it had suddenly become insignificant.

"I like you, Scott, and I wish the situation were different because you'd make one hell of a good academic. But forget what pop culture tells you about this job. Forget all that 'life of the mind' and summers off bullshit. You see anyone besides

Dr. Sutherland sporting tweed jackets and smoking a pipe? I'm happy to write a reference for any job you want, but graduate school? No way."

What do I do now? he wanted to ask. Instead, he focused on his professor's worried expression. History of the Novel was about to start, but it took all of Scott's resources to admit that he had to leave.

"Off with you, then. If anyone can make you forget your troubles, it's Dr. Sutherland."

Three

Katie sat at her mother's computer, attempting to protect the thirty-fifth president of the United States. She preferred playing games like this one, with random strangers, where she could be herself without worrying about what people she knew thought about her. She'd saved them all—Lincoln, McKinley, Kennedy, even Garfield—then MLK, Malcolm X, and RFK once she'd purchased the bonus pack. She'd saved them by herself and in multiplayer mode. Once, she'd even saved them with her little sister, who was hopeless at video games. After all of this, she began to feel—not bored, exactly—*limited*. She followed the historical simulations, fulfilled whatever role she was assigned, even tried being out-of-position or reacting slowly, just to recapture the thrill she'd felt the first hundred times she'd swooped in to alter the course of history. But none of it worked.

She was playing with a trio of college students from all along the east coast, and their leader, MajorTom, had assigned her the trail position, on the running board of the follow-up car. Totally pointless. While MajorTom and RedSoxSux raced to stop Oswald before the President came into view and Ernie_ from_Erie walked the route in front of Kennedy's limo, she was stuck bringing up the rear. Historically speaking, she knew she had an important role to play. The actual Secret Service member in her position had jumped down from the boring follow-up car and vaulted onto the back of the President's limo, thus giving him a close-up view of the chaotic aftermath of the shooting, and putting himself in harm's way if Oswald turned out to be the beginning of a larger attack. He wasn't, of course, though she tried to remind herself that the agent's heroism shouldn't be downgraded because of details he couldn't possibly have known in the moment. But no amount of research—and she'd done plenty of it—made the follow-up car seem exciting.

She could see Elm Street ahead. They would turn in preparation for entering the Stemmons Freeway and heading to the Dallas Trade Mart, where Kennedy was to have had lunch with a group of local leaders. Of course, Elm was also the location of the soon-to-be-infamous Dallas Book Depository, so before they made the turn, Katie (as nowhere_NC) stepped off the follow-up car and headed toward the President's limo.

MajorTom: NC, why are you out of position?

Some gamers, almost all of them guys, took the randomly assigned position of Team Leader way too seriously.

MajorTom: come in, NC.

The procession made the wide turn onto Elm. Crowds lined both sides of the street. Who had thought that such a tour was a good idea, no matter where it took place?

nowhere_NC: suspicious activity on Pres's side of street.

MajorTom: BOLO, Ernie. RedSoxSux and I are almost in position on our end.

The most controversial aspect of the game's latest edition was its occasional divergence from the historical narrative. When the gamers involved had a high enough combined success rate, the game could "go rogue." Suddenly, John Wilkes Booth might have an accomplice waiting outside Ford's Theater. She'd been involved in games where Oswald got a bullet in the back of the head just as someone dashed out of the crowd to lob an explosive at the President's limo. In the post-game debriefing, she'd seen an image of what was left of the car, Jackie Kennedy nothing but a bloody smear on charred upholstery.

She caught up to the limousine right before they pulled even with the Book Depository. She couldn't see the President's face, but she could tell from his posture that he was smiling, relaxed. His right elbow rested against the door of the limo, hand dangling casually. To his left, Jackie Kennedy looked out the other side, the perfect accompaniment to her perfect husband in her pink outfit and matching pillbox hat. Even though her success rate was ninety-seven-percent, Katie still hated the times she'd seen this poised, delicate woman scramble around the back of the limo, trying to hold the pieces of her husband together in her hands.

The President prepared to lift his hand again, to wave once more at the well-wishers. The graphics in the updated version looked so good on her mother's monitor that she could see his fingers tensing.

MajorTom: We've got Oswald! Say again, threat neutralized. NC, what about activity on the ground?

nowhere_NC: Going in for a better look. I see somebody in the crowd!

She stepped forward, drawing her service revolver at the same time. She could take her time now, let the President wave. Smiling, he turned toward his wife, who was saying something nowhere_NC couldn't hear with all the crowd and automobile noise. No wonder the Secret Service thought that an open-air drive through downtown Dallas was a good idea. Forget the Cuban Missile Crisis and the escalating events in Vietnam. How could anyone imagine any harm coming to this exquisite couple?

nowhere_NC raised her weapon and fired into the back of his head, right behind his left ear, still turned toward his wife.

With that, she became the rare person in the history of *The Service* to commit treason. Her father had told her that JFK almost single-handedly ended the tradition of men wearing hats, but both he and Dr. Delacroix still wore them, so what did that say about *their* fashion sense? The President's vanity must have been built into the game—unless she'd just discovered a glitch that she could announce to the internet—because even at point-blank range, his perfectly coiffed hair remained in place as the bullet bored into his skull and exited through his forehead. It continued through the seat in front of the President, lodging itself in poor Governor Connally's ass. "Oh, no, no, no," the governor said. "My God. They're going to kill us all!" That man couldn't catch a break, no matter who was pulling the trigger.

A voice from within the game announced: *The President Is Down. Repeat, The President Has Received A Fatal Wound. One Other Casualty Reported.*

RedSoxSux: What the frack?

Ernie_from_Erie: True that. NC?

MajorTom: We're waiting. . . .

nowhere_NC: There's activity in the crowd. I see at least three of them!

RedSoxSux: What's going on?

MajorTom: You see anything, Ernie?

Before he could respond, nowhere_NC turned toward Ernie_from_Erie, the point man in the motorcade, and fired once, twice, three times, bringing him down.

Player Three Is Down. Killed In Action, the game announcer said, in more measured tones.

MajorTom: En route. nowhere, do you have a bead on the shooters?

RedSoxSux: I'm not sure there is another shooter. I mean, I think it's nowhere.

MajorTom: What?

She was enjoying herself now, the sense of chaos and confusion was exciting. There was a good reason she called herself *nowhere*. Nothing nearly as interesting had ever happened in Elgin.

nowhere_NC: Definitely multiple shooters. Rendezvous east of the motorcade.

As her teammates raced down the hill, she took cover behind the lead car and began firing. When she ran out of bullets, she pressed the complicated series of buttons that reloaded the gun. She spun MajorTom around with a shot in the shoulder, and then put two more in his back.

RedSoxSux fired at her, scattering what was left of the crowd.

Katie took her time, protected by the front end of the bulletproof vehicle, waiting for RedSoxSux to come closer. Finally, when the woman had reached the sidewalk, nowhere_NC stood up and hit her in the head with her first shot, an achievement rare enough that if it had been Oswald, the group would have celebrated like they'd won the World Series.

MajorTom: What the—

RedSoxSux: You killed all of us!

Ernie_from_Erie: You *do* know we work *for* the President. Not the mob or the CIA or the Soviets.

nowhere_NC has logged off.

The thrill was sadly momentary, unlike the rush she got in the early days of playing the game. She knew people paid ridiculous sums for the new European version of *The Service*, but now that this experiment had failed to excite her enough, she didn't see the point. She certainly wasn't going listen to one of her parents lecture her about her misplaced priorities when she borrowed a credit card to order it online. Plus, she didn't want to use her own money. She hardly ever spent money, not that they noticed, and took as many babysitting jobs as they'd allow. Her savings account contained close to two-thousand dollars, but she'd need more, a lot more, if she was going to get out of Elgin.

Of all people, her own father stood between her and the opportunity to make more than the neighborhood cheapskates paid her to watch their brats. For some reason, he didn't think that high school students should have jobs. Instead, he wanted her to focus on her *studies*, on deciding what direction she wanted to go in life. But she hardly ever had homework, so what did he expect her to do, give herself assignments? She'd said those exact words to him the previous spring, when she'd asked for permission to get an after-school job. His brilliant solution had been to set up meetings with all of her teachers where he actually told them that she had *complained* about not having enough work to do. So while her father spent a week brooding over the school's low standards and threatening to come up with a *supplementary curriculum* for her, her teachers glared at her for making trouble, and her fellow students, who of course found out about what had transpired, kept their distance. In one afternoon, her father had ruined her entire life.

She spun the ergonomic chair away from the monitor on her mother's desk. She liked gaming here best because her mother's bad eyesight necessitated an extra-large screen, and the lone tree in their front yard, an ancient crape myrtle, blocked the sunlight from coming in the window. She felt like she was tucked away in a cave. Plus, sitting in her mother's study was like being in another house. Like their father, her younger sister was a slob. She left a trail of crap wherever she went, and as the days of the week passed, putting the most recent Saturday morning All-Family Clean-Up farther behind them, the clutter grew. Katie barred her sister from bringing anything into her room that she didn't take with her when she left, but no matter how vigilant she was, even her private space suffered.

Their mother, on the other hand, won the Battle of the Clutter every week. Katie would have called her pathologically tidy if it didn't sound like an insult. She kept no knick-knacks or keepsakes in her study because they'd only collect dust. Instead of school portraits and pictures from the holidays, the walls held bookcases and a few reproductions of photographs of the liberation of Paris. Unlike her father's disorganized bookshelves at school, her mother's books were arranged alphabetically by author—from Peter Abelard to Christian Wolff—and positioned so that their spines were even with the front edge of the shelves. Katie had once asked to borrow *Frankenstein* from her father for a school assignment, and after three days of nagging, he'd finally checked it out of the CC library, admitting that he couldn't "seem to locate" his own copy.

Her sister's piano was the only eyesore in her mother's neat world. Robin was a demon at the keyboard, a prodigy for all Katie knew, and she flung books of Fugues and Nocturnes onto the floor when she was finished with them. Stacks of sheet music threatened to spill from the top of the instrument, kept in check only by an electric metronome. She'd taped black-and-white, postcard-sized photographs of dead jazz musicians to the front of the piano for inspiration. Katie had no idea where a thirteen-year-old had heard of a guy named Meade Lux Lewis, but there he sat, smiling.

She moved to her mother's easy chair—her grading station—and looked at the stack of logic problems sitting on the ottoman before her. She knew her mother collected them on Mondays and returned them on Fridays—she'd been teaching this class since Katie had begun school; the schedule was as ingrained in her as her phone number—so when she flipped through the papers, she was surprised to see that more than half of them were still free of her mother's comments. Maybe her mother was *acting out*, as they'd said the previous summer about Robin when she'd tried to give herself dreadlocks. Since she'd been up late working on her sister's Halloween costume, Katie had noticed that their parents' arguing had increased. She had no idea what had happened the night before, but when her father had yelled up the stairs at her, she'd been genuinely frightened.

She'd only been in psychology class since the beginning of the school year, but even she knew that her mother's complaints about the *cubby hole of an office* she had on campus were symbolic of a larger problem. "First they put me in a closet," her mother would say. "But that's not enough. They have to be able to keep tabs on me, too. Or maybe the window is so I can be on exhibition." Katie had trouble following all of this, even after she turned off her sewing machine, but that didn't surprise her. It didn't make sense to her, either, that her parents spent the same amount of time working and taught roughly the same number of students, yet her father was a big shot on campus and her mother's office was the size of the family bathroom. She'd tried bringing this up, but her mother never wanted to talk about it.

That was fine with her. Katie had recently discovered that if she played the smiling, amenable daughter and kept Robin's nuttiness from calling attention to both of them, her parents left her alone. That morning, she hadn't even pretended to get ready for school. Her father had left early, before she'd gotten up, and her mother—well, her mother had lost much of her interest in her older daughter when she'd announced, at fourteen, that she intended to be a fashion designer. "You can be whatever you want," her mother used to tell her. "No limits!" But when she made her declaration, her mother said, "Aim higher!" After an attempt at changing her mind with *fun facts* about prominent women in *more challenging* fields, her mother had given up almost entirely on her. Being a lost cause had its benefits.

The last Friday of every month was known in their house as Molly's Day, which meant that after her mother taught her morning class, she drove to Asheville for yoga and whatever else she chose to do on her Special Day. Katie's father had instructed the girls not to pester—his word, as though *they* were the problem—their mother about it, that she'd tell them what she wanted them to know about her comings and goings. Surprisingly, her father had come up with the idea himself, as consolation for CC's decision two years earlier to increase their mother's class sizes by twenty percent without any increase in pay. After her father made her That Girl Who Wants More Homework, she had decided that an occasional Katie's Day sounded pretty good, too. She still had to put the finishing touches on her sister's Halloween costume.

Before that, she planned on taking a quick nap. She'd stayed up the previous night, waiting to see when her parents would come to bed, but by one in the morning neither of them had made an appearance upstairs. She'd slept fitfully, still bothered by her parents' tones, even though she hadn't been able to make out the actual words.

She pulled down the cardigan her mother always kept draped over her chair and wrapped it around herself, not bothering to put her arms through the sleeves. Her mother was thin, skeletal, so she knew her healthier proportions would never fit into it properly. If she tried, her mother would figure it out, even if it wasn't for weeks, and accuse her of trying to ruin her favorite sweater, the only wool item she'd kept after she'd gone vegan years earlier. That was the kind of confrontation that would ruin all her efforts at invisibility. Rather than risk that, she burrowed her hands into the pockets and tried to get comfortable. But when she balled her hands into fists to work them deeper into the fabric, her knuckles bumped against something hard and plastic. It was thin and round, with rough ridges that rubbed against her soft skin. She sat up in the chair, smoothed the cardigan in her lap, and pulled out the mystery object. It was a casino chip from Appalachian Spirit worth fifty dollars.

She held the chip in her hand, wondering if it was real and, if so, how fifty dollars could feel so slight. The disc was blue, with *$50* embossed in gold in the center, *Appalachian Spirit* spelled out in a circle around the outside. Her parents didn't gamble, didn't even play cards for fun—neither of them being much for the kinds of hobbies normal people enjoyed—so where had it come from? Maybe it was promotional, like the credit card replicas that came in the mail, but somehow she didn't think so.

Those cards were flimsy, with ridiculous names and obviously fake account numbers. If the chip were one of those, surely it would have been for some preposterous amount of money. Katie didn't have her mother's knack for analytical detective work, and she soon let the matter, and the chip, drop. She wasn't about to waste her free day puzzling over something that had no bearing on her life, not when she still had to dye the hat for Robin's Jackie Kennedy costume. Some days, she wondered how she was ever expected to make time for school.

Four

Everyone but Dr. Sutherland had arrived by the time Scott staggered down the two flights of stairs to room 115. The second floor had several cushy seminar rooms with large oak tables and comfortably padded chairs, but Dr. Sutherland preferred the plain, utilitarian classrooms on the first floor, with their long whiteboards and uncomfortable, creaky wooden desks. The class was already in a circle, the remaining desks pushed to the periphery, by the time Scott walked in.

Tony Hubble, one of Scott's roommates, stood in the middle of the circle waving his copy of *Pamela* in the air. "Who assigns a *new* book for Homecoming Friday?" he said. Tony was the one person in class who wouldn't have read the book no matter what day it had been assigned. He swore by *SparkNotes* and *Wikipedia*. "All my other classes were *cancelled*, but Dr. S. thinks, *How can I totally fuck up Tony's life the day before the biggest event of the semester?*"

Mary Lynn Carlisle—one of the Two Marys in class—agreed. "And it's *so* long."

"I only read until 150, on principal," Aubrey Benjamin said. "Sutherland assigns *way too much* reading."

"Right on," Tony said, offering her a fist bump that she ignored.

Mary Lynn turned to Scott, who had just gotten situated. He'd wedged another desk into the circle rather than taking the one available seat, which was next to Dr. Sutherland's chair. "I bet you read it," she said.

He only wanted to make it through the rest of the day and go back to his room, but he had to work the English department cocktail party that evening—he was a member of campus catering's "A-Team"—and now the entire class was focused on him thanks to Mary Lynn.

"It's a little slow at first," he mumbled. "But it picks up."

"*Slow?*" Derek Webber, Scott's other roommate, flipped through the pages of his copy. He claimed to never read for class, unless it was for Delacroix's, but his grades were almost as good as Scott's, and he'd won the annual poetry contest two years running. Sensing he hadn't impressed his audience, Derek added, "I actually *fell asleep* on page seven. Look, you can see where my pen dragged across the page." He held the book up proudly.

Tony scoffed. "You're screwed, man. You'll never be able to sell it back if you *write* in it."

"If you're *that* desperate, you could get it for free on Google Books," Mary Wardell, the other Mary, said.

"Mary W. speaks," Derek said.

Mary Wardell was the quietest member of the class, which wouldn't bother Scott if she wasn't also the smartest. Instead of listening to everyone complain about the book's length, he'd have preferred to hear about the color-coded tabs poking out of the pages of her copy of *Pamela*.

Too late. Dr. Sutherland appeared in the doorway, leather satchel at his side. Even after three courses with him, Scott was always surprised by how tall the professor was. When he stood, he loomed over everyone and only wrote on the top half of the whiteboards in a messy scrawl. Though he always began class among the circle of students, Scott had noticed that as much as the professor tried to encourage discussion, he grew impatient with wrong—or inane—answers and often spent three-quarters of the class at the podium, lecturing. Mary Lynn complained about this—this is a *seminar* class; we're not *babies*—but Scott preferred hearing an expert's opinions over the ill-formed remarks of his classmates.

"Big plans this weekend?" Sutherland said without looking up.

Aubrey threw up her hands. "Are you *serious?* It's Homecoming."

"That's right." Sutherland smiled. While Dr. Delacroix never smiled in class, Dr. Sutherland was downright profligate in that department. When he smiled, the ends of his mustache, which usually hooked around the corners of his mouth, stretched out demonically. The soul patch beneath his lower lip only exacerbated the effect. "Big game. Big Halloween party—"

"Big alums," Tony said. He'd talked of nothing but Evan Wykoff for weeks. They all played *The Service*, but Tony's dedication was legendary.

"Great opportunity for all of you to see what the future might hold."

"Totally." Tony said again, staring at the ceiling. "I've got some ideas Mr. Wykoff is going to want to hear. Ten years from now, I'll be the one coming back on a private jet to visit all of you peons. No offense, professor."

"Of course not," Dr. Sutherland said. "You and Evan have quite a bit in common."

"No way," Mary Lynn said.

"Like what?" Tony said, more serious than Scott had ever seen him in class.

"Like a C in this class."

"*Ouch.*" Derek clung to the sides of his desk, as though excitement alone might launch him into the air. He looked around for someone to high-five before his euphoria faded to embarrassment.

Mary waited for Sutherland to notice her raised hand before saying, "I heard you and Mr. Wykoff are friends."

The professor pulled at the lower portion of his facial hair, twisting it into a point. "Not exactly. But I can tell you something about Evan that no one knows." He paused, drawing in everyone. "*Pamela* is his favorite novel."

Groans from Tony, Derek, and Mary Lynn.

"Don't believe me? Ask him about it."

With that, Sutherland began class, but Scott took in little of what his professor said. He wasn't like Tony and Derek, who joked about becoming professors so they could wear whatever they wanted and have summers off, or Aubrey, who acted like it was a good fallback plan if she didn't make it as a YA writer. No matter what Dr. Delacroix had told him, he still wanted to believe in the life of the mind. If it didn't exist, why could he read Delacroix's arguments with Ishmael Reed in the letters section of *The New York Review of Books*, talk to Dr. Pagliarulo about her annual week in Santa Cruz for The Dickens Universe, or follow his professors' intellectual development through page after page of Google search results?

Even without paying complete attention, Scott could tell that *Pamela* mattered just as much to Dr. Sutherland as what was going on in the world now. "Readers found these characters so real that they became precursors to the celeb-reality stars of today. In the same way that reality TV molds minor celebrities and so-called ordinary people into pseudo-stars, Richardson used the artifice of these found documents to make Pamela and Squire B so believable that many readers couldn't help but be drawn in. Church bells all over England rang on the day and time of Pamela's wedding to Squire B—"

"—Spoiler alert," Tony whispered.

"People wrote to newspapers debating who Squire B really was and where the now-happy couple lived. All of this led

Henry Fielding—among others—to write a parody, *Shamela*, and then a sequel. *Joseph Andrews* copies Richardson's use of the epistolary style but shows Pamela's brother to be of very different moral fiber." Sutherland scribbled the titles and dates on the board. "Those of you who enjoyed *Pamela* will like these as well, for their playfulness. Those who disliked all the moralizing will enjoy Fielding's bawdiness even more."

Listening to his professor made Scott's head hurt. He wanted to have this kind of knowledge at his disposal, to share his opinions as confidently as Sutherland, who never seemed to consult his notes or stumble over a question. With that goal in mind, he dutifully transcribed his professors' thoughts into his notepads and the margins of his books. According to Dr. Delacroix, this was all pointless. The club wasn't accepting new members. Maybe he was right. Dr. Sessions, who'd started the year before, had a PhD from the University of Chicago but ended up at CC, not Duke or Davidson.

After twenty minutes, Sutherland had finally asked a question, something about why *Pamela* had been so popular. Scott ignored it, not wanting to clutter his mind with more of Tony's jokes or Mary Lynn's painfully literal interpretations.

Dr. Delacroix had no reason to lie to him, but what was he supposed to do now? If he were in Engineering or Business, he could have done internships. Education had student teaching and Nursing had practicums. But English? No wonder Evan Wykoff had turned to video games.

Scott heard what sounded like someone calling his name. When he looked around, he discovered that everyone, including Sutherland, was staring at him.

"Are you still with us, Mr. Kenney?"

Scott nodded.

"Then why do *you* think *Pamela* was so popular?"

He opened his copy. He'd underlined, highlighted, and notated portions of virtually every page, making such a mess of it that he no longer knew what was important and what wasn't.

So he settled for the title page.

"Seems to me we're ignoring the subtitle. *Virtue Rewarded.* Maybe readers found it inspiring to see a character like Pamela, who holds to her beliefs so strongly that she even converts Squire B. In doing this, she's *rewarded* both romantically and financially."

When he looked up from the book, he was greeted by blank faces all around. Maybe he wasn't cut out for this. Tony and Derek could always pull something out of their asses, even when they hadn't read so much as the book's back cover, but he was no good at thinking on his feet. He remembered something from Sutherland's lecture and added, "Or maybe they liked how controversial it was. People didn't want them to read it—"

Sutherland cut him off. "A word of advice, Mr. Kenney. Once you've made a good point, stop talking. Don't dilute it with conjecture."

He looked down, embarrassed. That's twice he'd been put in his place in one morning. But as with Dr. Delacroix, he realized, Sutherland had offered a glimmer of hope. Tony latched onto the second part of his comment, comparing *Pamela*'s readership to those who watched celebrity sex tapes, and while Sutherland did everything short of hitting him over the head to shut him up, Scott looked around the room. Everyone was looking at Tony—nodding in agreement, laughing at Sutherland's reaction—except for Mary, who stared at Scott as inscrutably as Dr. Delacroix had.

Five

No more fooling around, she decided. This month she really was going to yoga. Her resolve held all the way from campus until west of Hendersonville, when her phone rang. They couldn't afford a new-enough car for built-in Bluetooth, so she fumbled in her pocket and pulled it out just in time. Rocky Mount. This was it.

"Ms. Calloway," a vaguely familiar voice said. "This is Dean Whitmore. I have the pleasure of calling to tell you that you've been selected for the Philosophy department's Visiting Professorship."

She hit the brake pedal, narrowly avoiding the car in front of her, which had slowed to a crawl to allow others to merge onto the interstate. She wanted to scream at the driver, but even more, she wanted to call to god, mother nature, the universe, Dean Whitmore. After years of disappointment, something was going her way.

"Ms. Calloway?"

"That's wonderful news," she said. "Of course, I'll need to discuss it with my husband." She smirked at herself in the rearview mirror. As though she didn't know what his response would be. Still, she played up the hesitant charade, hoping to elicit more benefits from the dean.

She listened while Dean Whitmore enumerated the terms and responsibilities. It took a surprisingly long time, considering the precariousness of a visiting position, long enough that she was still listening when she blew by her exit and continued west. This was no time for yoga. It was time to throw dice.

Appalachian Spirit Casino was quiet on Fridays at lunchtime, just the way she liked it. By mid-afternoon, the place would be full of people who'd skipped out on work, hoping to begin celebrating the weekend early with a quick score. Though the revelry would continue in the face of losing streak after losing streak, a sense of desperation would fill the air. But that was hours away, and for now, Molly could enjoy the peacefulness of a half-empty casino.

Rikki, her favorite dealer, nodded to her and said, "Still up?"

Molly had four red chips in play, stacked on the 8. Though she tried to play rationally—as rationally as one could while betting actual money on a game—she couldn't help celebrating a little. A businessman in a baggy blue suit and tasseled loafers had bellied up to the table and begun barking "Hard eight!" with every roll, and she couldn't resist placing a bet against him.

The man rolled again, for the fourth time, the dice sailing above the table in the way he'd already been cautioned against doing, then ricocheting off the back wall and coming to a halt, showing a four and a three.

"Seven out," Rikki called.

The man slapped the table. "Son of a bitch! Thought I had it that time." He turned toward Molly and said, "You must be happy."

"Sure I am. I'm winning."

His wispy brown eyebrows shot up and his mouth fell open, powerless against the shock of an honest response. She got this reaction a lot, especially from strangers, who seemed to expect someone so petite to be suitably demure. She spoke her mind, always, except about where she was, forty miles west of where her family thought she went on her free Fridays, or when talking to Rob. In other words, she told the truth when the truth didn't matter and weighed her options when it did.

Why did she have to think of Rob? It was surely bad luck. She didn't know why she'd kept the job at Rocky Mount a secret for such a long time, any more than she knew why she'd blurted it out the night before. Part of that reticence came from the long odds. The last thing she'd needed was to have her family worried over the possibility of her moving five hours away when the position would inevitably go to some grad student from the Ivies looking for work while she finished her dissertation, just as Rob had predicted. But then she made the first cut, and the second, and had had to schedule a campus visit on her free Friday and claim car trouble to cover for having to spend the night. Thankfully, she paid the bills, so Rob never wondered where the money to fix the car came from, or went.

When it finally slipped out, it had felt like a relief, for the better part of twenty seconds, before Rob pounced. His enthusiasm and emotions often got the best of him, though in hindsight, she should have been prepared for this. She would need a better plan for when she told him she'd actually gotten the job.

She couldn't believe she'd hit him. She certainly hadn't meant to hurt him, merely to get him to stop talking. That had always been his problem; he talked too damn much. But this was blame-shifting, she knew. She'd hit him. As he'd said, she was supposed to be the cool-headed logician. Instead, *she'd* hit him hard enough to permanently warp her book and do who-knew-what to his head. He'd left before she could talk to him this morning—*apologize*, as little as she looked forward to that—and she couldn't blame him. Even Katie had seemed off, slinking around the house as quietly as possible. She hadn't even heard the girl leave for school. But she'd find a way to make it up to her, and to Rob.

"We'll see how you do," the businessman said, finally. "It's easy to place bets when you're not the shooter."

"You know why they call it a game of chance, don't you? Shooting, not shooting. Doesn't matter. It's all arbitrary." Unless you play the odds. That's what she liked about it. Taken at face value, craps looked like orchestrated chaos. It took three employees to keep the game moving smoothly: corralling dice and bets, figuring odds and paying out bets, managing the flow of the game. People like her besuited nemesis only thought about hard eights, boxcars, snake eyes. But if you dug beneath the surface, took the time to learn the game, you discovered that while you couldn't control the roll of the dice, you could mitigate the odds against going broke.

Molly made her initial bet, a line bet, and waited for the others, including her nemesis's predictable Don't Pass. Bets in place, the stickman, Julius, sent her the dice. Some people jiggled them excessively, blew on them, even held them up to an ear to note the quality of the sound they made. From talking to Rikki one day during her break, Molly had learned that the employees hated all of this because it slowed down the game. "I make more on tips than from salary," she'd said. "The longer each roll takes, the fewer the rounds, the less bettors make, and the less I get." Molly had never been a flashy shooter, but this comment had made her even more aware. She picked up the dice with her right hand, pinching them between her thumb and forefinger, tapped them once against the rail, and rolled them towards the back wall.

Rikki watched the dice land and said, "Eleven. Pass bet's a winner." She paid off bets and collected losses while Julius slid the dice next to the bowl containing the extras.

Molly removed twenty dollars' worth of chips from the stack

on the table, leaving fifty in play, and added them to the special pile to her left. That made two hundred. In the beginning, she'd bet with the hundred dollars she normally would have spent that day, between yoga, lunch, and a tour of the local bookstore. Over time, as she improved, she began setting aside more and more each month, until her buy-in total had recently reached one thousand. If she lost the money, she left, and started over at one hundred the next month. If she did well, she set aside money, little by little, until she had rebuilt her original buy-in amount. This she kept for the following month. The rest she gambled with until it was gone, or she had to leave, or she got tired of playing, though this last possibility rarely occurred.

She'd come to Appalachian Spirit Casino on impulse the first time. Before then, her free Friday had been dedicated to a yoga class followed by a nice lunch, but after a few months, this routine began to depress her. Having to drive an hour to find a restaurant that didn't treat her like a mental patient for wanting a vegan meal, or a yoga studio that wasn't a glorified senior citizens' center or meeting place for the Desperate Housewives of the Piedmont, it just reminded her of all she was missing living in Elgin. She would leave yoga rejuvenated, only to feel that buzz drain the closer she got to home. By the time she returned, she'd be as irritable as ever, sometimes even more so if she'd had a particularly good time. So when she found herself speeding by her exit one Friday, trapped in the passing lane by an idiot with a *Lake Life* decal emblazoned on the back window of her Jeep and a kayak wobbling on the roof, she didn't get upset, she just kept driving until she ended up at the casino. All those months of passing its billboards on the interstate must have worked, because she pulled into the parking lot without ever consciously deciding on it as her destination.

She chose craps with only slightly more deliberation. Poker was the hot game, most of the tables full even at noon on a Friday, and though she'd heard stories about card counting and blackjack, she wasn't interested in playing it safe, trying to turn the odds in her favor. That left slots, roulette, or craps. Roulette made her think of that ridiculous scene in *The Sting* where Robert Redford is cheated out of all of his money, and thinking about *The Sting* made her think of her husband, who loved the movie. And slots were for retirees and tourists, so that left craps.

It took her weeks to learn the game. She studied the employees' movements and watched the other bettors so intently she often failed to realize when it was her turn. She concentrated so hard she rarely spoke beyond the few exchanges the game required. For the first six months, she blew through her chips in less than an hour, until she finally rode another shooter's hot streak long enough to double, triple, quadruple her bank. She set aside most of the money, but spent some on her girls, treating Katie to a modest spending spree at a vintage clothing store in Charlotte and buying Robin the Thelonious Monk boxset she'd been begging for. Both girls were astute enough that she didn't have to tell them to keep the gifts between the three of them. She'd done similar things, periodically, in the year since that first windfall, though she'd spent more on the dresses, shoes, and jewelry she bought for herself during her Friday trips.

Even though the odds didn't add up in her mind, she put a place bet on the six, in addition to leaving money on the pass line. She typically played conservatively, sticking to the pass line when she was shooting, but something compelled her to loosen up. Maybe it was her way of celebrating the job offer, or the arrival of the annual masochistic rite that was Homecoming.

The six didn't come up on her next throw, but it did on the following one. She left the money in play, even the winnings, and hit the number again.

"Holy shit," her nemesis said. "Hot hand here!"

She tipped Rikki a twenty and took the rest of the chips off the six. She dropped fifty dollars' worth—it was so easy to forget the monetary amount of these colored discs, she'd learned over time, if she didn't force herself to remember—on the three.

"Got a good feeling?" The businessman was on her side now. He dropped a few bills on the table, which were changed into chips and placed next to hers.

She tapped the dice against the table once, her new buddy yelled "Big money," and she rolled. A one and a two. The same words Robin sometimes said before starting an impromptu piano recital.

While waiting for the dice to come back to her, she heard the cell phone inside her alligator clutch buzz. The purse was the last addition to her Friday outfit, the final piece necessary so that when she arrived at the casino, everything she had on was free of everyday associations. At the casino, she was no longer a wife, mother, adjunct instructor, or even a vegan. She was just Molly. Rob, she guessed, without looking. She didn't want to think about him, for fear he'd ruin her streak.

She rolled the dice again. A five. Everyone at the table—the dealer and stickman, other players, even Molly—turned in unison from the dice to the bets. She'd won again.

All eight spots around the table were taken now, the mid-afternoon lull no match for a genuine hot streak. The other seven waited for Molly to place her bet before doing so themselves. She stuck with the pass line for two rolls, disappointing her public, then went on another tear. She ran through all four outside numbers—four, ten, five, nine—parlaying her winnings into larger and larger bets. She'd never had a purple chip before, but when Rikki took five hundred-dollar chips and replaced them with the new one, she behaved like it happened every day. Two rolls later, she'd gone from purples to yellows, worth a thousand each, which she stacked on twelve, as absurd a bet as she could imagine.

"Boxcars!" her buddy said, crying out in near-orgasmic delight.

Her cell buzzed again, but she ignored it. She tapped the dice on the rail and tossed them, as casually as she might have swatted a fly.

Six

In Rob's estimation, whoever scheduled departmental meetings for Friday afternoons should have been left in the wilderness to die of exposure. Better yet, they should have been plagued with a slowly developing case of flesh-eating bacteria that flared up every Friday between two and four in the afternoon. Not that any of these fates would make him happier to be sitting in the Kreider seminar room, surrounded by his eight English department colleagues.

Betsy Mullins, their department head, stood before them, beaming a nicotine-tinged smile. "Word has it that our Evan Wykoff should be landing at any moment. He's flying his own plane!"

"Are you sure about that?" Herman winked at Rob and added, "I thought he was parachuting onto the field for halftime tomorrow."

Mullins had been at CC for thirty years, longer than almost anyone, and though she typically had a bemused, seen-it-all attitude, she couldn't help herself when it came to Evan. He, unlike the people seated at the table, unlike anyone at Confluence, had been mentioned by name in the Acknowledgements of her latest book, *The Play's No Longer the Thing: Shakespeare in the Age of the Multiplex*. Until the infamous TED talk, she'd enjoyed the privilege of being the young man's leading advocate. Her eyes gleamed at the mere mention of his name.

"Herman has a point," she conceded. "Even if he's making it at Evan's expense. We'll have two-hundred prospective students—two-hundred *potential English majors*—on hand tomorrow, not to mention the rest of the alums."

The rest of the alums. That summed it up, Rob figured. And it wasn't just his department that felt that way. At lunch in the faculty dining room, he'd fielded questions from junior professors, endured the reminiscences of those who'd had Wykoff in class, and noted how much more vigorously certain members of the administration attacked their food now that his return was imminent. It was a wonder they weren't putting the Young Genius on display.

Eleanor Pagliarulo, their resident Victorianist, said, "Any word yet on how the big announcement will be made?"

"Or what the announcement will contain?" added Tom Strelzik, professional grump, who taught Old and Medieval English.

Betsy gave them her best tired smile-and-head-shake combo. "Such discussions took place well over my head."

"But we're—"

She cut Eleanor off, patting her hand as she did so to soothe her friend's feelings. Betsy had been chair since Rob's second year at CC, creating her own fiefdom within Kreider Hall. But at least she knew how to run a meeting. "I've been assured by everyone from Evan to President Vessey that we're being taken care of. Now, unless we want to be here all afternoon, we need to cover a few pressing issues before the semester gets away from us." She turned to Leah Sessions, the department's newest hire, who, according to their printed agenda, had a new course proposal that needed to be approved.

Rob listened half-heartedly as Leah explained the need for Advanced Seminar in Reading, Writing, and Linguistics. Though he'd studied his fair share of literary theory, even spouted it occasionally in the classroom, he felt uncomfortable around those like Leah who worked *terministic screens* and *frame analyses* into everyday speech.

Listening to Leah do it so confidently among her colleagues clashed with what he'd been hearing lately through the common wall between their offices. He'd noticed it first in the mornings—Mondays, Wednesdays, and Fridays, to be precise—shortly after 10 AM. Without warning or preamble, the sounds of brass and stringed instruments and percussion would roar to life, as though he'd arrived late to the performance of a grand Soviet-era symphony. The first few times it had happened, the music was so startling that all he could focus on was wishing it away. Within ten minutes, it would do as he desired. But sometime late in the second week, he noticed another, quieter noise beneath the swell of violins, something human sounding, guttural. Crying, he realized, weeping. The kind of outburst that left one out of breath. It would go on for minutes at a time, until, finally, it stopped altogether. After another minute, the music would cut out as abruptly as it had begun, and the day would go back to normal.

When he began to notice it on Tuesday and Thursday afternoons as well, Rob checked the class schedule and found that the outbursts coincided with the end of Leah Sessions' first-year composition courses. He'd heard nothing but praise from English majors when he asked them about Leah, but though every professor in the department, with the exception of the chair and crotchety Tom Strelzik, taught two sections of composition each semester, he had no network through which to find out how she was doing in those classes.

"All those in favor?" Betsy said.

He looked around, figured if even Herman was in favor of whatever they were voting on, he'd vote for it, too. He raised his hand. So did everyone else, everyone but Strelzik, who opposed any new course that moved the department away from the language's Anglo-Saxon roots.

Eleanor Pagliarulo jumped in before Betsy could mention the next agenda item. "Since we're on the subject, my Special Topics course is going so well that I'd like to make Graphic Literature a regular offering, maybe even a requirement."

Betsy frowned at the agenda before her, which did not include room for Eleanor's spur-of-the-moment enthusiasm. But before she could say anything, Leah spoke up. "No offense, Eleanor, but is it rigorous enough to offer all the time?"

"What do you know about rigorous?" Strelzik said. "You let them write about television programs. Next it'll be rap lyrics. Too late."

Betsy finally looked up from her agenda. "I saw the presentations Leah's students gave, and she had them use TV shows so they'd feel more comfortable with the theorists they'd been discussing."

"Because we shouldn't expect them to feel comfortable *reading* anything, seeing how they're *English* majors."

"This isn't fair," Eleanor said, stifling her frustration behind the cuff of her sweater. "Don't turn my suggestion for a course that is at full capacity, unlike yours, Tom, into a . . . a *cudgel* for the same tired argument you make every month. I don't just teach comics. I teach Spiegelman and Chris Ware. And the field is exploding—*exploding*—with articles and books, which is more than I can say for the *Beowulf* industry."

"Eleanor, you're a real uniter," Herman said. "Ever consider running for office?"

She glared at him but kept her mouth shut. As everyone knew, she was up for full professor that year and Herman, who'd been granted that status upon his hiring, was on the tenure committee and therefore doubly untouchable. Plus, he'd made noise about running for department chair next year and might have the pull with Provost Blankenship to unseat Mullins.

"Is graphic literature all that different from illuminated manuscripts?" Rob said. "It's not like our curriculum couldn't use a little modernizing."

Eleanor said, "Welcome to the twenty-first century, Dr. Sutherland."

"It's purely selfish. If we don't keep our numbers up, we'll never get to replace Tom when he retires."

Tom looked up from his crossword puzzle. "I'm retiring? That's news to me."

"You just turned seventy-three. I assumed." Rob waved a hand in the air.

"My doctor says I have the heart of a fifty-year-old!"

"Let's table Eleanor's proposal until our November meeting," Betsy said. She hated tangents at her meetings. "We have a busy schedule this weekend, and I want to make sure everyone knows what's expected." She looked at Tom Strelzik and Annalise Granville, the early Americanist, who couldn't be counted on to arrive promptly to anything.

Rob felt the lump behind his ear. The cut had begun to scab over, but it still hurt like hell. He couldn't understand why Molly had done it.

They hadn't spoken since the night before. He'd waited until after his class to call, hoping she'd give in first. She never did. This time, she hadn't even answered. He'd hung up without leaving a message, unwilling to give her the satisfaction of a recorded apology. But two more hours had passed, and she still hadn't called.

"Are you listening, Robert?" Betsy said. "Diane in the President's Office says she didn't receive your RSVP for the reception tomorrow. I'm sure you'll want to be there, but she needs to know if you'll be using your plus-one."

He looked at Herman, who raised his eyebrows and, with a flourish of his left hand, showed him that the entire table was looking his way. Rob bowed his head, acknowledging everyone's attention, and then said, "What the hell. Sign me up for two."

Before Betsy could finish noting this, the door swung open, smacking against the wall and closing halfway again before Rob turned to see his younger daughter, Robin, standing there. She held her backpack by one strap—she wore out two a year by dragging them along the ground instead of wearing them like a backpack—and a tote bag full of sheet music and piano exercise books in the other hand. Hurricane Robin, Molly called her, for the way she arrived suddenly, took over an entire space, and left destruction—or at least a huge mess—in her wake.

"Where's your jacket?" he said.

Eleanor laughed. "Spoken like a true father. The poor dear's upset, Robert."

Standing up, he realized that she was hiccupping distraughtly, a technique she used to fight off a crying jag. He went to her as quickly as he could.

"I was just having fun!" she said, not waiting for him to get her into the hallway. "I thought we had a deal. If I showed him I could play it his way, he'd let me play it *my* way."

"Who, sweetheart?" he said.

"Faulkenstein," she sniffed.

Rob made his way around the table and put a hand on her shoulder.

Betsy said, "Where is your mother, Robin? We're in the middle of a meeting."

"Really, Betsy." Eleanor shook her head, looking around the table for support. "Have some compassion."

"I'm compassionate. But the administration, the alumni association, *and* admissions won't be if we don't get this weekend, right."

Rob knelt and embraced his daughter, who sniffled into his jacket. She burrowed in deeper, as she had as a toddler, until her face was inside the tweed coat, hidden from view. He could feel her chest heave with each asthmatic breath. "I'll be outside," he said, without even looking at Betsy for her assent.

As the door closed behind them, he heard Herman say, "We're all adults here, Dr. Mullins. I think Dr. Sutherland can survive the weekend without more guidance." God bless Herman.

With her bags in one hand and his free arm wrapped around his daughter, he crab-walked to his office, Robin still attached to him, her face against his ribs. She wasn't crying, not actively at least, based on the no-longer-expanding damp spot on his shirt. But with Robin, he knew the slightest setback—stubbing her toe on the entryway as she walked into a room, a momentary fright at the sudden appearance of an unexpected person—could unleash more waterworks. Katie was so much easier; even as a baby, she hardly ever cried. But Robin was loyal, funny, and already a good cook. He dropped her bags on the chair beside his desk and pulled her face out of his jacket. She blinked, adjusting to the light. The tweed's crosshatched pattern had scored her cheek and the side of her runny nose, which he wiped with his handkerchief. "You need to fix your beret yourself," he said. "I know you don't like the way I do it."

"Who cares. I'm not going anywhere."

"It's one thing if you don't mind looking uncouth at Bean Scene, but think about me. I've got a reputation to uphold."

"You're not supposed to take me there anymore," she said. "Mom says caffeine makes me *irritating*."

"I think the word you're looking for is irritable. But we can go. I won't tell if you won't." Only then did he think to add, "Where *is* your mother?"

"She didn't answer. Guess she's still in Asheville."

Of course. Molly's Day. He taught both summer sessions, tutored Faulkenstein's grandkids for the SATs so Robin could have free piano lessons with the best teacher in the area, and his wife spent a hundred dollars a month *recharging* in Asheville.

By the time they'd made the four-minute walk to Bean Scene, the cafe in the bottom of the student center, Robin had a spring in her step. The girl walked on her toes, bouncing off the balls of her feet. She recovered even more once she was seated at her favorite table, next to the window looking out on New Quad, a giant wedge of carrot cake before her and a cappuccino within reach. Mary Lynn Carlisle, one of his dimmer students, smiled at them from behind the counter, where'd she served their drinks and the largest piece of cake he'd ever seen. The young woman had made a fuss over Robin, telling her she wished she could pull off a beret and complimenting her on the vest she had on.

"I didn't know Katie made that," he said, nodding at the vest.

"Isn't it cool? She made it out of old ties."

"Where did she get—never mind. I don't want to know." He took a sip of his espresso and waited for Robin to say something about her piano lesson, but she behaved as though that crisis was in the distant past. "Ready to talk about Faulkenstein?" he said, finally.

"He called me 'a stubborn little girl' and said I'm not ready for the recital."

Robin had the gift of exaggeration, so he ignored the *stubborn little girl* remark. Faulkenstein had been teaching as long as Rob had been alive. Surely he knew such a comment was out of bounds, especially with someone so young.

"What did you do?" he said.

"What did *I* do?" She sat up, revived, practically lifted herself out of her chair like a gymnast on a pommel horse. The color rose in her cheeks, and she removed her beret, slapping it against her knee. "What makes you think I *did* anything? Just because I'm young doesn't mean I'm always wrong. And if I did do anything, it was exactly what Mom told me to do. I *reasoned* with him."

"When did you and your mother discuss this? This is the first I'm hearing—"

"They're called *Inventions* for a reason. It's not like Bach named them *Permanents*. I wanted to add my own creativity to the music. You know, make it more *personal*. Frankenstein has anger issues."

"*Faulkenstein's* family escaped East Germany as the wall was going up. Cut him some slack."

"Wynton Marsalis says Monk was the Bach of jazz, so I thought it would be cool to put a Monkish spin on the *Inventions*. And if Germany was so bad, why does he assign so many *German* composers? Bach, Brahms, Beethoven—"

"He's the most sought-after teacher in the state. You know how hard I worked to get you in."

"Schuman, Mendelssohn, Strauss. All German and all men. Mom's right. He's sexist *and* a fascist."

"I hardly think your mother used either of those words. And why didn't you tell me—"

"Fine. I added fascist. But if the jackboots fit. . . ."

"Where'd you hear such a thing? Forget it. I'll talk to Faulkenstein, see what I can do. But you have to be willing to listen to him." He waved off her attempt at interrupting him. "No matter what you and your mother think, you're not in a position to negotiate with Dr. Faulkenstein. You're the student. He's the teacher."

"I've been thinking—this was yummy, by the way." She tapped her fork against the now-empty plate. She'd eaten the entire piece of cake, hadn't saved him a speck of grated carrot nor a dollop of cream-cheese frosting. "I might quit."

"Not after all I've done for these lessons, you won't."

She rolled her eyes. "I don't want too much formal training getting in the way of my gift."

He couldn't help smiling at her choice of words and her seriousness. "Your gift?"

"Miles Davis only went to Juilliard for a year before he dropped out, same with Wynton."

"What are you talking about?" Try as he might—and he did try, very hard, no matter what Molly said—he couldn't keep up with all the trivia and names Robin spouted so comfortably.

"I've been taking stock—that's what Mom calls it. Looking at myself *dispassionately*. And what I've decided is—" She paused for effect, looked at him with those enormous brown eyes, the ones that typically flitted back and forth like a rabbit's but now met his dead-on. "What I've decided is, I might probably be a genius. A prodigy, at least."

"Not with that syntax."

"*Dad*."

"You're thirteen. Can you be a prodigy without a teacher? Even Van Cliburn stayed at Juilliard long enough to graduate." He was equally proud of himself for the reference and disappointed that his daughter didn't notice the effort.

"I don't want to be like him, just playing what other people wrote the exact same way they wrote it. I want to be like Monk and Andrew Hill and Cecil Taylor."

"Who and who?"

She ignored him. "I want to do my own thing. I can't do that if I'm Frankenstein's robot."

He searched her face for at least a hint of recognition of the joke she'd just made. Nothing. She was serious, intent on her belief in her own *genius*. What he wouldn't do for some of that confidence. The clock on the wall read 4:18, too late in the day to deal with Frankenstein—*Faulkenstein*, dammit—so why not go easy on his daughter, at least for the weekend.

"How's the new piece?" he said. His daughter was as dedicated a composer as she was a musician. "If you're as brilliant as you say, it must be really something."

"I'm taking a break. 'Theme and Variations on a Day in Williamsburg, Brooklyn' was too derivative of Ellington's chamber music and the underlying classical framework. I'm developing some new ideas, trying to break free of the constraints of traditional melodic and harmonic form."

"I have no idea what that means," he said, smiling to let her know it was *his* problem, not hers. "But I can't wait to hear it."

He thought about the recital, Sunday afternoon, the final event of Homecoming Weekend. It would consist of a few alums, many current students, and Robin, who was the teacher's prize student. He'd told her she was last on the program because she was least affiliated with the college, but in private, he'd admitted to Rob that she'd have the biggest impact this way. By going after everyone else, he believed she would rise to the occasion and dazzle everyone. *Dazzle*, from a man who was known for kicking out entire Music Theory classes for not working hard enough.

"What are you playing on Sunday?"

"You never remember." She rolled her eyes. "Beethoven's Piano Sonata Number Seventeen. The Tempest!"

"Sounds appropriate."

She smiled, giggling.

"You are going to play it . . . correctly?" He knew he was approaching dangerous territory, but in light of the afternoon's events, he couldn't help asking.

"*Moi?* But of course!"

Seven

Traffic thinned when she traded the Interstate for a U.S. Highway—*what, exactly, was the difference*, she wondered for perhaps the first time—so she tried her husband's cell again. Leaving the casino an hour earlier, she'd returned to a world of carefully plotted and lined parking spaces and natural light and sound. A world both more ordered and more unpredictable than the controlled environment of the casino. Inside, it had been easy to ignore the near-constant buzzing of her cell. She almost never gave in to the frenetic, overloaded stimuli of the casino, but this time, something had been different.

Even if she hadn't been winning, she would have remained in her seat, awash in the sounds of dealers' calls, clinking chips and dice, the beep-beep-booping of electronic games and slot machines. She'd found a release. But the real world beckoned, in the form of eleven messages—five from Katie, four from her husband, and even two from little Robin—and twice as many missed calls. She tried her husband's number but got his voicemail. Rob had spent over three-hundred dollars on his new phone and had signed up for the most elaborate data plan, but he never answered the damn thing. She had no proof—beyond intuition honed from almost twenty years together—but she figured he'd had his students show him how it worked. Neither of them was technologically inclined, the difference being that Rob never let that stop him from spending too much on gadgets that were too complicated for him to use. The sun had dropped below the trees in her rearview mirror. She left her husband a curt message explaining the obvious: she was going to be late. She was already late, not that she cared. She was speeding, almost recklessly so, but not because she didn't want to miss Robin's night to cook. She was speeding because the faster she went, the more the wind blowing in through the open windows buffeted her hair, face, and bare arms. Most of all, she was speeding because she had a purse full of bank-strapped bills that she'd won while almost everyone in the casino had looked on. The other tables had cleared so completely that, in time, even the dealers had left their posts to watch. She'd been on such a roll that if she'd bet on zero, she knew the dice would have come up magically blank just to satisfy her. It no longer felt like a game of chance but an organic relationship, one where those small cubes, feeling the desire she transmitted through her fingers, did whatever was necessary to please her.

The tiny dots kept adding up in her favor, so the chips kept stacking up as well. When the piles threatened to topple over, the dealer exchanged them for larger denominations, but the new chips multiplied. She was on the run of a lifetime. Even when she was in it, she knew she'd never experience anything like it again. Long ago, the English had called their form of craps Hazard, and she could see why. Winning at this rate felt so good that she could imagine coming back every day, chasing that high, until she was broke, bankrupt. She kept expecting the pit boss to call a halt to her run or use some casino trick to throw her off her stride. But when she'd looked around at the other bettors and her audience, she realized they were all feeling the same thing, if only by extension. How many borderline addicts had she pushed over the edge in a mere two hours? That thought had ruined her high, and she'd cashed out soon after, greeting the crowd's disappointment with a lame, "Might as well go out on top."

She'd been so far on top that once she'd signed the paperwork assigned with such a large windfall, she'd been accompanied to her car by a security guard, who'd remained beside her parking spot until she'd left the lot and turned onto the frontage road. The pit boss had asked her to stay until a journalist arrived. No one had ever won so much in one go at Appalachian Spirit, and they wanted to publicize the fact. But the last thing she wanted was more attention, so she'd demurred and headed for the doors.

The security guard, not the bank-strapped bills on the passenger's seat, had made her nervous. As though the sight of a middle-aged woman in her twelve-year-old station wagon rattling down the highway would tip anyone off. She blamed Rob, and all the heist movies he watched, for making her jumpy. Still, she pulled into a fast-food restaurant parking lot and buried her purse deep in her satchel. Any thief who was that thorough deserved the money more than its present owner, who'd simply thrown dice for a few hours while the chips piled up.

The traffic soon picked up again, so she took her foot off the accelerator and the car slowed twenty miles per hour in no time. She'd been going eighty-five. Now that she'd gotten herself back under control, she realized that the station wagon had been shuddering since at least Asheville. North Carolina drivers seemed to believe they were all on NASCAR teams—why else would they advertise their allegiances by sticking their favorite drivers' numbers to their bumpers? And they weaved between lanes at will, tailgating—*drafting*, they called it—for miles at a time. She'd been competing with the best of them until she slowed down. Now they weaved around her and zoomed ahead, pleased that one more car was out of contention for whatever prize lay beyond their imaginary finish line.

A yellow blur caught her peripheral vision, and she tapped the brake pedal again, eliciting a honk from the pick-up behind her. She moved into the far-right lane and then turned onto the exit ramp two miles later. She'd driven this stretch enough times to know that the yellow streak was an old sports car parked in someone's backyard with a FOR SALE sign on the windshield. Just that morning, she'd smirked at the faint digits below those two words, no clearer from the highway than they'd be if they were written in braille. But as she backtracked through Henderson County, sticking as closely to the highway as possible, she imagined herself reading the terrain and the landmarks by feel. No maps, no GPS. She needed to see that car.

She found the house fifteen minutes later, halfway down a street that dead-ended into a department of transportation storage area. The house Molly was looking for was dark brick, with smoke wafting from the chimney and lights blazing from the windows, porch, and the floods aimed at the carport. The houses on either side were similarly illuminated. It was Halloween, her daughters' favorite holiday. How had she forgotten? Even if she left now and sped the whole way home, she'd miss the unveiling of Robin's costume.

The girl loved a spectacle, and her big sister always indulged her, describing the costume as Robin sashayed down the stairs, like a low-rent fashion show. Somehow, Katie had convinced Robin to go as Jackie Kennedy, an improvement over the pop princess she'd insisted on being the previous year, even if it was an odd choice for a thirteen-year-old. She looked at the house before her once again, thought about the car in the backyard, and allowed curiosity to win out. She'd be home by the time Robin got back from trick or treating and, for once, she'd let her eat all the candy she wanted.

Weeds filled the flower bed in front of the house, broken up only by a rut of sandy soil running down the middle. Even in the near-dark, Molly could see that the gutters had gone untended for so long that something had begun to grow out of them. Two pumpkins, uncarved, stood sentry by the front door, the lone attempt at creating a festive mood, though she could hardly criticize. She hadn't decorated since Robin turned ten.

She rang the bell, waited, and was about to ring it again when the door opened. The entryway was dark, and it took almost a minute for Molly's eyes to adjust enough to make out the figure in the doorway. Before she could say anything, the woman said, "You're not Tina."

"My name's Molly. I'm here about the car."

"I thought you were Tina, from down the street."

"Sorry." She didn't know what else to say; the woman was so insistent.

"We're supposed to pass out candy together. It's almost time."

Enough about fucking Tina, she wanted to say. Instead, she smiled and said, "Is the car still for sale?"

"I'll get the keys." The woman remained in the doorway, looking over Molly's shoulder for a long time before she sighed and turned back into the house. Molly could hear kids gearing up for the big night, their tentative shouts and laughter like an orchestra tuning before a performance, and she hoped that the woman would return before Tina arrived.

"Here we are," the woman said, emerging once again from the darkness. The backyard sloped down toward the highway. Molly was unsteady on her feet, owing to the terrain and the heels she only wore on casino Fridays, and she had trouble keeping up with the woman whose flip flops slapped against her heels as she forged ahead. Molly usually changed back into her regular clothes at a rest stop on the way home but had forgotten in all the excitement. She thought about taking off her shoes—the woman was far enough ahead that Molly couldn't hear what she was saying—but she was down to her last good pair of hose and didn't want to ruin them. Her mother had been right: she was hard on her clothes.

She stopped at the driver's side door, next to the woman, who'd suddenly gone mute. Silence rarely bothered Molly but this woman seemed angry, hostile even, when she didn't speak.

"I always admire it when I pass by on the highway," she said. "It's beautiful."

"It was my ex-husband's."

"Then it's a piece of shit," Molly said, aiming for levity. "Let's bash in the windshield with a tire iron."

The woman laughed, really laughed. Snorting, coughing, the kind of laughter that only comes out of complete surprise. When she calmed down, she said, "No offense, honey, but I took you for a stuck-up, rich bitch."

The woman talked like she was decades older than Molly, but in the glow from the backyard floodlights, Molly could see that they might be the same age. It was difficult to say for certain. If life had treated this woman badly, she could have been a decade younger than Molly. At any rate, she was big in an athletic way, the type who maybe played softball and volleyball in high school, probably did something physical now.

"My ex bought it because he thought it was the same as the Mustang from some Steve McQueen movie. Turns out he was off by a year. Typical."

"I always liked McQueen," she admitted. "My husband prefers Paul Newman."

Molly shouldn't have been surprised that Rob would be a Newman Man. They both had the same kind of chatty bravado. She'd told a friend—back before they moved to Elgin, back when she had friends—that Rob had talked her clothes off of her with his jokes and disquisitions on everything from *Tristram Shandy* to The Smiths to Terry Gilliam movies. If he'd been a Steve McQueen-type, he'd have just ordered her to take off her clothes. His glowering look would have made conventional charm unnecessary.

"I don't care for either of them myself," the woman said. She rattled off details about the car that meant nothing to Molly, opened the hood, and pointed at the brand-new *blah* and the reconditioned *blah blah*. "My husband treated this car better than he treated me. Better than anything, really." She stepped back and looked at Molly. "You don't look like a racing enthusiast."

"Can't stand it. My parents dragged me to the Indy 500 every year when I was kid, but it was too loud." In high school, she went with friends, hoping for a good time and for alcohol. Every year, she ended up puking in the parking lot, accompanied by the strains of car engines that, in her drunken state, sounded like giant, mutated bees circling her head. But this Mustang wasn't the hollowed-out shell of a car designed solely to go fast on a track. Though older than her, its style was unquestionable, enduring. Attention had been paid to every detail, from the bucket seats to the black gear stick to the chrome detailing. And she liked that it had been driven, even if the most recent owner had been an asshole, that every time she turned the wheel, she'd feel how it had been worn smooth by the hands that had come before hers.

The woman quoted a price, adding, "That isn't negotiable. This and the house are all I got. If I don't get a good price for one, I won't have the other much longer."

What was she doing, pretending that buying this car was a realistic possibility? She was wasting this woman's time. Tina would be there soon, might be knocking on the door now, ready to begin their Halloween revelries. Here she was, behaving every bit the *rich bitch* the woman had taken her for, getting her hopes up only to walk away without giving the car another thought.

She'd been careful to keep these Fridays separate from the rest of her life. No one knew where she really went, not that she had to worry about Rob figuring it out. He was so inattentive that she didn't bother hiding the expensive dresses or shoes, simply placed them in the closet among their cheaper compatriots. The jewelry and accessories she kept in the filing cabinet in her study to protect them from Katie, who often raided her jewelry box without asking. But a bright yellow Mustang? She couldn't just pull it in behind the backyard wood pile, wait for her family to notice, and say, "That old thing?"

She looked up and saw someone, Tina presumably, coming toward them. She had to make a decision. But what decision was there to make? She couldn't buy the car. Walking around it one more time, she calculated how much it would cost her to keep it in a storage facility, how many months—years—she could afford with the leftover casino money, minus the cost of the car, which would take several of those bank-strapped piles. The point of her Fridays was No Strings Attached, not Add More Complications to Your Already Difficult Life. But if she bought it and pulled up at home, bye-bye free Fridays. She knew Rob well enough to imagine the self-righteous tear he'd go on. *So irresponsible. What if you'd lost? Gotten in over your head?* But that was the point. She could walk away right then and be the winner, the woman who kicked Appalachian Spirit's ass, who made *one big score* and really did quit. The Mustang would be her parting gift.

By the time Molly finished her circuit around the car, Tina was standing next to the woman, both of them looking expectant. "Fuck it," she said. "Is cash okay?"

Eight

Near the end of Prohibition, when politicians still cared about what academics thought, Elgin's mayor had struck a deal with the college president: in exchange for the latter's support of a law keeping the town dry, the former promised that the police would look the other way regarding alcohol consumption on campus during a select group of events each year, Homecoming foremost among them. When another mayor tried, years later, to rescind the deal, the college president, in his final act, created the CC Police department. Rumor had it the original officers swore allegiance to the college president above the mayor, the governor, even the President of the United States, but no record of such a pledge had ever been found. Regardless, the tradition continued to the present, where the English department faculty mixed with graduates from years ago in the State Room, all of them well-lubricated thanks to President Rowley's historic leadership.

Scott was behind the bar, studying the aging alums for a sense of what the future held for him. The forty and fifty-year folks were old enough to be his grandparents and completely exceeded his imagination. Even if most of them hadn't shunned the bar, he couldn't imagine what 60 or 70 would be like. Of those older ones who had come for the festivities, two were in wheelchairs, two more seemed to be suffering the effects of strokes, and one loudly enumerated his heart procedures: "I've had three angioplasties, a single and a triple, and a pacemaker. Been dead on the table twice. But here I am!"

If anybody could use a drink, Scott thought, it was that guy. His roommates couldn't believe he was working on the night of the annual Halloween party, but none of them cared about where the funding for their educations came from. Derek's family had enough money to cover his tuition, and he made up for the rest with first-generation-college-student scholarships. Tony went the opposite route. He went through student-loan money like a sailor on shore leave, applying for every offer that he saw. Not Scott. His parents had wanted him to go to NC State, like everyone else in the family, so when he chose CC instead, they told him he'd have to make up the difference in price, a little under twenty thousand. Per year. He'd been an RA for two years, despite his friends' calling him a narc, and a work study student all four years, first in the library and later for the English department.

But that still wasn't enough, so he worked four events per week for University Catering. He could make Tom Collinses and boxcars, mint juleps and Old Fashioneds, even cosmos and chocolate martinis for the younger crowd. He'd been counting on high volume at this party especially. Even though he was prohibited from doing so, he'd set out a tip jar to make up for his boss's decision to remove him from the other events he'd signed up to work. "You're a senior. Have a good time," the man had said, then chucked him on the shoulder as though he was doing him a favor by vaporizing the next week's grocery money. He hoped his boss was tied up with the other eleven such parties going on that night, many of them staffed by bartenders who couldn't tell a lime from a lemon.

Dr. Mullins appeared among the mingling masses, and led an attractive ten-year toward the bar. The woman spoke the whole way, flapping her hands, rolling her wrists this way and that. He'd never seen anyone get the best of Dr. Mullins in a conversation, not even Dr. Pagliarulo, who was typically by her side.

"Here we are," the department chair said, as though the walk to the bar had been an arduous adventure. "And this is one of our current crop. Shouldn't you be off enjoying yourself, Scott?"

"So everyone tells me." He smiled.

The woman said, "I'm sure the Halloween party will still be raging long after we've packed it in." She turned to Scott. "You do still have the party, don't you?"

Mullins jumped in. "I should know. Every year I ask them not to, but campus police still call me to let me know when they've gotten too many noise complaints to ignore it any longer."

The woman looked at him while Dr. Mullins went on about the importance of tradition, even if, like the Halloween party, it wasn't entirely wholesome. Scott didn't know what to do. Was it rude to ignore his professor—his work-study boss— who seemed lost in her own pontification? When the younger woman rolled her eyes toward the ceiling, setting one eyelid fluttering, he no longer cared about being rude. "I'm Scott Kenney," he said, as Dr. Mullins paused to take a breath.

"Renee Dunhill," she said. She thrust her arm forward and shook Scott's hand with a surprisingly strong grip. "I was just telling Dr. Mullins how the campus has changed. It's only been ten years, but New Quad was mostly woods when I was here. And that rec center! Have you tried the climbing wall?"

"I like sports at ground level." He poured them each a glass of white wine, refilling Dr. Mullins's instead of offering her a new one as he was supposed to do. He didn't want to spend all night washing dishes.

"We all expected to have you back before now for a book signing," Dr. Mullins told Scott. "Renee's quite the poet."

Renee gave Scott another look, this one not so humorous, more like an *I'm sorry you have to be here for this* slitting of the eyes. "The publishing world has yet to realize the best-seller potential of my double sestinas."

Dr. Mullins squeezed Renee's arm and said, "Look around you. 'Gather ye rosebuds while ye may. . . .' There's Michelle Nyburg. I didn't know she was coming!" With that, she disappeared into the throng, leaving Scott and Renee alone.

"That was pleasant," he said once he was certain Dr. Mullins was out of ear shot.

Renee shrugged. "Tact was never her strong suit, as I recall. When we were students, she told Michelle she 'lacked the intellectual rigor to survive at Georgetown Law.' Now she's a junior partner at the biggest firm in Atlanta. Maybe the tough talk inspired her."

"Maybe—"

Renee kept going. "She calls herself a feminist, but it was always the male students she doted on. And not just Evan. She claimed she was trying to push us more, but I wonder if she wasn't just pushing us *away*."

"You know those leaderboards at golf tournaments?" He leaned against the bar, warming to his position as the iconic bartender, lending an ear to a troubled customer. "Sometimes I wonder if she has one in her office with all of her students' names on it. 'So-and-so's leading at four-under-par while such-and-such turned in a bad reading journal and dropped three strokes.'"

She laughed. "Even after ten years, I have this narcissistic fear that she kept my paper on *The Spanish Tragedy* and reviewed it right before this party."

"You wrote about that too?"

"What's left to say about Shakespeare, at least when you're twenty-one?"

"I wish some of my classmates shared that view."

"The hubris of youth. We all had it. *No one's ever thought of Othello the way I do.* Fifteen minutes in the library, scanning articles, and you'll find someone with the same idea, expressed more insightfully, decades ago."

He opened beers for a trio of twenty-five years, then turned back to Renee. "So what's the solution? Only write about obscure figures and new books?"

"I have no idea. Maybe that's why I'm a poet. A community college instructor, actually. But I'm supposed to be asserting my creative, aspirational side."

"Says who?"

"My therapist."

He hadn't meant it seriously, had been trying to flirt, but he liked that she'd taken it at face value, which implied that she took him that way as well. He liked, too, that she wasn't embarrassed. His friends would have made jokes, to hide such honesty.

"How do you like it?" he said.

"Therapy?"

"Poetry. Teaching."

Two more people arrived, ordered martinis, and said hello to Renee. She hugged the woman, patted the man's arm when he reached out for a hug as well, and nodded while they talked about their kids and living in Charleston. Even over the sound of the martini shaker, Scott could tell she hadn't said half as much to them as she had to him, which he liked.

She had wire-rimmed glasses, like his older sisters' dolls wore—granny glasses, his father called them—but they matched her unfussy appearance and demeanor perfectly. She had on just a hint of makeup—blush and lipstick—and her chestnut hair fell straight to her shoulders where strands brushed against the purple scarf she'd wrapped around her throat, adding some color to her dark-gray dress. The couple picked up their drinks, dropped a dollar in the tip jar, and walked away, at which point Renee said, "I hate parties. I always latch on to one person and talk until I wear myself out. Then I try to leave without anyone noticing."

"I don't mind talking to you." *Don't mind?* What a lame compliment, he thought.

"You're working. I don't want to monopolize—"

Professors Sutherland and Delacroix appeared suddenly, both smiling broadly enough that Scott could tell they'd begun drinking before the evening's festivities. "Why are you working?" Sutherland said, affronted. "This is your final homecoming, until you return, triumphant, like Renee here." He paused to embrace her with one arm. "She just had two poems in *The Paris Review*. Do you subscribe, Herman? Incredible poems, particularly the second one. The image of those two couples—one young, one old—riding the train through the desolate west. Brilliant!"

Dr. Delacroix took two beers off the bar, dropped a five in the tip jar, and tried to tempt Sutherland out of his lingering embrace with the promise of a cold, imported lager.

"Mr. Kenney, I order you to go to the library first thing tomorrow and read those poems." Sutherland pointed at him with each word, glaring as though Scott was single-handedly responsible for whatever ills he was diagnosing. "This is the kind of accomplishment our department, *our school*, should be promoting, not the designing of yet another video game destined to end up on the scrap heap of—"

They all waited, against their better collective judgment, for Sutherland to go on, but instead he took a satisfied swig from his bottle and dropped what sounded like ten dollars' worth of change into the tip jar.

"I'm glad you liked them," Renee said. "Is your wife here? I'd love to see her."

Dr. Sutherland hung his head, suddenly depressed. "The elusive Professor Calloway isn't much for reunions, I'm afraid.

If I can get her to the game tomorrow, I'll consider it a personal triumph. She'd rather be at home wrapped in the warm embrace of family, or at least of the latest tome on analytic philosophy."

"There must be something to that, considering the rate at which she publishes."

"No doubt. But there's more to life than seeing your name among the contributors to a journal no one will remember in six months. What are the odds that any of us come up with something that will really endure? Renee, you're ahead of the game. Poetry is a truly worthy pursuit. But the rest of us? I don't know."

Scott couldn't help looking at Dr. Delacroix, who arched an eyebrow in response and said, "Shouldn't you save the oracular style for after the endowed chair?"

Renee finally slipped out of Dr. Sutherland's embrace. "I hear congratulations are in order. Word on the street is you're a shoo-in."

"Mere speculation," he said. "If anything, the administration would support it just to free up more space for classes on The Great Writers of Serial Television and The Twitterization of Contemporary Literature. I prefer to remain in the trenches, fighting the good fight."

"That's what it is, a fight?" Renee said, sounding more arch than Scott could ever imagine being in front of one of his professors.

"Dr. Mullins teaches Shakespeare almost entirely as a film adaptation course, Dr. Granville gave up teaching poetry years ago, and Dr. Pagliarulo hasn't taught a book without pictures since you were in school, Renee. Herman and I are practically the last holdouts."

Someone should tell that to Dr. Strelzik, Scott decided.

"You, my dear, represent the apex of the Golden Age at Confluence." Sutherland turned to Scott and added, "Mr. Kenney would have been at home among your cohort. You should see him struggle to appear interested in the inanities of his classmates."

"That's enough of that," Dr. Delacroix said. "You promised to introduce me to Ms. Nyberg."

Dr. Sutherland looked around the room, did a double-take, and said, "Michelle? Of course. She was on CNN the other week, talking about some wrongful-termination case she'd won. Come, Herman. Let me do the honors."

After Dr. Sutherland had gone, Dr. Delacroix leaned toward Scott and Renee, drawing them closer together. "It's possible that a bottle of fifteen-year-old Scotch was procured and imbibed by several of CC's finest before this party. Remember, what happens at Homecoming is forgotten after Homecoming."

Renee smiled. "I've forgotten already."

Dr. Delacroix nodded and chased after Dr. Sutherland, who seemed to be harassing Michelle Nyberg for committing a subject-verb error in her CNN interview.

Renee said, "He's the new African-American scholar?"

"Don't let tonight fool you. He's not usually this friendly."

"Fifteen-year-old Scotch does wonders for that. I should try it." She adjusted her glasses and looked around. "I wonder if the guest of honor intends to make an appearance."

"Aren't you all the guests of honor?"

She leveled her gaze on him in a way that made him understand how she managed her community college students. "We've been having a nice chat. Don't start bullshitting now."

"I heard he checked into his hotel a few hours ago, so I don't see why he wouldn't be here." He felt like a lap dog, eager to please after being punished for a minor offense.

"Probably waiting to make a big entrance." She held up her empty glass, waiting for him to refill it. "That's not fair. Some of the others—like Michelle—seemed comfortable speaking in front of people, but he had to turn it into a performance. Did you see his TED talk?"

He nodded. Hadn't everyone? It had over twenty-million hits on YouTube.

"He sounded like a British actor doing an American accent. And the story he told about Dr. Sutherland? Talk about revisionist history."

Everyone he knew liked Professor Sutherland. He was laid back in class, made jokes that were actually funny—unlike Drs. Mullins and Granville—and was always willing to supervise a new student club or play pick-up games in the gym. After Evan Wykoff's TED talk made the rounds, however, Dr. Sutherland became a near-mythical figure, a King Arthur or a Robin Hood. This was reinforced by his refusal to assume the mantle or in any other way change his demeanor. Scott admired him for this, especially as the hubbub began right after his friend Derek, upon winning the Academy of American Poets Prize, began walking around campus with a copy of Amiri Baraka's *Preface to a Twenty Volume Suicide Note* in the side pocket of his new denim jacket. By contrast, Sutherland seemed grumpy—pained, even—whenever anyone asked him about Wykoff. He complained about video games and told his students, "If you spent as much time reading—and not just for class, any literature will do—as you spend on *games*, you'd be amazed by how much you'd learn." Scott wanted to know more, but he didn't want to seem like a gossip, so he did what he figured a real bartender would do in his place. He kept his mouth shut, wiped down the bar, and waited.

"Unlike you and me," Renee said, "Evan was a Shakespearean par *excellence*, at least according to Dr. Mullins. He didn't just memorize soliloquies, he memorized *entire scenes*. And he was pretty insightful, no matter what he said in that speech. But he was too smart for his own good, at least back then. He liked to show off, which was fine in Mullins' classes, or even in Pagliarulo's and Granville's classes. And since Sutherland was young and—believe it or not—pretty cool, he thought he could do it with him too."

He almost interrupted her. Sutherland still seemed cool to him, even if staggering around the cocktail party throwing an arm around her was inappropriate.

"Sutherland squashed him like a bug. Every time he launched in with *Shakespeare this*—or *The Bard would never have*—Sutherland would shoot him down. Some of us tried to get Evan to shut up, to go along with Sutherland instead of arguing all the time, but he'd act put out and complain that his tuition paid the professors' salaries, so why shouldn't he say what he wanted to say?

"One day Sutherland had clearly had enough. He was obviously in a bad mood, but Evan didn't care. He whined about what we were reading—I think it was *Humphry Clinker*—and called it trivial. 'I've been rereading *Coriolanus*,' he said, 'and even though it's not a major work, by Shakespeare's standards, it's *a lot* better than this.' Sutherland glared at him, and then made eye contact with the rest of us, one by one. Evan tried to say something while he was doing this, but the professor raised his hand without looking at him, and Evan kept his mouth shut for once. Finally, Sutherland looked at him again and said, 'I appreciate your love of Shakespeare. I wish more people shared it. But oranges are not the only fruit.' I was just starting to understand what he'd meant when he launched into an incredible recitation of Coriolanus's 'O world, thy slippery turns' speech."

"He did that from memory?"

She smiled. "Someone checked it after class. He got it word for word."

"What did he do next?"

"He went back to Smollett. Like it was no big deal. In four years, it was the only time Evan looked defeated."

"That's—I mean—" He didn't know *what* he meant, only that the legend of Professor Sutherland continued to grow.

Scott scanned the room, found Dr. Sutherland standing in the corner, seemingly sober, talking to a forty-year. Sutherland wore a seersucker suit with a bow tie and a flower in the lapel on the first day of school every August, which Scott had always wondered about. Did dressing like Matlock really set the tone for the beginning of a new year? But maybe he did it for the same reason Clint Eastwood wore a Spanish poncho in all those spaghetti westerns. It looked a bit ridiculous, not to mention being too warm for the climate. Most importantly, it made it more difficult for The Man With No Name to draw his pistols. But if you've got a reputation as the biggest badass around, who cares what you wear. Anyone who challenges you is dead anyway.

Nine

The more she looked at the suit, the more disappointed she became. Instead of commending herself for knocking off a Chanel for $18.48, she couldn't help seeing the flaws. Even at night, the pink jacket's origins as a chenille bathrobe would be evident, she was sure. The navy collar and trim that she'd sewn over the robe's white piping wouldn't lie flat. Knowing Robin, she'd fidget so much that the collar would pop up like bad eighties fashion. And no matter how carefully she pinned the pillbox hat to her sister's hair, she knew Robin would mess it up the minute she bounded down the front stairs. The hat had been the most expensive item, the one thing she couldn't figure out how to fake, and she'd begged her sister all afternoon not to lose it. At least the blood stains looked good.

"Are you done yet?" Robin said, shifting from foot to foot. "Jamie and Jessica aren't going to wait forever."

"They're so nosy, they'll never leave without seeing you." The twins, who lived next door, were a year older than Robin and treated her like both a much younger sister and a fascinating specimen from a nearly extinct culture. "Besides, you want your costume to be—"

"I don't care about being *authentic*. I just want candy!" She tried to spin away from her sister, but Katie dug her nails into Robin's arm and held her still.

"One more dab," she said, twirling the paintbrush against the front of the skirt. She'd researched the exact placement online, and then spent an entire Saturday figuring out how to create the most *authentic* blood stain without actually opening a vein. While she ran the hairdryer over the spot, Robin fiddled with her cell phone.

"Why hasn't Mom called back?" Robin said. She flipped open the phone like one of those Star Trek communicators, then slapped it shut with both hands. *Thock, slap*. That's what Katie heard all the time. She almost wished her parents had given in and gotten Robin a smartphone like she'd wanted.

"Probably lying in a ditch somewhere."

Robin smiled. "Is the car on fire?"

"Eight-foot-tall flames," Katie said over the sound of the dryer. "Black smoke billowing all around."

"Everybody *back*. The gas tank's gonna blow!" Robin giggled.

She wished she could distract herself as easily. It wasn't fair that her mother could just disappear like this, *especially* on Halloween, especially at the beginning of Homecoming Weekend. And it wasn't just her mother; her father hadn't come home either.

A year earlier, their parents had decided that, in order to teach the girls independence, they would all share chores like cooking and cleaning. It sounded to Katie like another way to pawn off more work on the kids, but Robin had turned out to be a surprisingly good cook. What she lacked in skill and experience she made up for in novelty and enthusiasm. Within a month or two, Katie had begun looking forward to her little sister's Friday night dinners. For Halloween, she'd made Super Sloppy Janes, a combination of lentils, her own tomato sauce, and Dijon mustard on toasted buns. She piled soy cheese on top, then drowned them in some kind of barbecue-balsamic glaze whose specifics she refused to divulge.

She'd pouted all through dinner at the lack of adoring eaters, until Katie offered to make waffles in the morning, Robin's favorite breakfast. "When Mom and Dad wake up I'm going to dump a huge blob of Sloppy Jane on top of their plates," Robin said. They'd done the dishes together, even though it was Katie's night, waiting as long as possible before Robin got into her costume. "Do you think they forgot about Halloween?" she said, as though they were no-shows for her high school graduation, or her wedding day.

Before she could answer, the front door opened and Robin cried out, "Daddy!" Somehow, she could always tell the difference between the sounds each of their parents made when entering the house. Tagging along behind her, Katie bent down to pick up the pillbox hat that had fallen off her sister's head in her haste to show off her now-incomplete costume.

Her father said, "Why, Mrs. Kennedy, if I'd known you were coming, I would have been home sooner."

Robin giggled, which would have loosened the hat even if it had survived her hallway dash. More pins would be in order. "You almost missed Halloween!"

"Where's your sister?" he said. Then, louder, "Would Katherine the Great please report to the Grand Foyer. Your assistance is needed post-haste."

Katie stood at the top of the stairs overlooking the living room—the Grand Foyer. She started to say something: *Delusions of grandeur again, old man?* But she stopped when she realized they weren't alone. Her father stood in the middle of the room, leaning against a young man wearing a boxy tuxedo and an embarrassed smile. He was almost a foot shorter than her father, with tousled hair that had already begun to thin near the crown, bulldog cheeks, and a few extra pounds around the middle that were accentuated by the baggy tuxedo jacket. *Who would wear such a thing?* she wondered. No matter how formal the event, he'd look better in a tailored, department-store suit— even a sports-jacket-and-slacks combo—than he would in the most expensive, ill-fitting tux. Typical college student. She was surprised he wasn't wearing flip-flops.

"Robin, my dear," their father said. "What's going on here?" He waived in the general vicinity of the blood stains. Of course he did. Why commend his older daughter on her hard work when he could skip right to criticism?

"It's just like in *The Service*." The boy had a voice. Not a bad one. Deeper than she'd imagined considering his bland appearance. "That's exactly what she has on—"

"I don't mean the outfit," their father said. "I mean *that*." He poked one of the spots hard enough to make Robin wince.

"It's blood!" She twirled. "Isn't it awesome?"

"Blood?" He looked at Katie. *She* was always the one to blame. But this time she had him beat.

"It's a replica of the outfit she wore in Dallas. You know, November 22, 1963? I researched the exact placement of every splatter."

"But why not stick with the outfit pre-Oswald?"

"It's Halloween, Daddy. There *has* to be blood."

Katie ignored her sister, focused on the argument she'd rehearsed all afternoon, when she'd assumed their mother would be her opposition. "Without Oswald and the assassination, this suit is just another one of the many outfits that Jackie wore as First Lady. But after Oswald, it becomes iconic. Everyone's seen the photo of her climbing over the back of the convertible to protect her husband. With the blood stains, the suit is a piece of history." She wished her mother, the master debater, had been there.

"Incredible," the young man said.

"Because your thirteen-year-old sister couldn't possibly dress up as Jacqueline Bouvier Kennedy—later-to-be-Onassis—a split-second before arguably the most traumatic moment in American history?"

"Were you paying attention to what I said?" She studied her father. Red face, redder ears. Still leaning against the mystery man. "You're drunk," she said.

"That's immaterial." He looked around, like a sleeping dog jolted awake by a high-frequency noise. "Your mother knows about this? Where is your mother?"

"*I* wanted to go as Billie Holiday. Wear an evening gown with full-length gloves. And paint track marks on my arms."

"Mom said this is okay." Katie had been just as disappointed as Robin when their mother nixed the Billie Holiday idea. Oh, the possibilities!

"She said I wasn't *mature* enough. That Billie wasn't *appropriate* for someone my age."

Once Robin got rolling, Katie knew their father would give in, especially under the circumstances. The girl sang the opening to "Ain't Nobody's Business If I Do," pleading her lover to stay with her, even if he has to take all of her money.

"Enough," their father said. "Off you go. I'm sure the twins are dying to see what you've come up with this year." With that, he dismissed Robin from his mind and turned toward Katie. She hated how he did that. "Your mother still isn't home?"

She shook her head. Her father's student—at least she assumed that's who he was—tried to fade into the background so he could study the family photos on the wall unobserved, but she wasn't about to lose track of him the way her father had. He was really short, she noticed. "She never returned our calls."

"She left me a message an hour ago. Yoga ran late. Construction on 26. She wasn't clear. Bad connection, I guess." He ran his hand over his mustache, Gesture Number One in the Agitated Robert Sutherland playbook. "Is it just me or is yoga making your mom an even bigger flake?"

"Not a word I'd use to describe her."

"You're probably right. Of course you are. You're a genius, a revelation! Look what you did for your sister." He stepped back, wrapped an arm around the young man again. "Scott, I bet Katie here spent less than twenty dollars on that entire costume. Am I right?"

"Eighteen, actually."

He nodded, pleased. "That's why we're here. Young Scott has a party to go to."

"The legendary English Major Halloween Bash?" She'd heard about it for years, from every babysitter she and Robin had ever had. When she was ten, Cara Overby had spent an entire evening describing how drunk each person got and who'd hooked-up with whom. Finally, Katie had shouted, "My sister's six years old. She doesn't need to hear this!"

"Exactly. But Young Werther here foolishly chose mammon over fellowship."

"I was working the alumni cocktail party until Dr. Sutherland generously offered to find a replacement," he mumbled.

"Offered?" Katie said. "Insisted was probably more like it."

The young man—she thought his name was Scott—shrugged.

"You should see Herman behind a bar. He throws bottles around like Tom Cruise in *Cocktail!*"

She had no idea what he was talking about. "Doesn't Werther kill himself?"

"Quite right." Then, frowning, he added, "How did you know that?"

"I'm the dumb one in the family, in case you're wondering," she told the young man. "See? He doesn't disagree. Anyway, I probably heard you talking about it. Thomas Mann, right?"

Her father groaned. "Goethe! *Sturm und Drang?* Mann's not even the same century."

She knew that. She had read *Death in Venice* on her own, but whether out of stubbornness or immaturity—she wasn't sure which—she refused to tell her father the truth, that she actually paid attention to him, and to Dr. Delacroix. She read the books, stories, and poems that they discussed, at least the ones that sounded interesting.

"You want me to make this guy a costume? That's what you're saying."

"Precisely." Her father looked around again, losing interest already, now that he'd found someone else to pawn his student off on.

"Is there a theme?"

The young man ran a hand through his hair, though doing so made it look worse, not better. What was it with men and their hair? They criticized women for spending too much time primping, but they were the ones who couldn't keep their hands out of theirs—whether it be on their heads or faces—at the least hint of tension or discomfort.

"Authors and literary characters," he said.

"Brilliant!" her father said. "What about Shandy or Crusoe? Perhaps Tom Jones."

"'What's New Pussycat'?"

"Listen to my sweet, sweet daughter. Like the dentist's child with terrible teeth. If only I could get her to pay half as much attention to the written word as you do, Scott."

She bit her lip. She'd read *The History of Tom Jones, a Foundling* the previous summer, all 861 pages of it, which wasn't easy to do without her father finding out. If he knew about it, he'd have made her *talk* about the book, as though she hadn't fully *experienced* it if she hadn't yammered on about it with him and listened to a lecture on the historical context or its precursors and successors. Why couldn't she read a book without having to share her opinion of it with the world?

"Who's your favorite?" she said, ignoring her father. When the boy didn't respond, she added, "Don't worry about what *he* thinks. He can't grade your Halloween costume."

"I like James Baldwin, but of course I can't do black face."

"Of course not." Someday she'd have to ask Dr. Delacroix who the guy was.

"How about Faulkner?" he said.

Her father groaned. "You young people, so hung up on now, like nothing worthwhile happened before television. What's the point of contemporary literature? It'll be a hundred years before we know what's going to endure. In the meantime, you'll just waste your time on trivialities."

"So we should wait until we're a hundred years old to read anything recent," she said. "That's realistic."

"Read whatever you want, I don't care. Just don't *limit* yourself. And don't get me started on those silly video games—"

"Okay. We won't," she said. She grabbed the boy by the baggy sleeve of his tux and led him upstairs. The fabric was scratchy, even cheaper than it looked. She hoped it had been imposed on him.

It felt strange having a boy, a stranger, in her room. Thanks to her recent ostracizing at school, she didn't have many people over, period. Now she couldn't help wondering how it looked to an outsider. What would this kid think of the Grace Kelly and Jean Seberg posters, of the photos she'd cut out of *Vogue* and *Paris Match*? The explosion of fabrics covering her sewing table, leftovers from Robin's costume? *Of course the scraps are pink*, he'd be thinking, *and the walls purple. How girly.* She almost corrected the thought aloud. Lilac. The walls were lilac, a *light* shade of lilac. Very subtle. Mature. So what if she was into fashion? She wasn't shallow. Fashion was important, no matter what her father thought, style an indicator of what mattered to a society at a particular time. Not to mention being big business, which this country could use, considering how crappy the economy was. Within thirty seconds of entering her room, she was ready to give her father's student a piece of her mind, then throw him out, all before the kid had even opened his mouth.

Finally, he spoke. "So, is your dad okay?"

"Duh. He's drunk."

"Yeah, but—I don't know. He hasn't seemed like himself all night."

What do you know about who my father is, she wanted to say. Instead, she went for an inscrutable stare, a pose she'd been working on in the mirror. She'd learned that—at least with her parents—silence often got her results more quickly than talking did.

"On the way here, he told me I should *tap Renee Dunhill's ass*."

"He didn't say that!" All the times he'd ranted about pop music, R&B, hip hop, for contributing to the *degradation of language. Why can't you be more like Robin*, he'd say.

"All I asked was if her poetry was any good, but instead of answering, he went kind of nuts. He said something about how she'd always had a first-rate mind, but now she's got a first-rate rack too."

"He actually said *rack*?"

"How am I going to get that conversation out of my head?"

"What about me? All of a sudden my father's a perv. No wonder he likes Fielding so much."

"You've read Fielding?"

"A little." More than a little. *Tom Jones*, of course, but after she'd read *Pamela*, to find out what her father was always raving about, she read both *Shamela* and *Joseph Andrews* to remove the bad taste of Pamela and Squire B's bizarre romance from her literary palate. It had worked. *Joseph Andrews* had moved into her top-ten. She'd bought a cheap, Dover edition at the Mall and hid it under her mattress. Sometimes, when she couldn't sleep and had already gotten complaints for revving up the sewing machine too late at night, she'd pull out one of her favorites—*Joseph Andrews, Jane Eyre, The Bluest Eye*—and read a chapter here or there, until she was tired.

"We read *Tom Jones* for Dr. Sutherland's class. It's kind of wordy. I don't mean long. A book should be as long as it needs to be. But parts of it seem tangential, unnecessary, like Fielding was getting paid by the word. Like the opening chapter of each book—"

"That's my favorite part!" The enthusiasm had come out before she could tamp it down. She hated when that happened. Unlike Robin, she preferred to keep herself controlled. "The narrator is hilarious. *You may be as smart as Shakespeare or as dumb as some of his editors.* Something like that. When he goes after his critics, it's like he already knows exactly what they're going to hate about his book but doesn't care. He's like, *screw you if you don't get what I'm doing.*"

Scott was staring at her in a funny way. Not the look she'd been going for. More *quizzical*, she thought, if that was a word. After thirty uncomfortable seconds, he broke eye contact and said, "You're supposed to be the dim bulb?"

"I'll make you a deal," she said. "I'll get you suited up for this party as long as you don't tell my father about any of this."

"You *hide* the fact that you read great literature from your parents?"

"It's complicated." Instead of explaining that her mother found fiction—all fiction—trivial and that her father championed it so ardently that the phrase *too much of a good thing* came to mind, she said, "You mean you don't keep secrets from your parents?"

Before Scott could answer, a car engine roared into the driveway. An unfamiliar engine. The car's horn sounded once, twice, a third time. If her sister hadn't left for trick-or-treating twenty minutes earlier, Katie would have assumed it was her. She was always doing things like that: ringing doorbells for no reason, blaring their cars' horns just to see what a certain rhythm sounded like, how much pressure was needed to produce a particular volume.

Since Katie's bedroom faced the back of the house, she walked past Scott, still mute, out the door, and down the stairs to the living room, where the noise had roused her father from an inebriated snooze. He rubbed his eyes with the palms of his hands, and then flattened the hair at the back of his head as though he were expecting President Vessey to be at the door.

"Did you call for a ride, Mr. Kenney?" he said, looking past his daughter to the boy at the top of the stairs. When Scott shook his head, her father said, "Since we've been summoned, we best not disappoint."

Katie noticed right away that the nap, brief as it had been, had helped him sober up. He was still a bit unsteady, but much of the manic quality—what Robin always referred to, approvingly, as *Daddy playing silly-buggers*—had drained from his demeanor. He tugged at the front door twice before realizing it was locked, then flipped the deadbolt and turned the knob. In the doorway, squinting into the car lights in the driveway, he said, "What in the fuck. . . ." She couldn't make out the rest.

She followed him out the door, almost trampling him when she saw her mother (it *was* her mother, wasn't it?) lounging oh-so-casually against the front bumper of an antique sports car, like a car show model or the photo of Miss August on the calendar at the Xpress Lube. The car was bright yellow with round headlights that looked like unblinking eyes trained on her father's sad-looking Mazda in the carport. It had been polished to a sheen, like the high heels dangling from her mother's feet. The engine ticked while it cooled down, the only noise other than the revelry of trick-or-treating all around them.

"*Mom?*" she said, not sure where to begin. Her mother didn't move. She had on a navy wrap dress Katie hadn't seen before that plunged enough in the front to make it look like she had cleavage. To Katie's embarrassment—and later, pride—she'd outgrown her mother's hand-me-down bras in seventh grade. The light above the carport reflected off of her mother's stockings (*Stockings?* on Molly Calloway?) and drew Katie's attention to the pumps that completed the outfit. Her mother never wore heels, equated them with Chinese foot-binding whenever she saw Katie wearing them, but there she stood, in a pair that Katie had also never seen. She felt like she'd come across a picture of her from another time, before she was a wife and mother.

"Are those *leather?*" was all she could think to say since her mother seemed content to remain mute, letting her self-satisfied smile do the communicating.

"Alligator, actually. I've got a matching purse in the car." She said *car* casually, as though she meant their ancient station wagon, the one Robin had thrown up in countless times on trips through the winding mountain roads north and west of Elgin. She had bedded down in it at the drive-in, before it closed, watching *Toy Story 2* and *The Incredibles*, among others, before sleeping through the second, more adult half of the double-feature.

Her father, struck dumb for one of the few times in memory, kept looking at *her*, as though she had something to do with this. Finally, he said, "You're stealing cars now?"

"You caught me." Her mother smiled; when was the last time she'd seen her actually *smile?* "The American Philosophical Association is just a front for organized crime. We logicians take care of the grand theft auto division."

"And our place is the new chop shop?"

"Only for the southeast."

"Of course."

"Why is this funny?" Katie said. She couldn't take it any longer, her parents' eagerness to turn everything into a joke, especially in front of Scott, who was absorbing it all from the porch. She could imagine him regaling everyone at his Halloween party with stories about Dr. Sutherland's fucked-up family.

Her parents turned to her almost in unison, wearing similar expressions of irritation, as though she were a rude audience member at the theater who insisted on joining the actors in their scene. As though *she* were the problem. "Mom left this morning in the wagon," she said. "And now she's in *this*. But you two have to show how cool you are, so you can't have a *normal* conversation about what the fuck is going on."

Even cursing didn't snap them out of it. Her mother blinked a few times and then said, "I thought you of all people would be happy about this. Now you'll have something of your own to drive."

Her father said, "This is for *her?*"

"I can't drive stick," she said.

"No one but me is driving it. The wagon's in Hendersonville. We can pick it up tomorrow."

"How did you pay for it?" Katie looked at Scott, lurking in the shadows, before continuing. "I mean, I don't remember you and Dad discussing it. Isn't that what couples do?" Late and overdraft fees, debt consolidation, these were terms she'd heard courtesy of her parents' bickering.

"She's right. We should have discussed this."

Her mother batted away their concerns like so many harmless flies. "I saw it from the highway coming back tonight. It used to belong to this woman's ex-husband. She was selling it cheap to piss him off. I offered a few hundred and she took it. Happy?" The father-daughter jury remaining silent, she added, "This is the first time in history that such an amazing deal was met with such disapproval, especially from the young lady who stands to benefit—who's that?"

At first, Katie assumed her mother meant Scott, still on the porch, but following the direction of her mother's pointer finger, she saw what looked like a two-headed blob coming up the driveway, obscured by the dark patch between the streetlamp and the light above their carport. Once the blob came out of the darkness, she realized that it was Mrs. Humphreys, from down the street, with a hand clamped to the back of Robin's neck. From the look on her sister's face, the grip hurt. Combined with the loss of her hat, she bore the solemnity of the widow Kennedy on Air Force One, witnessing Johnson's swearing-in.

Mrs. Humphreys didn't bother with pleasantries. "What kind of parents allow their child to leave the house like this?"

"As one of our most famous first ladies? Her sister spent weeks on this costume. It looks great." Her mother could shift gears even faster than her new car.

"It has. . . . She's covered in—" Humphreys took a small flashlight from her coat pocket and shined it on Robin's torso. "She's covered in brains, for Pete's sake."

Katie's mother shot Mrs. Humphreys a look both so quick and so deadly that it put Oswald's work to shame. "It's Halloween, Sheila. I've seen half a dozen zombies and twice as many vampires, all with far more blood than this."

"But this is a thoroughly tasteless and inappropriate costume! Why not dress as one of the Twin Towers, with a plane jutting out of the side?"

Not a bad idea, from a purely theoretical standpoint. It would be an incredible challenge, for a designer and a seamstress, but alas, it was probably too soon.

"Wasn't your daughter a trampy cheerleader last year?"

"Based on *a movie character*. There's a difference."

"The *difference* is that *my* daughter's pubescent body is covered." Katie had to give her mother credit.

Mrs. Humphreys stared, mouth agape, then turned to Katie's father who was trying to slink off in the same way Scott had when the whole thing began. Where was that kid? Had he vanished?

"That is a hateful thing to say. My daughter blossomed early, like I did, and it was no picnic for either of us, not that you'd know anything about that. How is it that with nothing more than common sense I can see that you shouldn't trivialize a tragedy like this, while you people with all your degrees think it's a joke?"

"She has a point," her father said. "The costume *is* in questionable taste. Thank you for helping us to see that, Sheila."

Katie watched her mother shoot an even deadlier look at her father, and then step forward to take Robin's hand. None of them, not even Katie, had noticed in the midst of the great debate that the young girl was crying, silently. When she wiped her face with the back of her hand, the smeared blood-spray colored her cheeks like rouge. Softly enough that Katie had to strain to hear it, her mother said, "Thank you for ruining a thirteen-year-old's Halloween. If you ever lay another hand on one of my girls, I'll break all five fingers, one at a time." It took all of Katie's restraint to keep from cheering.

Ten

His buzz was gone, leaving him disoriented and irritated. He followed Molly into the house at what he hoped was a safe, nonthreatening distance, not out of fear for his safety but out of genuine hesitance. They hadn't spoken since the previous night, nor had they even been in the same room. But somehow—he thought of it as husbandly intuition—he knew she expected an audience.

She strode into the living room, placed her new car keys on the end table by the reading lamp in the near corner, and dropped into the easy chair. With her legs stretched before her, he noticed the high heels, a style he couldn't remember her wearing since their wedding.

"You'll have to get some driving shoes, for a car like that. Something in a dark leather, to match the trim. Oxblood?"

"I was thinking flashier, a nice scarlet."

"You, flashy?" He knew they shouldn't joke, that Katie was right about that, and about so much more. But he couldn't help himself. They'd argued enough recently.

"I know. It's out of character, isn't it?"

"What about gloves?"

"Naturally." She held her hands up for consideration, waggling her fingers in the air.

He sat down on the ottoman before the chair, hunching forward. He did his best to make eye contact, but Molly evaded his gaze, her eyes roaming the room like a stranger taking in their shabby surroundings for the first time.

"Last night. . . ." he said, finally, not sure how to continue. He could hear Robin's stereo going upstairs, playing something percussive, making even Katie's snooping unproductive.

"Let's not," Molly said.

"We need to. That was. . . ." He sighed, even as he knew that a dramatic reaction would get him nowhere with his wife. "I don't know why we can't get along."

"The million-dollar question."

"Maybe you should take that job, if they offer it to you. A little space and all."

"Absence makes etcetera, etcetera?" She still didn't look at him, training her eyes over his shoulder, at something in the distance.

"What do you think?"

She finally made eye contact. He couldn't tell if she had tears in her eyes or if it was just the dappled light streaming through the crappy lampshade.

"I can't remember the last time you asked me that."

"I'm not a monster." He wanted to take her hand in his, to caress it.

She smiled, though he refused to take it at face value.

"You're no bed of roses, yourself," he said. He flinched, involuntarily, as he said this, which seemed to wound her worse than the comment.

"How about we retreat to safer ground?" she said. "The Mustang, for instance. It's been completely overhauled, with custom *this* and refurbished *that*."

"Slow down. All the technical terms are straining my meager intellectual abilities." He felt relief at their renewed banter.

She looked down at her hands, in her lap. Her skirt had ridden up a bit, exposing much of her thighs, which he tried not to leer at. "I didn't mean—if I taught twelve classes a year, I wouldn't have time to publish either."

"You'd still find a way. Guess I'm too lazy."

"We have different priorities."

Not knowing what else to say, he yielded to her interest in the Mustang. "So the car: midlife crisis?"

"I'm not that old. Forty's the new thirty, right?"

"Go much lower and the administration will be after me. Remember Ben Szymanski?"

"Wasn't the girl nineteen? Even for you. . . ."

He gritted his teeth, trying to keep the words from escaping his mouth, but in the end, he lost. "You can't help yourself, can you? Pick, pick, pick."

She tried to stand up, but he leaned forward, blocking her path. He didn't mean it aggressively; he only wanted to keep her from running away again.

Robin's album stopped, and they waited for the next one to begin. When it did, he couldn't help taking it as an omen. She'd played the soundtrack to *Elevator to the Gallows* enough times for even him to recognize it.

"I thought we'd declared a truce for Homecoming?" she said when he refused to let up.

"You're the one who violated those terms."

"So I did."

It was as close to an apology as he was likely to get, so he slid back on the ottoman and let her stand up. She didn't go far.

She picked up the keys, seemed to be weighing them against an invisible burden in her other hand. The dress looked good on her, mirroring her angular form but softening the edges.

"If you let this drop," she said. "I'll take you for a ride tomorrow. Robin says it looks like something Miles Davis would have driven, if he'd stooped to buying domestic."

"I'd rather you stay here now and talk to me."

She shook her head, regret showing on her face. "I'm not ready. Not yet. But soon."

He nodded, releasing her from his company. Instead of her study, this time she climbed the stairs toward the kitchen and made the turn to their bedroom.

THEY'D ONLY FOUGHT LIKE THIS once before, in the months leading up to Robin's conception. Back then, the disagreements had been exacerbated by Katie, of all people, the exceptionally demanding three-year-old. Everyone had told them life would get easier as their daughter got older, but two was harder than one, three more difficult than two. He came home from ten hours at Confluence exhausted, with nothing left to give. But Molly wanted his return to mark a break for her, after she'd spent all day catering to their daughter's eccentric needs. She wasn't teaching yet, so they couldn't afford a babysitter to offer a reprieve.

He'd arrive close to six and collapse on the same couch they still had, only to have his wife practically drop Katie in his lap. "You want dinner?" she'd say. "Then deal with her."

Only once had he balked, handing Katie back to Molly.

"I can't do it," he'd said. "I spent seven hours doing student conferences. I'm all out."

She'd pushed back her shoulders and set her jaw. She bounced Katie, crying, on her hip. "If you ever want dinner again, you'll take your daughter and *play* with her."

That was the beginning of their shared kitchen duties.

It wasn't that he didn't love his daughter, or his wife. He just didn't understand why she had to be occupied every minute of the day, why she couldn't be satisfied playing alone on the floor for a few minutes. Try as he might not to, he blamed Molly, who he thought doted on the girl to excess. She instilled in her such an expectation.

They'd had it out several nights later, when they'd both had time to stew over his refusal. As always, it was late, after ten-thirty, almost an hour past his productive period. Molly had started it in the bathroom, where they'd been brushing their teeth.

"I need more help from you," she'd said. "I'm not your servant."

"And I'm not a machine."

"Which is why you can't play with your daughter for thirty minutes a day?" She spat toothpaste into the sink. "It's not much to ask, considering."

"What happened to division of labor?"

"So it's perfectly all right for you, the man, to go out in the world while I stay home and do all the stultifying work to keep you happy when you return?"

"You make me seem like a Neanderthal." He replaced his toothbrush and leaned against the sink. She often accused him of using his size to show off, but he didn't know what else to do. He'd been over six feet since he was thirteen.

"It isn't the 1950s."

"Fine. Go out and get a job. We'll put her in daycare."

"Philosophers aren't in high demand around here."

The eternal argument. It wasn't his fault they'd ended up in Elgin. Any port in the storm, he often reminded her. The job market was such a storm. "Two bad that heart attack didn't take care of Trillo. You could have had his classes."

Thinking about it now, he couldn't believe they'd been having what amounted to the same argument for thirteen years. Molly's sacrifice. It depressed him enough that he poured a tall drink, and then another. He'd been right about the weekend. It would take all the alcohol he could handle to make it through.

Eleven

"I'm not sure this is a good idea," Scott said. Most immediately, he meant taking the seventeen-year-old daughter of one of his professors to a college Halloween party. On a grander scale, what he'd seen that evening had made him wonder if Dr. Delacroix wasn't right in warning him off pursuing a PhD. If Dr. Sutherland and Professor Calloway were anywhere close to being examples of what graduate school did to one's psyche, he wanted to stay far away.

"You can't back out now," Katie said. "I've gotten dolled up."

She'd outfitted them as Nick and Nora Charles, a couple he knew nothing about until she mentioned Dashiell Hammett, whose movie *The Maltese Falcon* he'd seen in Film Studies. "He wrote books, too," Katie had scolded him. The second scolding he'd received in a quarter of an hour. The first had come after he'd fled the scene between her parents for what he thought was the relative safety of Professor Calloway's study. There, he found a wall full of books, almost all of them hardback, though without dust jackets. Each one, at least five hundred, had been alphabetized. Most seemed to be philosophy, based on their titles—he recognized few of the names—with a smattering of theology and history. He'd intended to read every title, if it would get him away from the sight of his professor, drunk off his ass, arguing with his wife, who seemed to have turned up with a classic car without discussing the purchase in advance. But how was that possible, for one half of a couple to do something so significant without the other knowing?

He understood his professor's point of view, especially in light of how crappy Dr. Sutherland's ten-year-old Mazda was, not to mention the dilapidated state of their house. He hadn't taken more than a dozen steps without encountering a stain on the carpet. The walls, filled with nail holes, needed to be repainted, and the kitchen and bathroom—*one* bathroom, for four people, three of them female—were in desperate need of an update.

He'd made it as far as H—Habermas, Hegel, Heidegger— when Dr. Sutherland's daughter slipped into the room without his noticing. When he finally looked up, she said, "What are you doing in here?"

"Just trying to give you all some privacy."

"You better not be enjoying this," she said, stepping between him and the bookcase. "And if you tell anyone what happened—"

"I won't," he said, "honest." He backed up as she moved closer, until his backside brushed up against Ms. Calloway's desk.

"I bet your family is just as fucked up as mine," she said.

He thought about his older brother, who lived in his childhood bedroom and worked restocking vending machines, and his father, who'd been downsized so often he should have been invisible to the naked eye. He couldn't disagree.

They'd left the study for the safety of Katie's bedroom as soon as they heard her parents on the front walk.

"Hey," Katie said, bringing him back to the present. "You still with me?" She clinked her martini glass against his tumbler, both pilfered from the Sutherlands' kitchen cabinets. According to Katie, the costumes were leftovers from her school's performance of *Anything Goes*. Thankfully, she was a stickler for details, so his suit and both of their overcoats were wool, which came in handy during the forty-minute walk from the Sutherlands' to the English House.

Standing at the edge of the driveway, at last, Scott just wanted to take a bath and go to bed. But every window in the house was illuminated, even his bedroom window, and music from inside and conversation from the back porch filled the air. Scott held out his arm, trying to seem gallant, but Katie hung back, letting him lead the way. "As you wish," he said, trying yet again to be accommodating, but sounding robotic instead.

When they reached the bottom of the porch steps, Tony and Mary Lynn burst through the back door, unlit cigarettes in their hands. Mary Lynn jumped, startled, and her cheerleading skirt flounced indecently. Looking up at her, Scott got a quick glimpse of her red panties. Or what there was of them, a v-shaped swatch that tapered to almost nothing between her legs.

"Dude," Tony said. "About time you showed up. The cocktail party get rowdy?" He was dressed as Hunter S. Thompson, complete with a white cowboy hat, sunglasses, and bomber jacket. He had a cap gun in one hand and a plastic cigarette holder in the other.

"Like you wouldn't believe. Dancing on tables, lampshades on people's heads."

Tony snorted. "Even your fantasies are outdated. No wonder you like that *Pamela* crap."

"Better to go for the totally original, alcoholic has-been, right? You wore the same thing last year, I might add."

"Oh." Mary Lynn said. "He told you."

Even when he stood up for himself, it backfired. He was serious when everyone else was joking, sincere when they were ironic. He couldn't win.

"Who are you supposed to be?" Mary Lynn said.

"Nick and Nora Charles," Katie said, with a bow. "At your service." Scott had almost forgotten she was with him.

Mary Lynn didn't even try to hide the way she scoped out Katie. She started at the top of her head, covered by what Katie had called a Stella hat, and then worked her way down her face and overcoat to the legs that were far more shapely than Scott had imagined before seeing her in a dress and stockings. "I don't know you," she said.

"I'm Scott's cousin. I can't believe he didn't tell you I was coming." She swatted him on the arm and added, "My name's Katie. I go to Wake Forest."

"Fancy," Mary Lynn said.

Katie didn't miss a beat. "Are you Lolli Pop or Jaw Breaker? I can't remember which is which."

"You know the Kōhaku Twins? Cool. I'm Lolli Pop, the sweet one."

"The Kōhaku Twins?" Scott couldn't help feeling out-of-the-loop, as though everyone else was speaking a different language.

"Dude," Tony said.

"It's manga," Katie said.

"Do you know Casey Armbruster?" Tony said. "He and I went to high school together."

Katie shook her head, doing a remarkable job at pretending to consider the name. "Doesn't ring a bell. They keep us pretty busy in Fashion Design."

"Too bad. Casey is *crazy*."

"Who's the other twin?" Scott said, trying hard to maintain eye contact. Mary Lynn's cheerleading costume was supposed to be one of the old-fashioned, conservative ones, except that it was several sizes too small. Her ribs pressed against the slender top every time she inhaled, which also caused it to ride up enough that two inches of perfect flesh showed at her waistband.

"Mary Wardell, of course."

"Man, she is *hot* in that spandex get-up," Tony added.

They both laughed at Scott's confusion, then Mary Lynn said, "You're too easy. Aubrey's Jaw Breaker."

Scott took Katie's arm for real this time and pushed past the jokers and into the kitchen. A dozen empty wine bottles stood beneath the kitchen table, which held reinforcements—wine, vodka, whiskey, a bottle of tequila covered in dirty fingerprints— and a smattering of red pistachio shells. The room was hot, stiflingly so, and when he looked around, he saw that someone had set the oven to broil even though nothing was inside it.

"Nice friends you've got," Katie said, taking off her overcoat. She'd warned him that the dress was a bit too flapperish for Nora Charles, but it was the best she could do under the circumstances. It was black with silver fringe that swished against her knees, along the hem line, and a modest V in the front that accentuated her chest even as it covered it completely. When had every young woman he knew become so attractive? He was the same slightly paunchy young man he'd been when he'd arrived at CC, but the girls he'd started with, like Mary Lynn, had transformed from pale, skinny coeds into full-fledged women. Now he was faced with Katie Sutherland—note that last name, he reminded himself—a seventeen-year-old—note her age, he also reminded himself—who could easily pass for a college senior, and not just because of her poise and fashion sense.

"Tony's not so bad, as long as there aren't any girls around. And Mary Lynn. . . . Well, you met her."

"If you can't say anything nice?" Katie smiled. Even her smile was great, he noticed.

"You want a drink? It seems a shame to carry these things all this way and not put anything in them." He poured the old-fashioned glass half-full of whisky and topped it off with a couple of ice cubes.

"Anything clear and non-alcoholic."

"Clear?"

"Like a martini. For character."

He gave her club soda and said, "Now we enter the lion's den."

1970s era Stevie Wonder blared through the house, courtesy of Derek, DJing for the third straight year, which made it difficult for Scott to say anything to Katie. Instead, he just pointed whenever they approached a cracked floorboard or waved in the direction of something he thought might be of interest. Sophomores he didn't know had congregated in the hallway, sitting against the walls and stretching their feet before them, which left almost no space for them to walk.

English House had passed down from senior class to senior class for eighteen years, alternating roughly between men and women, and the decor matched the current random assortment of tenants. They passed movie posters for *Reservoir Dogs*, *Amelie*, and *The Matrix*, a retro Guinness ad, and several years' worth of WordFest banners in varying degrees of intactness. Each room was painted a different color, the living room walls different shades of green—mint, chartreuse, lime—depending on what colors were cheapest when the walls needed to be touched-up. The furniture was much the same, as cohesive as the storeroom at Goodwill, where much of it had been found.

Derek, in 60s-era Amiri Baraka proletarian garb, complete with watch cap, nodded at Scott when he and Katie entered the room. He was perched on the arm of a threadbare captain's chair, talking to Genevieve Browning, a junior, who was lost amid the chair's sagging cushions and Derek's intensity. Before Scott could return the nod, Mary appeared next to him, definitely not in spandex, and said, "Poor girl. Holly Golightly was the wrong choice for this crowd. Derek's the third guy to go after her."

"He's been fawning over her ever since she recited the opening of *Howl* at the poetry reading last month," Scott said, shaking his head in his best approximation of *rueful*. Around

Katie, he couldn't help behaving as though everything he did was on display. "He told me she's got the voice of a chain-smoking fallen angel."

"Ah, the soul of a poet."

Katie leaned around Scott to look at Mary, on the other side, and said, "Audrey Hepburn's like blood in the water for guys. I went to a party as Sabrina last year. The effect wasn't far off."

Scott could imagine. He reminded himself, for the tenth time, of Katie's situation. That's what he was calling it, her situation; it saved him from going into all the ways she was off-limits.

Mary looked at Katie for a second and said, "Hepburn had the perfect combination of sex goddess and girl-next-door. But Genny probably just thought the clothes were cool." Scott couldn't figure out the implication, if there was one, in her assessment. "I'm Mary, by the way."

"How many of you are there? You're the third Mary I've heard about in fifteen minutes."

"Second, actually." Scott had no idea how to explain without potentially offending Mary, who could be prickly. "Mary Lynn and Tony made a joke about you being dressed as . . . what's her name?"

"Jawbreaker," Katie said.

"Right."

Mary looked away, surveying the room. "I wouldn't be caught dead in that get-up."

Scott studied her. She had on the same thing she'd worn to class. Jeans and a green cardigan over a beige t-shirt, the lone addition being an adhesive name tag. Beneath *Hello, My Name Is*, she'd written *Not Marian Evans*. "George Eliot. Clever."

She smiled. "Thought I'd get into the spirit this year."

"I don't get it," Katie said.

"George Eliot was a pen name. Marian Evans was her real name, though she didn't like to use it, even when she was famous."

"Cool," Katie said.

"I'm not much for dressing up. But you two? Wow." To his surprise, Mary seemed genuinely impressed by their outfits.

"Katie's a seamstress, and a designer. She did these—"

The front door banged open, revealing Randy Burkas, standing before them, posed like Superman. He'd been growing a beard for weeks, claiming it was for his costume, but he'd shaved it down to a mustache and soul patch sometime after classes had ended that day. He had on a corduroy blazer with brown slacks barely a shade lighter—giving the effect of a truly unfashionable suit—and a dark brown tie. He'd grayed his hair at the temples and done something to his shoes to appear taller. "Settle down now," he said. "And cut all this Stevie Wonder nonsense. Ever heard of The Smiths? New Order? *That's* music." As he walked into the house, Scott noticed a copy of *Tristram Shandy* peeking out of a front jacket pocket. It was Dr. Sutherland's favorite book, as The Smiths were his favorite band, and brown seemingly his favorite color.

Mary rolled her eyes. "I guess we know who'll win the costume prize."

He tried not to, but he couldn't help looking at Katie, who was staring at Randy so intently she didn't notice Scott, right next to her. He brushed a hand along her bare arm, aiming for concern, and whispered, "You okay?"

"I got my dad to stop wearing brown-on-brown when I was, like, ten," she muttered. "This guy's too cheap to spring for something classier. A good houndstooth—"

Aubrey emerged from the bathroom and raced toward faux Dr. Sutherland. As much as he tried not to, Scott couldn't help watching her sports-bra and short-shorts clad figure bounce past him, Lycra allowing everything to jiggle seductively.

"Ah, the Halloween tradition," Mary said.

Derek materialized next to them, throwing an arm around Scott. "I don't know about you all," he said. "But I, and the entire Black Arts Movement, support them."

"That's what it's all about. Forget artistic respect or basic human rights. Focus on the tits."

"Why, Mary Wardell, I do believe you've learned something at this decadent, over-priced institution of higher indoctrination." Derek patted Scott on the shoulder and left, calling, "Dr. S, can I talk to you about an extension on my *Crusoe* paper?"

Randy scoffed. "I finished my dissertation while my wife was eleven months pregnant. Do you mean to tell me you can't complete a measly five-page paper by the agreed upon date?"

"You must be totally lost right now," Mary said to Katie.

"I'm catching on."

"Randy's doing a comprehensively inaccurate portrayal of Dr. Sutherland, our History of the Novel professor," she said. As an aside, she added, "I liked what you said in class, Scott. But I'm not convinced the subtitle's as optimistic as you might have it."

"How so?"

"Think about that phrase, *Virtue Rewarded*. What if virtue is just a means to an end?"

"I'm not sure I follow." He often found himself in this position with Mary.

"Here's Pamela, relatively poor, hired as a servant, with nothing to offer in terms of eighteenth-century exchange culture *except* her virtue."

"So it's a test? Squire B only marries her because she remains virtuous for so long?"

"Not exactly."

Katie jumped in, stepping between the two of them. "If she sleeps with the squire right away, she's like every other woman he goes after. Waiting makes her special."

Mary nodded. "Therefore, she's *rewarded* with marriage and all the gifts that come with it, just like she would have been if she and her family had held a greater position in society."

"Kind of cynical," he said.

Mary looked at the ceiling, frustrated by how slow he was to come around. "Has anyone ever been as goodie-two-shoes as this chick? Even Dorothea Brooke is tempered by the whole Casaubon-Ladislaw love-triangle. But Richardson's got Pamela so far up on this pedestal that there have to be cracks somewhere."

"I hadn't thought of it that way," he said.

"You should. How about right now, while Katie and I get another drink."

Left alone, Scott looked around the room, at the group of sophomores clamoring for attention from Randy Burkas-as-Dr. Sutherland, at the student-poets listening to Derek recite one of his poems. Tony and Mary Lynn hadn't come back inside, which wasn't a surprise, considering how many mornings of late he'd awoken to find her eating breakfast in their kitchen in nothing but one of Tony's retro hockey jerseys. He could have sworn he'd heard them going at it one night up on the roof, above his bedroom.

He realized, standing in the middle of his living room, that he would have been more comfortable working a catering event or sitting in the library, inching his way through the canon in preparation for the GRE subject test—though what was the point after his meeting with Dr. Delacroix? He didn't mind talking to these people before and after class, but he had no interest in engaging them in a meaningful conversation, not even Derek, with whom he'd often stayed up late debating the merits of Pound and Eliot. The superficiality wore him out. Not one of them, except perhaps Mary, could listen to his graduate school conundrum and offer anything more useful than, "Dude, you're obsessing." And if they couldn't help with the big stuff, why bother discussing anything?

Randy had retaken the spotlight. "You ever notice," he said. "That Dr. S is a pair of six-shooters away from looking like a Wild West gunslinger?"

"Yeah!" someone Scott didn't know said.

"Totally," came from another such person.

Scott couldn't help himself. "Aren't the guns, by themselves, the definition of a gunslinger?"

Randy frowned. "That's enough of that Mr. Kenney," he said, doing his best imitation of Professor Sutherland's deep voice. "We're having a serious discussion. We don't need you fucking it up with all your *thinking*."

"You know *Deadwood?*" one of the sophomores said. "Dr. S would have made an awesome Sheriff Bullock."

Genevieve Browning shook her head. "I hate historical stuff. Isn't there enough going on right now for Hollywood to focus on?"

"What I'm *saying*," Randy said. "Is that Dr. S is almost cool."

"I bet he was a bad-ass in college," Derek said.

Randy saluted that comment with a tip of his beer bottle. "That must be why a certain co-ed has a big-time crush on him."

"I do not!" Aubrey said. "And what if I did? He's kind of cute, for an old guy."

"Have you seen him at the gym? He hits the treadmill so hard it sounds like it's going to collapse." Genevieve demonstrated, her ballet flats slapping against the hardwood floors.

He turned and saw Mary W and Katie in the doorway, listening. Katie looked a little troubled by the way Scott's fellow students were discussing her father. He walked over to address what was going on, but she spoke before he could say anything. "My sister's way into jazz. She played me this song by some Mingus guy called 'If Charlie Parker Were a Gunslinger, There'd Be a Whole Lot of Dead Copycats.' I'm not sure who Charlie Parker is, but it seems like the same could be said of your Dr. Sutherland, if he found out about this."

Scott sucked on ice cubes, the whiskey long gone, and wondered if this was a threat. When he'd invited her to the party, he hadn't thought about what would happen if her parents' names came up. Of course, he hadn't thought that dumb-ass Randy Burkas would show up dressed as her father, either.

"Dr. Sutherland knows who here is worth his time and who isn't," Mary said. "And everybody knows about Aubrey's crush. She's done everything but write *I Love You* on her eyelids."

Tony Hubble came into the rooming, surprisingly unencumbered by Mary Lynn's presence, and said, "You guys hear that somebody killed Kennedy?"

"Yeah," Mary said. "Lee Harvey Oswald. Then Jack Ruby killed him."

"Unless it was all a CIA or mafia or communist plot," Scott said.

"Don't forget Bobby Kennedy," she added. "Considering how much he loved LBJ, I'm sure he was dying to get his brother out of the way."

"I'm serious," Tony said. "Somebody in *The Service* walked right up to the president and—*blam!*" He slapped the doorframe for emphasis. "There goes JFK's head."

Mary turned to Scott. "Don't tell me you play that game, too."

"It's a stress reliever," he said, not adding that until his sophomore year, when he'd taken Dr. Delacroix's African-American Literature course, it had been a grade reliever as well. He was the only person he knew who got better grades in upper level classes than he had in the general education requirements he'd barely passed his first three semesters.

Mary shook her head. "Assuming this is worthy of discussion, isn't the whole point of the game to protect the Commander-in-Chief?"

"Exactly," Tony said "Though if they ever add the Reagan shooting, I'm going to save that Brady dude and let the president fend for himself."

Scott said, "So why would someone kill Kennedy? It doesn't make sense."

Tony's passion, which he never held for class, came out as he said, "Must be a real nut job. Even the racists and the white supremacists have left Lincoln alone. But this guy wiped out his whole *team*."

"Probably looking for attention," Mary said. "Everybody wants their fifteen seconds of internet glory."

"Or he was bored with the game," Katie said. "I can see where it might get repetitive, if you play it enough times."

"Sorry," Tony said, "but you'd still have to be seriously deranged to want to blow the smile off that purdy face." He frowned, looked to either side of him, and then added, "Anybody see Mary Lynn?"

"I'm with Katie," Mary said. "That game has got to get old after a while. How many ways can you possibly save Kennedy or Lincoln?"

"'There are more things in heaven and earth than are found in your philosophy, Horatio.'"

"Look at Tony," Mary said. "He learned something in four years of college."

Twelve

After throwing up for the second time, Rob went looking for Herman, his reluctant host. If asked, Rob would have cited his colleague as his closest friend, but he hadn't realized until he'd appeared on his doorstep around midnight the night before that he'd rarely been inside Herman's house. A low-ceilinged, brick one-story formerly owned by CC, the college president had given him a sweetheart deal as the final enticement during his hiring. The inside wasn't much to look at, even in Rob's hungover state, just a series of plain rectangular rooms, all painted white, containing smatterings of furniture.

He couldn't remember everything that had been said the night before, couldn't call to mind every detail of the two hours of butting heads that had preceded his flight to Herman's. Just thinking her name—Molly—made him angry. After a few drinks, he'd sought her out, deciding that they needed to have it out, at least about the damn car, for real this time. But the smug, bemused way she had looked at him as he asked her, repeatedly, what fucking world she lived in where one spouse bought a car—an obviously expensive, antique one, no less—without ever mentioning it to her partner infuriated him. *Partner.* When he'd hit on that word, emphasized everything it *should* mean, she'd ratcheted up the condescension.

"That's the most that can be said of us," she'd said. "Even on a good day." He'd been about to disagree when he realized that would only egg her on further "Look around, Rob. We're only partners in the way two strangers who get trapped together in an avalanche are."

What's the avalanche, he'd wanted to ask, our children? Our relationship? But he'd known better, remained mute in the face of her ridiculous metaphor. Instead of speaking, he'd pounded even more whiskey, one after the other, until the buzz from the cocktail party was back, until it was definitely not a good idea for him to get behind the wheel and drive the thirteen minutes to Herman's house, which he'd done anyway.

He couldn't find Herman anywhere. He'd wandered every room, poking his head in the man's bedroom, where he'd found the bed made and the shower faucet dripping. His friend's breakfast dishes lay in the sink, and the coffee pot was full of fresh coffee, but Herman had vanished. Finally, he opened the basement door, and found himself assaulted by a *shucking* sound that pulsed like his throbbing head.

"So this is where all the money goes," he said, standing on the landing halfway down the stairs. Most of the semi-finished basement was dedicated to an enormous model train layout, the kind Rob had only seen in Christmas displays at the mall. Four or five—he couldn't keep the number straight—trains worked outer and inner loops around an impressive urban landscape. It didn't contain miniature trees or grass, but it was filled with buildings—houses, factories, high-rises, stadiums— and a grid of streets. Even two of the walls had been covered with landscape-style wallpaper.

Herman sat at a drafting table overlooking the entire operation. But he had his head down over a yellow legal pad where he was madly writing with the Montblanc he reserved for his scholarly work. A stack of books—all of them about Ann Petrie, his latest obsession—sat to his left, just beyond an enormous beaker of coffee. The man hadn't been kidding about having graphomania.

"I would have put odds on you sleeping through the entire day's festivities," Herman said, not looking up. "Hope I didn't wake you."

"You mind? Those things sound like they've bored a tunnel through my head."

Herman reached over to a laptop on the edge of the layout, hit a few keys, and the trains eased to a halt. "They help me think," he said. "Like white noise."

"You never told me about this."

His friend studied him; one of his patented smirks creeped up from his lips to the corners of his eyes. "You think it's fun being a Black professor at CC? Try adding *model-train enthusiast* to your rep."

"I'd say *obsessive*."

He dropped the pen on the notepad and swiveled in his chair. "That's what I mean. What's his name, over in Modern Languages, has a dozen Spanish guitars, goes to Seville every summer to study with some octogenarian, but *I'm* obsessive. He's just a devotee."

"I'm too worn out to argue."

"Speaking of which, put down that coffee and get some orange juice. You need vitamins, not caffeine."

"I think I need to die." He'd meant for it to sound funny.

He smiled. "That's one way to go."

"Did I say anything completely idiotic last night?"

"Nothing I haven't heard before."

"Tell me about this thing," he said.

Herman stood up, walked him around the layout, which was a scale representation of the Pittsburgh of his youth, in the early-sixties. He'd paid handsomely for replicas of Forbes Field, former home of the Pirates and Steelers, and Pitt's Cathedral of Learning, where he'd spent his undergraduate days. He had laid all of the track himself, arranging lines on three levels so that he could run up to six trains at a time. Idle locomotives sat in the round house, ready to be called into service, and more trains lined the shelves opposite the layout. Rob guessed there must be at least three hundred.

"How long did this take?"

"I'm still tinkering. Might strip it all down and update it. Today's Pittsburgh is more attractive. Could be nice to have that for a change. Anyway, it's about the work, not the end result."

"Thanks for putting me up."

"Forget it." Herman sounded friendly but didn't look away from the layout.

"I didn't know where else to go."

Herman looked disgustingly refreshed, light-blue button-down shirt and pressed gray slacks, leather Oxfords on his feet. "You might want to consider bowing out on some of this weekend. You look like you could use a respite."

"A respite?" It came out sounding weaker than he would have liked.

"Unless you want your breakdown to happen in front of all these students and alums."

Breakdown? Was that what was going on? If anyone was having a breakdown, it was Molly. That fucking car. Coming home two hours late, in an outfit he'd never seen before, the type of clothes she'd never worn, not on their early dates when they were trying to impress each other, not to their wedding, or her classes at CC. He'd have to check with Katie, but he suspected she hadn't been wearing one vegan item when she'd turned up. Katie. Robin. He needed to find out how the girls were holding up. But first, he let Herman lead him upstairs for a Bloody Mary and a big breakfast.

Herman removed vacuum-sealed hash browns from the freezer, cracked three eggs into a bowl, scrambled them with a flourish of whole milk, salt, and pepper, and poured them into a sizzling pan. The kitchen seemed to be the one room that had been updated, with polished, stainless steel appliances. A row of copper-bottomed pots hung above the island in the middle where Rob sat, drinking alternately from a tall glass of orange juice and a slightly shorter one filled with tomato juice and vodka. Every time he took a sip from the juice, Herman topped it off.

He and Molly used to do this sort of thing for each other in graduate school. They'd met during her first year, when he was serving as a peer mentor. Even at twenty-two, she'd had more poise and focus than most of the advanced PhD students in his department, and he was charmed by her decision to go into philosophy. She was obviously bright, with a working knowledge of everything from physics to economics, yet she'd chosen the least practical, highest-risk field he could think of. Once they'd moved in together—by spring break of that year, though he didn't give up his lease until after school ended— their townhouse became the epicenter for the high-achieving, hard-partying sect of the Graduate School in the Humanities.

Most nights, study groups convened in their living room while, in the two bedrooms, smaller groups listened to ABDs read from the latest chapters of their dissertations. Everyone secretly hoped for a positive response from Molly, who flitted from room to room, always asking the pertinent, challenging question no one had thought of. Meanwhile, Rob mixed drinks, refilled bowls of chips and dip, railed against scholars who treated Laurence Sterne as the first postmodernist, discussed the traditional approach to the history of the novel and several newer, even more fascinating, revisions. Every day had brought new discoveries—thanks to his reading and his new relationship—and no matter how hungover, he awoke hopeful and energized, if only to face back-to-back sections of first-year composition. Even on a good day, his reserves were low now.

"Eat," Herman said. Rob had zoned out, not realizing that

his breakfast was off the stovetop and on a plate before him. "You need to soak up all that whiskey."

The hash browns were perfect, the eggs a mass of peaks and valleys. "I haven't had animal products in years. Molly says she can smell a deli sandwich on me if I get it for lunch. Now that she's flouncing around in alligator-skin pumps, maybe that ban has lifted."

"You're not missing much, in terms of deli sandwiches. Tell me when you really want to go off the rails. I'll make you a *coq au vin*."

"I didn't know you were a foodie." He grimaced at the term, afraid that he'd offend his friend, as he had with the *obsessive* comment.

"After thirty years on my own, I'm done eating fast food and microwave dinners," he said. "And cooking for yourself means if you mess up, no one's the wiser."

"I never do anything alone anymore." Another pathetic comment.

"Again, you're not missing much."

Herman's curtness pushed him away from the precipice of a pity party. He seemed so well-adjusted, both resigned to and satisfied with his lot in life. Rob had been too, he thought, but now he couldn't separate acceptance from denial.

"Tell me about this car. You weren't making any sense last night."

"It's a yellow Mustang. It's looks like the one in *Bullitt*. It'll probably be the end of me."

"Doesn't have to be." Herman scooped a forkful of potatoes from the corner of Rob's plate. "Assuming she really did buy it from a private dealer, she wasn't going to get a bank loan on the spur of the moment, so she must have figured out a way to swing the cost."

"She claims the woman wanted to unload it cheaply to spite her ex. But doing that in this economy? When she could easily get thirty grand for it?"

"Must be a hell of a car."

"That's the other thing. How's it going to look when she starts cruising around campus in it? She drives too fast as it is." He thought of the tickets, a glove compartment's worth of them, that she'd gotten over the years, most of which had been forgiven, at least the ones from campus police, once they found out she was married to a professor and not merely a lowly adjunct. "I can just picture her flying down River Run, taking the turns on two wheels. She'll be worse than the undergrads."

Another smirk from Herman. "She won't be boring."

"Are you saying I'm boring?"

"We're both boring. Most people here are. Maybe Molly's the last of the true eccentrics."

"She hit me on Thursday night," he admitted. "With a book, not her fist. But it was a big fucking book."

Herman didn't laugh, though he did smile, which Rob appreciated.

"I honestly can't remember how it came to this."

"Little by little, I imagine."

Rob had meant that one instance, but Herman took the long view so readily it made him wonder how many people had been noting the deterioration of his marriage from afar.

"I called her on her shit one time, and she drilled me. Turns out she had a job interview on the other side of the state, which she sprung on me only once she was confident she was going to get the job."

"At least she's doing something."

"Planning her escape. I know her job here sucks, but I've done everything I can think of to make her life better. And she rewards me with secrecy and a bullshit Mustang."

"It'll put Strelzik and his old Jaguar in its place."

"I'm glad you're amused."

Herman sat up and removed the napkin from his lap. "What do you want me to say? Let's go talk to social services about filing spousal abuse charges? Get a restraining order against your big, scary wife? You've got a foot on her. You should have ducked."

"We were practically right next to each other."

"That's your first mistake, getting within arm's reach." Herman cleared the plate and utensils. "You want anything else?" After Rob shook his head, jarring loose another bolt of pain, Herman added, "So this job?"

"It's at Rocky Mount."

"Good school."

"That's what I said, right before I mentioned that it's five hours away. She's got it in her head that just because she's got more publications than Harold fucking Bloom, they're going to give it to her without a PhD, at which point she'll abandon us."

"She said that?" Herman turned away from the sink to study him.

"I'm a professional literary critic. I know how to read between the lines. If she forgets about us so thoroughly that she can rationalize buying this car, how insignificant will we be when she's hours away? She'll have a boyfriend within three months."

"Better him than you, from the sound of things. You don't have to answer this, but what, beyond habit, is keeping you two together?"

"You wouldn't understand. You don't have kids."

"Neither of you seem that preoccupied with yours." He turned on the sink, letting the water heat up before scrubbing the plate in his hand.

Rob realized that he hadn't checked on Robin before he'd left, had no idea where Katie was. For all he knew, the pair had taken their mother's keys and were joyriding around town.

"I'm not giving up," he said. "Not after twenty years."

"Then tell me what's worth saving."

It had to be an illusion. The lump behind his ear felt like it was throbbing. He refused to give in and touch it. Instead, he stared out the window, where a black bird dive-bombed a hapless squirrel. He wasn't trying to ignore Herman. He just didn't know where to begin. How could he sum up twenty years? Maybe if he were a poet, like Renee, he could pinpoint a handful of moments and assemble them into something meaningful. But as a wildly hung-over academic, he lacked the resources.

Thirteen

K atie watched the sun creep along the floor through slitted eyes, illuminating massive dust bunnies she hadn't noticed the previous night, and fresh wine and beer stains so thick she could feel their stickiness from across the room. She was still drunk, though not on the two glasses of mixed-berry vodka she'd finished. She was drunk on kissing, on what a book her mother had once given her called *heavy petting*. It had gone on for hours, it seemed, buried among the coats on Scott's bed. Later, it continued in the hallway before ending on the couch in the living room once their hosts had announced their intentions to go to sleep. By that time, the party had broken up, the roommates off in their various directions, with various hook-ups, all except for poor Scott. Even that idiot dressed as her father had left with someone. She could still conjure the red-wine taste of Mary's mouth, the woolly feel of her tongue, and the wooden look of her teeth. She'd never made out with a college student before, and only kissed two girls previously, but these minor imperfections made it even more memorable, more lascivious.

Mary stirred, drawing her closer beneath their blanket, and Katie opened her eyes all the way. Scott's roommates, Derek and Tony, stood in the doorway, staring so intently she was surprised she hadn't felt their eyes on her sooner. She pointed toward a chair across the room and whispered, "Hand me my dress," relishing her power over these young men.

Tony, barefoot, in baggy shorts and a green, long-sleeved T-shirt that read, EAT BERTHA'S MUSSELS, brought the dress to her without making eye contact. Her shoes were missing, along with her stockings—no loss, now that she remembered how many runs she'd gotten the night before—so she shifted out of Mary's embrace and stood before the guys in her slip, newly confident. She'd always liked her body. A lady out of time, that's what her father called her when he saw her at her sewing machine, one of Robin's scratchy Art Tatum recordings on the stereo. She pulled the dress over her head, shimmied it into place, and zipped it up at the side. Too bad she hadn't put the zipper in the back. She figured she could have gotten Tony and Derek to fight over who got to zip it up.

In the kitchen, she sorted through boxes of cereal until she found one that didn't look like a relic from the previous year's tenants, poured a heap of it into a bowl, and discovered that the refrigerator contained no milk, and little besides leftover beer—foreign and domestic, regular, light, and ultra, dark and IPA. She crunched Frosted Flakes and tried to remember how she'd ended up half-naked with homely Mary. The girl was smart, no doubt about it. Katie had enjoyed listening to her debate *Pamela* with Scott. Their give-and-take, how engaged they were even at a party filled with loud music and too many people, proved what bullshit Randy's performance as her father had been. If he could get two people this interested in a 250-year-old novel, he couldn't be the buffoon he'd been portrayed as.

At some point she'd begun drinking, not something she did regularly. She remembered talking about Virginia Woolf, Mary's favorite writer. Katie had read *To the Lighthouse*, one of the few novels her mother actually admitted to enjoying, and they discussed the weird middle section, which Katie hadn't been able to work out. "It's like the house itself is telling the story," she'd said. "But why not jump forward and fit all of that in as you go along?" Before she could follow-up her own question, she realized that Mary was standing much closer and staring at her lips. She'd seen the same look on the faces of boys from school, back when they invited her on dates and to dances, before she'd become a pariah. She knew what it meant. Shifting to one side, she let her hip come to rest against Mary's—where had this confidence come from, she'd wondered at the time—and when Mary had reciprocated, she'd reached out and rested a hand against the small of her back, lightly enough to seem accidental in case she was rebuffed.

She wasn't. Soon they were on their way down the hallway, hand-in-hand, looking for an open room. They stumbled across Tony and Mary Lynn in one bedroom and a couple she hadn't met in another before ending up in Scott's room. She had no idea where he was and didn't stop to consider whether or not she'd be hurting his feelings. Mary was too good a kisser, and before she knew it, she'd stripped off the I Am Not Marian Evans name tag, along with the sweater it was attached to. Mary's full breasts, corralled beneath a distressingly unfashionable bra, pressed against the thin satin of Katie's dress, and within minutes, they were all over each other.

Minutes, perhaps hours, later, the party began to break up, people pulling their coats from beneath the young women's bodies. Katie couldn't remember getting to the couch but assumed they'd crab-walked, lips still pressed together. She wasn't sure where such overwhelming desire came from—from listening to her parents' fight, from the sudden awareness of how lonely she'd become, from the headiness of being attractive to someone so much older and more mature? Her parents would have told her to be introspective, to analyze her feelings, to get to the root of this atypical behavior, but she pushed them from her mind and dove further into Mary's mouth.

Scott shuffled into the kitchen in jeans and a t-shirt. When he saw her, he looked away, and though she followed him around the room with her eyes, he kept his down, focused on whatever he was doing—pouring coffee grounds into a filter, adding water to the carafe, filling a mug, anything that kept him away from the table. With his back still turned, she said, "Sorry about last night. I mean, I know I came with you and all—"

"It's not like we're together." He'd interrupted her too quickly.

"I know, but. . . . Would you mind turning around, so I can see you while we're talking?"

"It's okay," he said as he shifted from the counter to a seat at the table. "I was doing you a favor, remember? You wanted to get out of the house. Forget about. . . ." He waved a hand in the direction of her home, where everyone—even her father—must have been awake by now. Had they noticed she was missing yet? "I'm glad I could help," he said.

She studied his face. He looked puffy, his eyes rimmed with red, but she couldn't tell how much of it was sleep deprivation. She hated feeling so full of herself, assuming that he was into her and therefore disappointed that she'd chosen Mary instead. But she'd seen the way people looked at her—not just at school, but in town, even some of her father's colleagues, though not Dr. Delacroix, who always behaved like a friend, not a pervy uncle—especially in the last year or so. Her mother had warned her about this when she'd bought Katie her first bra, a thoroughly embarrassing conversation at the time but one that had turned out to be prescient.

"The slightest hint of sexuality and men will look at you as a pair of tits, a nice ass, or a pretty face," she'd said. "Figure out which ones see more than just those individual parts and get rid of the rest of them." That's what she liked about Dr. Delacroix.

Even more, that's what she liked about other girls. They might size each other up, but they weren't beholden to cup sizes or some plasticized, feminine ideal, to use her mother's term.

Scott spoke first. "Does she know?"

"She still thinks I'm your cousin."

"Are you going to tell her?"

"I haven't decided." Truthfully, she'd intended to slink off after she got dressed. She wasn't certain she'd ever be ready to go back there. If only there were some way to rescue Robin, some humanitarian sibling relocation program.

"You know what we were talking about last night, about *The Service?*" she said. "I was the one who shot Kennedy."

"No, you weren't." He poured a cup of coffee and sat at the table. When she didn't respond to his challenge, he said, "*You* killed Kennedy?"

She told him her username and avatar and described how it had happened in enough detail that he'd know she was telling the truth. "I don't know why I did it," she said. "I was bored. I was annoyed at the people I was playing with. I was tired of everyone online always wanting to play Kennedy."

"No one realizes that even Garfield and McKinley can be fun if you do them right."

"You just have to think about it, challenge yourself to try a different approach," she said. "I could tell that everyone had lined up perfectly, the way they always do, and that we were going to get Oswald. Then everyone would be all, 'That was a close one!' and 'Way to go, team!' But if you watch the Zapruder film or read about how it actually went down, you see all the chaos and confusion. I wanted to feel that excitement again."

"Did it work?"

She shook her head. "People just got *mad.* I knew they wouldn't understand, so I logged off. I think that was my farewell to *The Service.*"

"Maybe you could talk to Wykoff. Seeing how he looks up to Dr. Sutherland, he'd probably be happy to hear your ideas."

"Shit. I didn't even think about him being here." She imagined explaining that she had screwed up his game; surely he had heard by now. She imagined him taking back the big donation her father had been obsessing over. "For now, let's keep this between us," she said.

"Maybe he'll write you into the next edition, make a meta version where gamers have to stop both Oswald and Katie Sutherland in order to win."

"Yeah, right." She trusted Scott, though she couldn't say why. Though he'd been weirded-out by her encounter with Mary at first, he seemed to be coming around. She didn't see him as a gossip, so she told him her suspicions. "My Dad never said one word about Wykoff until after that video went viral. Then he started talking shit whenever he saw me playing *The Service*."

"I understand." She listened while he described the story Renee had told him, about Evan Wykoff, obnoxious Shakespearean. "I've had three classes with your father, and he's never done *anything* like that. Maybe he's softened with age."

"I always thought he was being a snob. But it sounds like he really doesn't like the guy."

Scott shrugged. "Maybe he'll storm the stage this afternoon."

"That would be awesome."

"What would?" Mary stood in the doorway.

"I was telling her about Dr. S., what he said about Evan Wykoff yesterday."

"Why is everyone so obsessed with him?"

"I said Dr. S. might rush the stage in protest."

When Mary walked by, on her way to the coffee maker, she brushed her fingertips along Katie's shoulder blades. Katie shivered in response.

"Doesn't sound like Dr. S.," Mary said. "Might have to get Randy to do it for him."

"You don't think he could be confrontational?" Katie said. As strange as it felt, she liked knowing how others saw her father. He had the teaching awards and tenure, but if teaching was a performance, as he said, then his students had the best sense of what he was like away from home.

"He does really great in a room full of students, where he's obviously the authority. But in the real world? I bet Ms. Calloway—his wife—deals with everything and pays the bills."

"But she's an academic, too," Scott said.

"It's different for women. They still have to work so hard just to be treated equally. Men like Sutherland see being professors as extended adolescence."

What the fuck do you know? Katie wanted to say. *My father might act like a fool, but he really cares.* Instead, she said, "Sounds like the people here last night like him, anyway."

"As long as you trust the inmates' assessments of the asylum."

"That's not fair." Finally, Scott had spoken up. "We've both had dozens of profs. How many can you name who are better in the classroom? As for outside it, we can't know for sure." He glanced at Katie. "You're just spouting stereotypes."

"Jeez, Scott. I didn't mean to offend. I'm just saying it's harder for women. Our idiot classmates call Professor Calloway *Mrs. Sutherland*, as though there's something wrong with her asserting her identity, especially when she's smarter than her husband."

"But she doesn't compare as a teacher."

Mary dismissed this line of argument. "Not when she's stuck teaching logic all the time."

"I had Sutherland for Freshman Comp, and it was obvious then that he was great."

Good for you, Katie thought. She tried to lighten the mood. "Maybe Mary just has a crush on Professor Calloway."

Mary didn't blush. "She is hot. But I like my women with a bit of a figure."

Katie smiled. Mary wasn't her usual type, but she liked hearing that she fit the bill just the same.

Fourteen

The Library and Technology Center opened early on Homecoming Saturday to accommodate alums who wanted to explore the college's latest addition, but Scott was still the only person waiting when the doors were unlocked at nine. A half hour earlier, once Katie and Mary had left, he'd gone to *The Paris Review* website to read Renee's poems, only to find that they were paywalled. He didn't know enough about literary journals to decide whether or not this was a good thing. Perhaps she was a big deal, and the editors kept her poems in reserve to entice people to pay for the journal. But some of the free poems from the latest issue were by a recent Pulitzer Prize winner.

Climbing the stairs to the library's second floor, he felt just as mixed-up as he had when he'd set off on his quest. Not because of Katie Sutherland. Well, not because of her *exclusively*. He'd known from the start that she was off-limits. She was four years younger than him, and a minor on top of that. And she was Dr. Sutherland's daughter. She'd turned out to be more substantial than he'd first thought, with her obsession with fashion and her bedroom walls filled with cut-outs from glossy magazines. She seemed so relaxed, even at the party, among people she'd never seen before. And he'd been surprised by her opinions about books and video games, especially once Mary had arrived on the scene.

Now he couldn't remember *why* he'd declared her off-limits. Perhaps it had to do with his roommates' assessment on their way out the door to the weekly Saturday morning Ultimate Frisbee game. "No offense, dude," Tony had said. "But your cousin is hot."

Derek concurred. "I don't normally go for white chicks—" a total fabrication, at least on campus, where he'd have dated his way out of eligible partners by the end of sophomore year— "but that girl could start a war between city-states. Like Helen of Troy?"

He hadn't declared her off-limits for any principled reason, he decided, but preemptively, because he knew she was attractive enough to be completely uninterested in him. But then she let Mary maul her while half the English department looked on. Scott hated the way Tony and Derek talked about women, *You know that Nursing major with the ass like a ripe peach? Man, I want to set up camp in Holly's rack and just live there.* As he'd watched the new couple leave his house that morning, still hand in hand, he'd decided to view the night before as a call to arms. Enough sitting on the sidelines, enough waiting for what he wanted to come to him. Going after Renee seemed almost feasible. And he was counting on her poetry being his angle.

He walked along the shelves of Current Periodicals, passing *Pediatric Nursing, Parade*, and *Parenting Today* before coming to *The Paris Review.* The newest copy sat face-out, the remaining copies from that year stacked beneath it. But this one looked nothing like the image he'd seen on the journal's homepage. The one with Renee's poems was red, with a black-and-white image of an old-time lamp post, at night, in the mist and rain, like something out of *The Third Man*. This one was green, with a photograph of kids running on a graffitied playground.

Though the Library and Information Technology Center had been open more than a year, Scott would forever associate it with massive piles of dirt, constant hammering, and a mechanical pounding so loud that it woke him from a dead sleep every morning, even from the other side of campus. They'd broken ground the summer before his freshman year, but a variety of problems pushed the completion date back almost a year. This meant that Scott had spent more than half of his college years listening to dump trucks and cement mixers doing their thing, the all-hours shouts of laborers, and, above all, the idling and revving of engines, the beep-beep-beeping of vehicles moving in reverse. Even now, standing amid the polished glass and gleaming metal of the finished building, the thought of all that noise almost drowned out its grandeur.

Downstairs, he learned that the library had received the latest issue but hadn't processed it yet. "The webcams in the multimedia lab have been on the fritz," the librarian told him. "In order to get those back online, we've had to triage." When he asked if he could see the issue long enough to read a few pages, the librarian frowned. "I'm not sure where it is."

He left the librarian, passed the Friends of the Library breakfast in the first-floor café, and headed out the door. From the library steps, he could look down the row at the Engineering and Business buildings, to his left, and the enormous Performing Arts Center, on the right. Across from the library sat the Student Center. He'd heard that it would be the next building to be replaced, though he wasn't sure why.

If anything, the Humanities or Social Sciences buildings should be replaced. Neither was handicapped accessible above the first floor. Every Monday morning, the water in the bathrooms was orange with rust. And both buildings were cold when they should be hot, hot when they should be cold, and so humid that the walls beaded with sweat in the spring and early fall. No, the ten-year-old Student Center, that was the problem. Once they built a new one, CC would be right up there with Duke and Chapel Hill.

For the first time, he understood the dazed looks on the faces of alums when they came back for Homecoming. In only four years, the school had opened the Library and Information Technology Center and the new Performing Arts building, enclosed the open end of the football stadium, and added a wing to the Student Recreation Center. He couldn't imagine what it would be like to have graduated twenty-five years earlier, when New Quad was nothing but a tree-lined knoll and the football stadium was a green field with metal bleachers on two sides. At the rate they were going, in ten more years the entire school would be a series of space stations, orbiting Mars.

When he arrived in front of Kreider, he was somewhat surprised to find the door unlocked. The Kreider computer lab had closed to force students to use the new facilities at Ledbetter, so there was no reason for the building to be open so early on a Saturday or for Dr. Sutherland's car to be in the lot out back. But there was no reason for Scott to be there either. No reason except for his quest to find those poems. Childe Scott to the Professor's Office Came.

His knock was greeted by a half-groan, half-throat clearing that he took for a *come in*. Inside, Dr. Sutherland sat at his desk, one hand gripping a coffee mug, the other pressing a chemical ice pack to his forehead. Sutherland offered the better part of a smile and said, "I rallied for a bit this morning. Must have taken the last of my reserves."

"Can I get you anything?"

"No," he said. Then, pausing to think about it, he added, "What do you give a drowning man?"

"A life preserver?"

"I'll have one of those."

Scott tried to hide his discomfort. He could still smell alcohol on his professor. He took the seat that Dr. Sutherland offered with the waggling of his fingers. The professor was pale, a look exacerbated by uneven gray stubble. The only other color on his face came from his bloodshot, watery eyes. The man looked like hell, bad enough that he should be in bed, not sitting upright in his office with a stack of papers before him.

Dr. Sutherland noticed the direction of Scott's eyes and said, "My students would prefer I did this drunk, but hungover is the best they're going to get. And, just so you know, I'd never do this with papers from a seminar."

"Not that it's my business, but I usually feel better if I, you know, throw up?"

"Feeling my mortality, I suppose." He sighed. "I don't care what anyone says about age being just a number. As soon as I turned forty, it was like a door closed behind me, barring me from everything I used to enjoy. Don't look at me like that. I'm serious. One night of hard drinking and look at me."

"There have to be positives, right?"

"My kids, for sure. You met them, right?"

He nodded, refraining from dredging up any of his own memories from the night before.

"The older they get, the more fascinating they become. Just yesterday, Robin announced that she's *maybe-probably-definitely* a genius on the piano. She spouts off the names of old jazz guys like they're family members we see every year at Christmas."

"And Katie?"

"I wish she'd choose something more serious to be interested in, but when I was her age, I thought I'd be a psychiatrist, so who knows? She's a hell of a seamstress, though, and more focused than ninety-five-percent of my students."

"So your kids, that's something. And your job?" Scott knew he didn't have to bother, but he'd always been a pleaser, the giver of pep talks and the lender of an ear.

"I feel too lousy to bullshit, so here it is. The unvarnished truth. President Vessey and his underlings assured us that the Great Recession would be a boon for us, that we'd end up with all the kids who could go to pricier schools but were now nervous about the debt. It would be like an intellectual stimulus package, and all we had to do was keep our tuition reasonable and wait for the applications to roll in."

"Isn't that kind of harsh?"

"I used to think so. The attitude now is, why should someone spend a hundred grand on college if it doesn't prepare them to step right into a six-figure career? On the first day of the semester, I actually had someone ask me how taking my survey of British literature was going to help him. In his mind, everything outside of his Business Administration or Mechanical Engineering classes is extraneous. Why read Boswell's *Life of Johnson* unless you're training to be a raconteur?" Sutherland flipped the ice pack over and pressed it against the back of his head. "I swear to God, this headache is *moving*. We need to talk about something else, something more pleasant."

"Why did you decide to become a professor?"

"That's better," he said, though Scott wasn't sure if he meant the subject matter or the ice-pack. "Second semester of my freshman year, I took a British lit course with this old guy, Eric Hoagly. He was short, barely five-five, and bald, with this enormously bushy beard. He wore threadbare sweaters with leather shoulder and elbow patches and corduroys with holes in the back pockets from where his wallet sat. A truly comical figure. As he paced the room lecturing, without ever referring to his notes, he'd oh-so-casually dip his fingers into the bags of candy sitting in front of the students and pop a jelly bean or two into his mouth or crunch on a peanut M&M."

"How did people react?"

"Are you kidding? We loved it! We brought so much candy I'm surprised we didn't make him diabetic. What I admired was the way he carried himself. My science professors behaved as though they were chained to their textbooks. Forget wandering around the room during a lecture. They couldn't step away from the podium. Hoagly cared enough to truly know the subject matter, and even when he taught something he admitted he didn't care for—Blake, say—he did it with enough passion that we ended up liking it *for* him."

"That's how I feel about Dr. Delacroix," Scott said, without meaning to. "I mean, I like your classes—"

"We're being honest here, right? He's a hell of a teacher and an amazing scholar." Sutherland dropped the ice pack to his desk. "What are you doing here, this early on a Saturday?"

"I came to get my car," he said, trying not to look as uncomfortable as he felt. "When I saw *your* car, I thought—"

"Nice of you to check on me."

That's not what he'd meant. Scott hadn't considered Dr. Sutherland's feelings on his way up the stairs. But he knew better than to disabuse the man of the notion. He said, "Remember last night, how you said Renee Dunhill had some poems in *The Paris Review?*"

"A talented woman. She was well on her way even as an undergrad. Never had any confidence, though."

"The library's copy isn't available, so I was wondering if I could borrow yours."

"Of course," Sutherland said, heaving himself up out of his chair. "It's around here somewhere."

That's what Scott had been afraid of. Dr. Sutherland's disorganization was legendary. At various times, the professor had joked that he'd arranged the books by height or color or in order of purchase, but no such system, no system at all, seemed to prevail. As the two of them scanned the shelves, Sutherland from the top, Scott from the bottom, he found back issues of *The Paris Review* wedged into various places, but none from the most recent three years.

"You've got quite a collection," he said, to interrupt his Professor's grumbling.

"Started reading it in college. Back then, I fancied myself a budding writer. Where the hell is that damn thing?"

"It's okay, really. Maybe someone else has it."

"In this department? Half of them read nothing but fantasy novels. The rest, like Dr. Strelzik, prefer their reading, even their *pleasure* reading, with a whiff of mustiness and decay." Sutherland pulled a book from the top shelf. "Here it is! Wait, this one's from *last* fall. Some excellent work in it, though, if you're interested."

"I mainly want to read Renee's poems."

"In ten years, I'll be telling some smitten coed all about *you*."

"I'm not smitten," he said, though he could feel himself blushing from his ears down to his throat.

"You just happened to be wandering around campus on Homecoming morning in search of a semi-obscure literary journal with no ulterior motive?"

He smiled. "Maybe a little smitten. I thought if I read her poems, I'd have something to talk about with her."

"I never took you for a Casanova, Mr. Kenney, but that's an excellent strategy. Unfortunately, your strategy is running into the harsh reality of my organizational system."

"I'm not trying to sleep with her," he said. He was only so direct because his professor seemed to be giving him half his attention. "She seems interesting in a way none of the girls on campus are."

"Don't sell them short." Sutherland handed him a stack of books without looking, and then continued. "If interesting is what you're after, you can't do much better than Mary Wardell. That young lady has all kinds of ideas."

"I know," he said, trying to beat back the image of Mary and Dr. Sutherland's daughter tussling on the couch in his living room.

"I'm writing a recommendation for her for grad school. Unfortunately, she's gone over to the dark side. Composition Studies. That's where the jobs are, but considering how much she likes Fanny Burney, I thought I had a budding eighteenth-centuryist in my midst."

"She's going to grad school?"

"And Derek's applying in creative writing. But I'm sure you knew that."

"Yeah." He set the books on the corner of Sutherland's desk. The man seemed to have forgotten that he'd given them to him, filling in the space they'd opened with books from another shelf. When another stack of books came his way, Scott said, "I should probably be going."

"What about you, Mr. Kenney? Considering grad school?" Before he could respond, Sutherland added, "Herman and I think you're plenty talented."

He set the new stack of books on top of the previous ones, resisting the urge to knock them all to the floor. *Are you guys messing with my head on purpose,* he wanted to ask. Twenty-four-hours earlier, Dr. Delacroix had dashed the one hope he'd had for life post-graduation. Now, Sutherland acted like he and Delacroix were the founding members of the Scott Kenney Fan Club. "

I know you're enamored with contemporary literature," his professor said. "But you could always fold that into a broader interest in the development of the novel. Twentieth-century literature is a saturated field."

More books came his way. If he didn't get out of there soon, he'd spend all of Homecoming helping Dr. Sutherland reorganize his office.

"It's been a while since someone wrote a historical survey of the novel that truly grapples with race. Herman would know better than I, but I'd say you're in a good position to do something to correct that oversight."

He couldn't take it any longer. "Dr. Delacroix doesn't share your opinion, actually." While his professor was turning his bloodshot eyes on him, Scott added, "I mean, he's not as *enamored* with the grad school idea as you are."

Sutherland sighed and said, "You know why Dr. Delacroix is here, don't you?"

"He filled me in."

"The phrase, *putting your money where your mouth is* comes to mind. But his opinion isn't shared by all. Jobs do exist."

"So why...." He didn't know what question to ask first. *Why did Dr. Delacroix flat-out refuse to help me? Why didn't I cast my lot with you in the first place?*

"Don't think about it too much. At least, not yet. For all we know, you'll hate graduate school and leave early, like the famed Evan Wykoff." Sutherland paused before adding, "I think I need to throw up again."

Dr. Sutherland pushed past him before he had time to get out of the man's way. He hit Scott's shoulder hard, sending him backwards into the piles of books. Sutherland didn't even stop. He swung open the door and rushed down the hallway so quickly that the door slammed shut with the momentum of his flight, leaving Scott alone, surrounded by twenty-five years' worth of books that spanned the history of English literature.

He stooped to collect the books that had fallen and found the latest issue of *The Paris Review* tucked between a book on rakes in the eighteenth century and a series of lectures dedicated to a long-dead Defoe scholar. He scanned the Table of Contents, confirmed that Renee's poems were inside, and headed for the door.

Fifteen

When she'd found out she was pregnant with Katie, Molly had been a twenty-four-year-old philosophy graduate student, the only woman in her year, one of three in the program. Like the others, she'd dealt with the sexism, both of the casual and creepy varieties, that was seemingly inherent in her field. The male professors typically fell into one of two camps: those who ignored her as an intellectual being and those who actively sought to get in her pants. So when her gynecologist confirmed what multiple pregnancy tests had already indicated, she sought out her two female professors for advice. Rob had frozen at the news. He alternated between panic at the thought of having a child and fear that he, always *he*, would never get to finish his all-important work.

Dr. Praeger, the more senior professor, looked at her with disappointment. "I hope this wasn't planned," she said, once it had sunk in. Molly could barely shake her head under the Aristotelian's withering gaze. Dr. Praeger sighed, took off her glasses, and studied Molly. The woman, in her late-fifties, had perpetual bags under her eyes, and Molly could see the circles, likes bruises, and broken capillaries that accompanied those bags. It all felt like visual proof of the adage that women had to work twice as hard as men to get ahead in academia. Finally, Dr. Praeger laid her hands flat on the desk and said, "I was going to put your name up for a Belt Fellowship, but now. . . ." She shook her head. "I suppose Erin will have to do. Unless you're going to. . . ." Dr. Praeger didn't bother to finish the statement, merely dismissed Molly without another thought.

The department's other female professor, Dr. Hullett, closed her office door as soon as Molly announced her news. "Jesus, Molly. What are you going to do?" she said.

"That's sort of why I'm here."

"*I'm* not planning on having a baby until I get tenure. *You* haven't even finished coursework."

She did the math quickly, knowing that Dr. Hullett had begun teaching the same year she'd been accepted into the graduate program. The older woman would be thirty-eight when she got tenure, in her forties by the time she reached full professor. Molly would be twenty-five when her baby was born.

"Have you told anyone else?"

She knew she couldn't tell her about Dr. Praeger without risking a crying jag—she'd become so emotional lately, no longer the Ice Queen—so she lied. "I thought you would be the best person to talk to." But she could tell already that just because she was younger than Dr. Praeger didn't mean that she would be more sympathetic.

And why should she have been? Molly had sat through seminars where PhD students treated Dr. Hullett as though she were the cleaning lady, an unnecessary intrusion, not the professor. Students who deferred to the male professors on everything from thesis topics to the best place to get a drink after class referred to Dr. Hullett by her first name and commented freely on her attire. At least Dr. Praeger had attained stature simply by surviving twenty-two years at the

University. Where the older professor pulled no punches, assumed that all graduate students were simpletons until proven otherwise, Dr. Hullett tried soft power. She had her students over for dinner. "Not a bad cook," one of them had told Molly, "so she has that going for her."

In her office, she gaped at Molly with a combination of fear and confusion she hadn't seen even on Rob's face. The woman looked as though she worried the condition might be contagious. "You can't tell anyone," she said.

"It'll be obvious, after a while."

"Not if you have it taken care of. You *are* having an abortion, aren't you?"

Molly truly had considered it. As pro-choice as she was, though, she felt that something more than mere inconvenience should be at the root of that decision. She could plead financial hardship, but she knew that for all of his scholarly pretensions, Rob would drop out of school and dig ditches if that were the only way to support them.

"You're braver than me," Dr. Hullett said. "Congratulations, I guess."

The bigger she grew, the less attention anyone paid to her, as though the more physical space she took up, the less room there was for intellectual engagement. The more predatory of the male faculty—*the Kings Leer*, Rob called them—seemed to forget she was even in class once she'd expanded to elasticized maternity-jean proportions. Once, as an experiment, she'd kept her hand raised for an entire class period, just to see if Dr. Longley would call on her. He didn't even bother passing over her, simply ignored her entire side of the room. The same went for her fellow students. She was the best logician among her cohort, but she found herself frozen out of reading groups and went unconsidered when students were putting together panels for conferences. "You've got enough on your hands," she was told. Or, "who's going to breastfeed your little one if you're at Berkeley with us?"

Once Katie was born, she did her best to keep up. Rob, who had pledged to do half the work, quickly grew impatient and begged out of diaper changings and middle-of-the-night feedings to finish preparing for his exams. "Once I'm ABD, I'll have more time," he promised. But then he had deadlines for his prospectus, and for chapters of his dissertation, and constantly came upon Calls for Papers. "If I don't put myself out there," he said every time they argued, "I might as well give up. I'll never survive the job search otherwise." She wanted to remind him that she was still, technically, a graduate student as well, that she'd received a university fellowship her first year, not just the departmental funding that he'd made do with, and now she was limping along at half-pace while struggling to keep Katie clothed and fed.

Her dirty little secret was that she liked taking care of Katie, that as much as she acted put-upon whenever Rob spent the weekend in the library or came home late from a departmental function, she could barely stifle her jealousy whenever he did chip in. She wanted to do everything herself, experience each milestone in Katie's development. She liked being the one who could decipher their daughter's needs. And Katie responded in kind. She was Molly's shadow, opting to be held by her mother, or to follow her around once she was crawling, even when Rob did try to dote on her. But the more time she spent with Katie, the further behind she fell. She barely completed the requirements for an M.A. before she timed-out of the program and was only a few courses into her PhD when Rob got the job at CC. In retrospect, maybe she should have taken Rob up on his offer to take care of Katie while she remained at grad school. But she'd been loath to miss-out on so many milestones and had convinced herself, at the time, that she wouldn't regret the decision.

Then Robin came along, and Molly was in danger of becoming what she hadn't wanted to be: a professional Mom. All anyone wanted to talk to her about were her kids. At

University events, she found herself exiled to the wives' corner, discussing which grocery store had the best deals on dry goods or the freshest produce and parsing the latest episode of *Dora the Explorer*. No matter that by then she was teaching two courses per semester while juggling the vast majority of the child-care responsibilities. Even her colleagues greeted the appearance of each of her articles with the kind of astonishment they would have shown if the family cocker spaniel were to suddenly begin speaking Elizabethan English.

Nevertheless, she'd survived the elimination of her department precisely because she was so inconsequential; the school could pay her measly adjunct salary without feeling the pinch a tenure-track line would have necessitated. Meanwhile, the girls grew older, both of them in school, and Molly became so prolific that the chair of Social Sciences had hinted on more than one occasion that she was making the full-time faculty look bad.

She'd been presenting at a conference outside Atlanta the previous spring when the chairwoman from Rocky Mount had approached her about the visiting professorship. No guarantees, the woman had said, but Molly's publication record and more than ten years' teaching experience might make up for the lack of a PhD. And the visiting appointment was the tip of the iceberg. If all went well, the school would be opening another tenure line in the near future. An established candidate would have an inside track. Molly hadn't realized how much she'd coveted such a position until that conversation. Suddenly, her introductory logic courses became depressingly insignificant. The relief she'd always felt at avoiding university service turned into frustration at her inability to help shape the direction of the school.

She couldn't explain why she'd kept this from Rob. Perhaps it had to do with how satisfied he was with his place at CC. Years ago, before Robin had been born, he'd talked about the school as a stepping stone. Neither of them wanted to be academic guns-for-hire, jumping from job to job every time a better offer came along, but that didn't mean they had to stagnate. Surely if he'd been a little more ambitious, Rob could have lifted himself out of the inertia that had kept them in Elgin for so long. Every time he won a college award, or advanced in rank, she felt a little less hopeful, until she feared she'd spend the rest of her life teaching the same classes, semester after semester, forever being known as Mrs. Robert Sutherland, hanger-on. The job at Rocky Mount was a chance to get out.

Such thoughts occupied more and more of Molly's waking hours as she graded another set of mediocre logic problems, buoying her spirits when the burdens of family life got her down. *I'm doing this for all of us,* she'd almost convinced herself.

This refrain ran through her mind while she sat at the kitchen table on Saturday morning, missing half of her family. Molly had never wanted to be the type of overbearing mother who expected her daughters to tell her everything, to be her best friends. Her own mother had ruined their relationship with the pressure of such an illusion. But she hadn't realized how easy it was to take a hands-off approach until that strategy backfired and led to Katie disappearing for an entire night. Here it was, almost ten o'clock, and Molly was still waiting for the girl to come home.

She couldn't help blaming Rob. The Mustang was bound to be a tough sell, but he'd gone off the deep end over it. She'd tried to coax him into her study, where they could continue fighting in private, but he was so wound up he wouldn't listen. He pointed toward the window, toward the car, and then at her outfit. "The All-New Molly Calloway. Unencumbered by husband and children, she'll be free to tool around Rocky Mount in her sports car. Too bad it isn't a convertible."

She'd looked down at her purse, on the couch, where the rest of her winnings lay nestled among stray tissues and the scraps of paper that collected throughout the week. She considered throwing the bank-strapped bills at her husband, either to get everything out in the open or as the final shock, the one that would send him completely over the edge. Instead, she gathered her purse and school bag together and walked toward the study.

Now, Robin tried out chord progressions on the piano in that study, letting each collection of notes ring until it died out before moving on to the next one, repeating the same series of chords, with only minor alterations, over and over, until it was all Molly could do not to scream at her to stop. The girl had been quiet, despondent, since the night before. Amid the chaos, Molly had failed to look in on her in time, and once she'd calmed down enough to see how her youngest was holding up after Mrs. Humphreys' intrusion, she'd found Robin asleep, on top of her bedspread, still dressed as Jackie Kennedy.

She was about to get up and go into her study, sit down at the bench next to her daughter, and promise they'd spend the day together, when she heard the front door open. From her perch in the kitchen, she could see the lower half of the entry-way, where Katie padded across the carpet barefoot, high heels in one hand, pantyhose in the other. Her feet were covered with grass clippings and dirt. Katie climbed the stairs and lingered in the hallway. Thanks to the split-level design of their ranch house, she couldn't get to her room without passing the kitchen.

"I hope you had a good time," she said when the girl finally emerged. She had on the same dress from the night before, a Katie Sutherland Original, and it was clear that the dress, at least, had seen better days. Her daughter, though, looked remarkably fresh.

"Where's Dad?"

"You were with that boy, Steve?"

"His name's Scott. Jesus, Mom. He was in your class."

Thankfully, Robin had stopped with the chord progressions and moved on to a Bach fugue.

Katie moved into the room, leaving a trail of pine needles in her wake. She poured the last of the coffee into a mug and added almond milk, her movements as graceful as a dancer's, as calculated as a stage actor's. When she continued on to the freezer, where she removed a slice of bread from a bag, Molly had had enough.

"You've had all night to come up with an excuse, so it better be a good one."

Katie shrugged, her back to her mother. She had broad shoulders, accentuated by the backless dress. Molly remembered them fighting over how low cut it was, negotiating the amount of skin it had to cover with the assiduousness of warring countries discussing reparations.

"I'm waiting," she said. When Katie still didn't respond, she added, "Forget the damn toast."

The girl sighed—it must be hard, having such a schoolmarm for a mother, Molly thought. Finally, she said, "I went to the English party with Scott. I thought you and Dad needed some space."

"And here I thought you were being irresponsible."

"It's not like I'd planned it. And in case you're wondering, you scared the shit out of Scott."

"Poor boy." She tried not to smile. She remembered him now, how meek he'd been in class. "I figured you, of all people, would appreciate the addition of a third car to the family."

"You're right. My life will be totally different now that I have a crappy station wagon of my own." She crunched on her toast. "You run Dad off?" she said.

"Your father left shortly after you did. He at least told me where he was going."

"Somewhere far away from here, I imagine."

"And miss the adulation of Homecoming Weekend?"

Katie gave her a remarkably withering look, for her age. "You should have heard all the people last night who went on about how Professor Calloway's logic class totally changed their lives."

"That's right," she said, warming to a familiar topic. "If they're not up on their desks reciting poetry, the teacher must be shit."

Katie shrugged again and started to stand up. Molly grabbed her wrist, firmly, until she settled down again.

Robin had moved on from Bach to—was it Schubert? One of the Impromptus?

"And don't worry about the station wagon. It's going to be a *long* time before you have to slum around in that old thing."

As always with her daughters, the minute she felt like she had the upper hand, she grew remorseful. Katie was a good big sister, more responsible than the majority of her students. She thought about all the babysitting Katie had done over the years, unbidden, the intense concerts she'd sat through in the study.

At the piano, Robin abandoned her lessons altogether, moving on to a rollicking, bass-heavy version of "St. Louis Blues." Her tastes had become increasingly avant-garde, but occasionally she still let loose with some of the stride piano that Molly preferred listening to.

Looking down, Molly realized she hadn't let go of Katie's wrist, had been stroking the inside of it, idly, with her first two fingers, as she had when the girl had been a cuddly toddler, curled against her watching *Sesame Street*. Before letting go, she offered her best attempt at a truce. "I wouldn't have cared that you went, if you'd asked. I went to the occasional college party at your age, too."

"For purely analytical purposes, I'm sure."

"Naturally." Smiling, she added, "I was trying to solve the alcohol-hangover dichotomy."

"I'm not hungover." The denial combined with a flicker of a smile. "Not compared to *Dad*."

Now they shared a full-fledged smile, the kind of conspiratorial look that Rob often complained about. "I'm already outnumbered," he'd said recently. "Don't go turning Robin against me, too." It wasn't Molly's fault that he asked for it, poked fun at Katie's fashion sense and whined about the *hen house* he lived in.

"I'd be amazed if your father can focus on a line of print right now without needing to vomit."

"Thank God he isn't here, then."

Robin trudged into the room, stomping even without shoes on her feet. She marched to the beat of the tune she was humming, something jaunty and angular, most likely Thelonious Monk, her favorite pianist. At least he'd been her favorite a week ago, which was no guarantee. "Where is Daddy?" the girl said. "I'm almost ready to debut my new piece." She didn't wait for a response. She sang, "bump-ba-*dum*" repeatedly and pirouetted out of the room. It was impossible not to love her. The good feeling was infectious, leading Molly to ignore her disappointment with her older daughter.

"What do you say we go for a ride," she said. And Katie, who had previously shown nothing but disdain for her mother's latest purchase, agreed without hesitation.

Sixteen

Banners flapped in the breeze that swept through the open end of Old Quad. Standing on the front steps of his building, Rob had to struggle for a moment to stay upright even though his equilibrium had returned to normal and he'd endured the past hour without resorting to caffeine, ice packs, or vomiting. He'd also graded half a dozen more papers and avoided Betsy Mullins, who'd been trolling the halls in search of more warm bodies for the department's Visit Day table. As much as he appreciated Herman's hospitality, he wasn't about to waste two hours sitting with him while they answered questions about why the department didn't offer credit for AP scores.

Instead, he gathered his coat around him and set out for the Faculty Dining Hall. The buffet table sat against a glass wall looking out on the Student Dining Hall, and though he'd told himself not to, Rob couldn't help studying the faces at the smattering of occupied tables. He'd told himself not to because the last thing he wanted after spending the morning grading horrid papers was to run into the writers of such disastrous prose. Since it was the morning after Halloween, however, the undergrads were still tucked in their beds. The tables were full of alums who had made the nostalgic, albeit culinarily suspect, decision to eat breakfast in the cafeteria.

Rob stopped in front of a table overlooking the quad, where a group of ten-year grads sat sipping coffee while powdered eggs congealed on the plates before them. The group looked up in unison, all of them noting their old professor with smiles and shakes of their heads, the two men among them standing up to greet him.

"Dr. S.," Trent Fulton said. "We weren't sure you'd still be upright after last night." Trent had married a fellow English major, Judy Koestler, in the University chapel the weekend after graduating. She looked to be six months pregnant, by the bump pressing into her lap.

"You were in rare form last night," Corey Diski, the other man at the table, said as he went to fetch a chair.

"I wasn't that bad, was I?" Rob looked from Trent to Judy to Renee Dunhill, the last, and quietest, member of the quartet.

"The last I remember," Trent said. "You were reciting 'Ozymandias.' After that, it gets a little foggy for me, too. That young man behind the bar had a very liberal way with the liquor."

"Scott," Renee said. "He was nice."

"You made quite an impression on him as well," Rob said. Renee blushed.

Judy saved him from doing himself any serious harm. "We still haven't seen your wife. Is she here?"

"Judy still owes Ms. Calloway a paper on first-order logic."

Judy slapped his arm. "I'm fairly certain she's forgotten about that by now, Trent."

"I wouldn't count on it," Corey said. "Remember the way she hounded Michelle when she missed the midterm?"

"She had mono!"

Rob cleared his throat. "If I recall, she didn't want Ms. Nyberg to lose out on Phi Beta Kappa. She meant well, in her way."

"Sorry, Dr. S. Sometimes I forget that you two are married."

"I understand completely," he said.

Renee squinted at him over the top of her coffee mug, showing off a pair of budding crow's feet. "Trouble at home?" she said.

"Not at all," he said.

Rob's former students fell quiet, eyeing each other as they fiddled with empty coffee cups. While Rob knew he'd talked to Renee the night before, he couldn't remember what they'd spoken about. As for the other three, he wasn't sure that he'd seen them since the Koestler-Fulton wedding ten years earlier.

The more he thought about the night before, the foggier his memory became. He remembered enjoying a few too many glasses of Scotch with Herman, vaguely recalled switching to beer at the cocktail reception, and then . . . nothing. Until he woke up, at home, to the sound of Molly's latest purchase in the driveway.

Thinking about it raised his ire all over again. Her ridiculous explanation, the even more ridiculous sum of money she claimed she'd paid for it. But if it had cost what it was worth, and she truly had gotten it from the previous owner, where had the money come from? He shouldn't have had so much to drink, certainly shouldn't have compounded the problem by adding whiskey to the fire once he and Molly had begun arguing.

The group had moved on to discussing Evan Wykoff, who'd been missing from the previous night's festivities and had yet to make an appearance.

"President Vessey has him squirreled-away," Corey explained. "He doesn't want to give him a chance to reconsider his big gift."

They all looked to Rob, either out of anticipation or suspicion, he wasn't sure.

"Seems to me all the i's should be dotted by now," Trent said.

"So none of you have seen him?" Rob said as casually as possible.

"I got a text last night," Corey said. "Reminding me that we're all supposed to sit together at the game."

"As though we're the ones who might forget," Judy said.

Renee shook her head. "He's got a lot on his mind."

"I'll trade places with him."

Judy's gaze passed over her husband and settled on Renee.

"Have you heard from him, Professor?" Corey said.

"I'm as in the dark as the rest of you," he said. Rob remembered Evan and Corey as being inseparable as students, the rare case of first-year roommates who actually hit it off. He'd never understood why. Corey Diski, who went on to be a Fulbright scholar before entering seminary, had been so much more earnest than his compatriot, the kind of young man who asked for summer reading recommendations from professors, and then came back in the fall prepared to discuss the suggested texts. He always had one more article to read, one more point to consider, before he put pen to paper, as opposed to Evan, who was never at a loss for opinions of his own, who seemed burdened by the need to consider outside sources.

Trent had been the hanger-on from the start, the average student who took his association with his smarter classmates as confirmation of his own intelligence. He'd latched onto Judy in the same way. They'd been classmates in Rob's Introduction to Literary Theory course. Unlike her husband, Judy had been able to keep up with Corey and Evan, Renee and Michelle Nyberg, the sharpest group he'd encountered at CC. In fact, they'd ruined the course for him. He could even remember some of the topics of their final essays: Renee on Modernism and Bloom's *Anxiety of Influence*, Corey's Deconstructionist reading of Revelation, even Evan's unoriginal psychoanalytic reading of *Hamlet*.

" . . . was the last time I saw him," Corey said. "It must have been a year ago."

"You see each other often?" Renee said.

"We try to, but now that he's gone Hollywood, he's harder to get a hold of."

"That last movie wasn't half bad," Judy said. "Did you see it, Professor?"

"Refresh my memory," he said. He knew he hadn't seen it, though not solely out of snobbery. He rarely made it to the theater, and when he watched something at home, it was most likely not of his own choosing. Still, he drew the line at mindless action movies.

"It's the first adaptation of the Arthurian legend that holds up to Bulfinch," Judy said. At least she still remembered something she'd learned at CC.

"Be that as it may, I rarely make the viewing choices at home," he admitted.

"How are the kids?" Renee said. "Robin must be getting ready for college by now."

"Katie, actually. And she's more interested in fashion school than in anything academic, I'm afraid. It's positively killing her mother."

Judy sat up straighter. "Fashion can be intellectual, can't it?"

"Spoken by someone who reads *InStyle*," her husband said.

"What about serious books?" Rob said, trying to avert a marital spat, even if it wasn't his own. "What's everyone been reading lately?"

"No time," Trent said. "Between work and the kids, we're tapped out by the end of the day."

Corey nodded along. "My parish recently began a volunteer challenge with Habitat for Humanity. Just the thought of holding a hammer gives me callouses."

"And you, Renee?"

"I just read Rae Armantrout's latest collection. It made me want to give up, it was so good."

Rob felt utterly without hope. Here were the brightest minds he'd taught in the last fifteen years, and they were comparing poetry to movies. If this was all his influence came to, what was the point, he wondered.

"I heard Evan's next game is going to be a horror-suspense one. Maybe he'll do a take-off on *The Turn of the Screw*, Professor."

Rob glared at Trent, who seemed oblivious.

"Actually," Corey said. "They're working on a game about Afghanistan and Iraq. You didn't hear it from me, but I believe it'll be called *Jihad*."

"Catchy title," Trent said.

Renee shook her head. "Isn't there enough war in the news?"

"First-person shooters are all the rage," Trent, the expert, said. "And who doesn't want to take out a bunch of Taliban pricks?"

As the group devolved into a debate about video games and violence, Rob said his goodbyes. Outside again, he turned up the collar of his sport coat, meager defense against the wind ripping through the quad, and headed back to his office. At some point, he had to go home. He'd been wearing the same clothes for close to thirty hours, and he could smell the alcohol seeping out of his pores. A shower and a change of clothing were in order. But not yet.

Seventeen

Her mother downshifted into third gear, and the Mustang lunged forward, gripping the asphalt as it came out of the turn on the twisty county road. They were surrounded by fields of cotton and hay and cow pastures that went by in a blur as Katie concentrated all of her mental powers on keeping the car on the road. Her mother had turned into a maniac.

Gravel sprayed from beneath the passenger side tires as they veered onto the shoulder, and her mother turned to her and said, "I'm not scaring you, am I? This car just wants to *go*."

"And Dad thinks I'm the one he needs to worry about it." She hadn't meant to bring up her father so soon, but she pressed on. "I wonder what he's doing right now?"

"Probably sleeping it off at Herman's. That's where he was headed, Ms. Nosy Pants."

"I didn't mean it that way."

"Of course not." Her mother shifted into fourth. The engine growled in response. "Since you weren't here to eavesdrop, you were just curious."

"I don't eavesdrop. I mean, not on purpose. It's a small house."

"Tell me about it." She didn't know how to read her mother's expression. Maybe she was distracted by keeping them on the road. Maybe she knew just how much sound carried in their small house. Maybe she regretted every part of her life that had led her to Elgin.

They must have been going sixty-five, at least, though Katie refused to look at the speedometer, out of fear, and embarrassment at the prospect of getting caught.

"I know you heard us the other night. Any thoughts you'd like to share?"

"I couldn't hear that much," she lied.

"It's a small house, remember?"

"You've been arguing a lot."

The car slowed, and her mother flipped on the turn signal. In fifty yards, she made a right into a country cemetery, which she navigated in second gear, thank God. The last thing Katie wanted was an accident in a graveyard. She imagined plowing through rows upon rows of tombstones, sending them flying in their wake while the Mustang's tires threatened to dig up the long-interred. At the top of the rise in the back of the cemetery, her mother depressed the break and let the car idle in neutral.

She said, "This is for your ears only. I've received a job offer, at Rocky Mount."

"Is that in Greenville?"

"Beyond Raleigh."

"That's hours away!" She hadn't meant to, but she knew she sounded panicked. She didn't like listening to her parents argue; that didn't mean she wanted one of them to walk out.

"We're still talking ifs. *If* I accept it." She played with the gear stick, wiggling it back and forth the way she shook the mouse when her computer wouldn't respond quickly enough.

"*As if* you'll let Dad convince you to stay."

"I'd be back on weekends." She could tell even her mother found this to be a lame defense.

Maybe it was the shock, but somehow Katie doubted this. She knew her mother. Once she got used to being on her own, they'd never see her. It would be as good as a divorce, from all of them.

"You can't leave," she said, fearing she'd cry if she continued. She cleared her throat and stared out the window, at the uneven rows of tombstones. Plastic flowers in uniform pinks, blues, and yellows sat in the vases at the head of each plot. "I know we're fucked up, but you can't—"

"Listen to me." Her mother gripped the wheel. "I've been here for fifteen years, waiting for your father to do something, *anything*, to make our lives better."

"Who will look out for me and Robin?"

Her mother laughed. "You're practically out the door. As for Robin, she's tougher than she seems. She'll surprise you. Trust me." When Katie remained silent, her mother added, "She wouldn't be the first kid in history to live in a one-parent household."

"So you admit this is it. The D word."

"I don't know."

She waited for her mother to say something else, but for once, Molly Calloway remained silent. She knew her mother had suffered, but she didn't believe that her father hadn't done what he thought was best for *all* of them. She knew—from his caustic remarks and the eavesdropping she had, in fact, been doing—that the job market wasn't exactly booming. And surely by now he was making good money. Their house was a dump, their cars prehistoric, so they must be saving most of his paycheck, she figured. And while she knew her mother didn't make much, at least it was something.

"I think you're being selfish," she said, finally.

"I think you don't know what you're talking about." With that, her mother put the car in gear. "Let's talk about something more pleasant," she said. "Like the looks on the faces of all those yokels when we blew past them."

Katie shook her head, trying to bring herself back to the present. All she could think about was how long it had been since she'd seen her mother this happy. Not when she received copies of the journals she published in. Not during Robin's concerts. Not when Katie debuted her latest fashions. Not even when her father had cancelled his summer school class to take the family to New Orleans when she was fifteen. Even then, her sister had them waiting in line outside of Preservation Hall so they could stand in a firetrap listening to a bunch of geriatrics play what she called *authentic jazz*.

No, she hadn't seen her mother so happy since she was small. Back then, the four of them used to do impulsive things like New Orleans all the time. Her parents would skip their classes to take the girls strawberry picking, her father lugging baby Robin around in a harness, or they'd spend the weekend traipsing around some Civil War battlefield, Katie complaining about how *bored* she was, not realizing that she'd look back on those sunburnt, mosquito-filled trips as the good times.

As her mother brought the Mustang back to what she called *cruising speed*, Katie realized that, unless she came up with something soon, her mother would vanish.

"I know about the casino," she said. "I found a chip in your cardigan."

"You little snoop."

"I wasn't looking for it. You should be more careful."

"Doesn't matter now. This car is my goodbye present to all that."

"So it did cost more than you said!" She felt like a prosecutor catching out a cunning witness.

"I didn't say that."

"I don't hear you denying it." She couldn't believe she'd been right. The casino idea had come to her out of the blue, a long-shot that was only worth the risk on account of how much she feared she was about to lose.

"Between us, yes, it did cost more. But I didn't take one dollar out of our bank account, so it might as well have been free. I've been playing with house money for the past year. That's how good I've gotten."

"So why quit?"

"Just that I get bored, too." Her mother wouldn't understand about *The Service* even if she tried to explain it. Either she'd blow it out of proportion, call her daughter a budding sociopath, or she'd behave like what Katie had done was of no consequence, a childish reaction to a juvenile video game.

"Anything else you've uncovered, nosy?"

Katie didn't like the way her mother said this, as though everything they'd discussed was merely a series of silly jokes. She enjoyed being taken into her mother's confidence. But her mother seemed to look at it all as inconsequential, as though lying about her whereabouts, gambling with what Katie could only assume was thousands of dollars, and planning to abandon her family were minor details.

They passed an empty field containing an enormous hay bale with a smiley face painted on its side. It reminded her of her father, who often stuck his head in her door and said, "Cheer up. It's not that bad," if he saw her scowling at her sewing machine or frowning over homework. She detested this almost as much as her mother's blasé attitude.

"I think that's enough for one day," she said in response to her mother's question. She hadn't meant to, but she'd parroted the remark her mother gave at the end of class. When she was little, if she was home sick from school, her mother would drag her to Confluence. She'd sit in the otherwise-empty front row of her mother's logic classes coloring or reading to herself while her mother put her students through their paces. Each time, she would notice how her mother's enthusiasm and optimism waned in reaction to her students' inability to answer questions, to ask their own questions, to generally do more than merely occupying space in the room for fifty minutes at a time. By the end of class, when her mother had failed, once again, to infect her students with a love for logic problems in all their glorious complexity, she'd take off her glasses, sigh loudly, and say, "I think that's enough for one day."

"Then let's enjoy the ride home. Robin doesn't know what she's missing."

Robin. What was she going to do about her sister? How could she leave her alone with her father, who would most likely descend into depression without their mother around? She'd been fighting with her parents over her wish to go to design school instead of a traditional college, due to both their academic snobbery and their desire that she attend one of the schools that offered tuition-exchange with Confluence. She knew that design school would saddle her with loans, but she didn't want to be saddled with guilt, too, at the thought of her sister and her father alone in their crappy house. Robin was like an exotic flower—beautiful, temperamental, and in need of constant attention. Without Katie around to feed her enthusiasms and prune her doubts, she feared the girl would begin to wilt. And her father, as much as she loved him, wasn't the most intuitive perceiver of his daughters' needs. Her mother shifted into fourth gear and let out a yelp as the car surged forward. She had her window down, the breeze buffeting her hair and the sleeves of her sweater. She'd gone back to her usual cotton. Katie had no idea what had happened to the previous night's outfit, but she wished the change had been more substantial than just her mother's clothes.

Eighteen

When he pulled into the driveway, he was disappointed to find it empty. He'd been dreading a confrontation with his wife for so long that the lack of one irritated him almost as much as their argument had. He hadn't worked out exactly what he'd intended to say, but he knew it was going to appeal to whatever sense of family loyalty she still possessed, mixed with a heavy dose of falling on his own sword. He was prepared to accept any amount of blame, so long as she kept their foursome intact and stopped acting like a woman on the verge.

Inside, he found Robin asleep on the couch, curled on her side, hands cupped beneath one cheek in an angelic pose straight out of a Renaissance painting. He tiptoed past her and up the stairs, shutting the bathroom door behind him.

Dressed in khakis and the burgundy sweater his daughters had given him for his last birthday, he made his way back downstairs where Robin had roused herself enough to sit up and turn on the television. He couldn't remember the last time they'd all been awake without the droning of the idiot box as accompaniment. To his surprise, the minute he entered the room, she turned off the TV and looked out the window, at their next-door neighbors' house. The twins were in the yard raking leaves with their parents, the four of them chattering away, making Rob feel like even more of a failure as a parent.

He sat down next to his daughter and tried jostling her with his shoulder, a lame attempt at getting her attention. He waited a few seconds, and then said, "I'm sorry about last night."

Robin continued looking out the window, where the quartet was engaged in collecting the leaves on a large blue tarp. It would be days before the city sent someone to collect the ones they were leaving at the curb, long enough that one good wind storm would eradicate most of their hard work, but still the family seemed happy, so damned happy.

"It had nothing to do with you," he said. "Your mother and I—we aren't seeing eye-to-eye right now."

With that, Robin got up, ignoring his tugging on the hem of her sweatshirt and walked into her mother's study where she headed for the piano. Rob knew that if he didn't follow her, she could be in there for hours, between practicing and composing. He tossed Molly's cardigan on the floor and sat in the easy chair adjacent to the piano, a spot conveniently situated so that he could keep an eye on both his daughter and the driveway.

"Where are they?" he said, once his daughter had begun picking at the keys. He knew she was feeling out a new melody by the way she circled back around one basic idea, adding a few notes each time. She did this with only her pointer fingers, though Faulkenstein, who he had yet to confront about the previous day's incident, insisted that she always play with proper hand positioning.

"Mom took Katie for a ride in the new car."

"You didn't want to go?"

She blew her bangs out of her face. "Even I wouldn't fit in that backseat."

"So they left you here?"

"I have too much on my mind right now."

Too much on her mind. That had always been Robin's problem. In elementary school, they'd begun sending her to a therapist because of her anxiety. She worried about everything, both the present—what would she have to do at school that day, would the twins approve of her outfit at the bus stop—and the future—what would high school be like, would she have to change clothes in front of the other girls for gym class? The therapist had recommended visualization and breathing exercises, had suggested sports as a way to wear out her body and brain, but the only thing that had worked was piano. "Want to share?" Rob said. "I'm a pretty good listener."

The melody completed, Robin began playing block chords with her left hand as accompaniment. It still sounded rough, but Rob could hear hints of the frisson that would lead to a pristine finished version. The chords echoed the right hand that bounded up and down the keyboard, moving with an ease he'd spent hundreds of hours trying to produce on the basketball court when he was her age, to no avail.

"Just want to be alone," she said.

"Not on Homecoming, you don't. I'm meeting Dr. Delacroix for the game. Why don't you come with me?"

"I'll be in the way." She wouldn't look up, no matter how repetitive her keystrokes were.

"Hardly," he scoffed. "You'll save me from listening to him drone on about his model trains."

A slight pause this time. "He's into *trains?*"

"Can you believe it?"

"Sounds kind of cool, actually."

"I'll have him give you a tour sometime."

She crashed down on the piano with both hands, her foot slamming the sustain pedal at the same time. Sound filled the air around them, reverberating in his eardrums. She lifted the pedal and fired off a rapid run up and down the keyboard, the notes a cacophony that made little sense to him even as he knew they were exactly the ones she meant to play. She went on this way for the better part of a minute, then slammed the lid shut and hopped off the bench.

"I don't want to see his stupid trains," she said.

By the time Rob had gotten out of his wife's easy chair, Robin was halfway across the room, headed for the door. This was turning out to be more difficult than he'd imagined. In truth, he hadn't thought much of Robin in the last twenty-four hours, though he knew he should have.

"So we'll skip the game," he said. "And do something else. Whatever you want."

"I'll pass," she said.

Before he could respond, he heard Molly swing into the driveway in the Mustang. The engine growled, revving as it climbed the abbreviated incline leading to the carport. He didn't know whether he should follow Robin or wait for Molly and Katie. Why did everything have to be fucked up all at once?

Robin looked out the window at her mother and older sister, who had climbed out of the car and were walking up to the front door, then left the room and headed upstairs to her room. Rob let her go, opting to wait for the rest of his family in the living room. The door opened, and his wife and daughter entered silently, Katie first. She made for the stairs without wasting a look in his direction. Meanwhile, his wife took her time removing her coat and hanging it in the entryway.

"I see you had the same effect on Katie that I've had on Robin," he said.

She turned and said, "I told her about Rocky Mount. It didn't go over well."

"I can imagine."

"What's your excuse?"

"I don't know why Robin's so surly. Strike that. She thinks we've all forgotten about her. Except maybe her sister, who encouraged her in last night's fiasco."

"This isn't about the costume," his wife said. "She may seem oblivious, but she's the intuitive one. I'm sure she senses that something's wrong."

"Why don't we fix it, then."

She dropped into the chair opposite him and shook her head. "For once, I'm not going to let you trample my needs."

"That's a bit grand."

"Not from where I'm sitting."

"You make me seem like the villain in some Victorian novel."

She raised her chin. "I wouldn't know."

"Of course not. Your work is far too important for such trivialities."

"There you go," she said "Trying to pick a fight."

"You walked in here looking for one. Not me."

Molly slipped off one of her shoes, massaged the heel of the foot with her palm. When she showed no interest in responding, he said, "You wear out your shoe gunning the engine?"

"I was the picture of restraint. Just ask Katie."

"I'm sure you impressed her with your sense of responsibility."

She put the shoe back on and smoothed the creases in her slacks. She never wore jeans, a choice Katie supported, unlike her husband who was accused of dressing like a homeless person most weekends. She seemed thinner now that Rob was really looking at her, something he hadn't done much of lately, fearing that even a lingering glance would unleash another diatribe. Now that he thought about it, he realized she'd increased her yoga of late.

He didn't know what to say. Regardless of her attitude, he was typically the appeaser, the one who came up with elaborate ways to quell her frustrations, like Molly's Day. A truly dumb idea, he now realized, it had merely led, more than a year later, to the presence of that ridiculous car in the driveway. He may not have been willing to uproot the family and start over at another school, but at least he looked for solutions within their confined situation. Now, he had no interest in giving in. He couldn't keep his wife from pursuing that job, but he didn't have to let himself be steamrolled.

He looked out the window, noticed that all four of his neighbors had stopped raking leaves to gawk at Molly's sports car. Elgin was small enough that by Monday morning, he figured everyone would know about the Calloway-Sutherland family's purchase.

"I have grading to do," his wife said, though she made no move to get up.

"I do too. But it's Homecoming. Day of sloth. And truces, if I recall."

"Forgive me if I'm lacking in school spirit."

"I spoke to some folks this morning who would like to see you, school spirit or no."

"Sure you did." For once, she actually made eye contact. He couldn't tell if she was studying him out of a desire to know whether or not he was telling the truth, or merely to make him uncomfortable.

"Don't believe me, then. And imagine the surprise on the current crop's faces if the elusive Molly Calloway made an appearance at the football game." He feared he'd offend her with this characterization, but she smiled instead. Not much of one, but enough that he took it as a triumph.

"If you can convince the girls, I'm game," she said.

Nineteen

Scott met his roommates outside the football stadium where they made the long march to the student section on the far side of the field. Along the way, they stopped at the concessions stand to fortify themselves with hot dogs and soft drinks. But all Scott could think about was the copy of *The Paris Review* sitting on the passenger seat of his car. Though he'd had it for two hours, he had yet to read Renee's poems. Every time he cracked the spine, something got in the way. His roommates had to show him the blue Cs painted on their hairless chests. His mother chose Homecoming Saturday as the occasion for an impromptu phone call. Even Mary Wardell had pestered him with a series of texts demanding to know where he was hiding his cousin.

The stadium was a sea of blue-and-white banners and clothing, PG-rated versions of the latest dance and hip-hop tracks audible above the noise of several-thousand fans. Most games were sparsely attended. Not Homecoming. Scott saw virtually everyone he knew. He saw classmates and fellow work-study students, all of them decked out for the game in Confluence sweatshirts and windbreakers. He wished he'd changed into something with some school spirit, but it was too late. Instead, he gawked at his professors, in the typically empty faculty section opposite the students, noting that even Drs. Strelzik and Granville, who rarely showed up for English department functions, were in attendance.

Mary Wardell crashed through the crowd around them and marched up to Scott. "Where's your cousin," she said, breathless. "I thought she'd be with you."

"Check out Mary," Derek said. "I didn't realize you even knew where the stadium was."

Tony slapped Derek on the back and added, "She's here for purely anthropological purposes, to see college students in their natural environment." Spoken by someone who attended one football game a year and went home every other weekend of the semester, where he let his mother wash his clothes, prepare his meals, and, quite possibly, do his homework for him.

"Don't you mean *sociological?* Anthropology is for cultures other than your own."

"Cultures other than your own?" Tony said. "That's exactly what I'm talking about."

Mary flashed her middle finger in Tony's direction, before pulling Scott away from his roommates. What she didn't understand was that having Tony and Derek talk shit in front of her was an improvement over the snickering that typically went on behind her back. Dr. Delacroix referred to Scott's roommates as "the peanut gallery," and he was right.

Once they were out of earshot of the others, Mary said, "Where's Katie?"

"She's not big on football," he said, making up the excuse. "She had some studying to do instead."

Mary had dressed up, wearing tan corduroys and a striped sweater, minus the holes and overly stretched sleeves that characterized most of her clothes. She'd even done something with her hair, working the unruly mane into a braid that hung between her shoulder blades.

Before either of them could continue the conversation, the entire student section was abuzz with activity. At first, Scott assumed the football team had made their way onto the field, but the commotion was too great for the appearance of their 2-5 team. He looked around him, noticing that everyone had turned in the direction of the near sideline, where President Vessey strode, purposefully, next to a short, thin man in a billowing overcoat too warm for the mid-60s weather. Even from seventy yards away, Scott noticed the geometrically precise part in the man's hair and the effort it took Vessey to keep up with him. Evan Wykoff had arrived.

"Take a look at that," Derek said, slapping Tony on the shoulder. "On a scale of one-to-ten, she's at least a thirteen."

Tony nodded, without taking his eyes off the field. "It pays to be the best."

Scott had been so busy watching Wykoff and President Vessey make their way toward the stands that he hadn't noticed the woman behind them. Tall and leggy, she seemed to glide along the Astroturf on four-inch heels, her dark skirt showing off the shapeliest calves Scott had ever seen. As she negotiated the metal risers, Scott could have sworn he heard the clicking of her heels from the other side of the stadium.

"That is reason enough to give up English and go into video-game design," Derek said. If this were one of Dr. Sutherland's novels, Scott's roommates would have been in a full-blown swoon.

She followed the men into the stands and took a seat behind Wykoff, who had joined a group of English alums Scott had met the night before. Including Renee Dunhill. President Vessey shook Wykoff's hand, nodded at the woman, and headed to his regular seat at the fifty-yard line.

Wykoff shook hands and high-fived with the alums around him, who had converged on him like proverbial moths to a flame. But unlike moths, they continued to hover nearby without getting burnt. One of the poorer tippers from the night before threw an arm around Wykoff's shoulder while his pregnant wife snapped a picture with her cell phone. Others crowded into the background. Wykoff took more pictures and shook even more hands, patting some on the back, hugging others, and offered a wave to those too far from him to reach personally.

"I'm going over there," Derek said. "I feel a poem coming on."

"I'll give you twenty bucks if you do," Tony said.

"You guys are pathetic," Mary said, but even she was focused on the spectacle. So was the entire student section, which missed the long-awaited arrival of the football team, cheerleaders in back-flipping tow. The team ran onto the field, looked up at the quiet stands, and then ambled toward the sideline, having suffered their first defeat of the day.

Wykoff took off his overcoat, positioned it on the bench, and sat down. The captains of the two teams met in the center of the field for the coin toss, but Scott had no idea who had won. He was too busy watching Renee, three seats down from Wykoff. She sat between the bad tipper's wife and another woman, the lawyer she'd introduced him to the night before. Michelle Something. Renee wore another scarf, this one a pale blue somewhere between Confluence cobalt and the washed-out color of the sky. Like Wykoff's mystery guest, she had on a skirt, though hers hung loose about her thighs and stopped mid-calf. Her sweater matched the blue of her skirt. He'd have to ask Katie what made this choice look stylish instead of bland. Assuming he saw her again.

"You guys are pathetic. The game is on the field, Scott," Mary said.

"I'm not—I mean—Forget it." How could he explain that he was pining—not lusting—after a different somebody than the one Derek and Tony continued to discuss. "It's not what you think," was the best he could do.

"Sure," she said. "I'm going to buy an overpriced water. You want anything?"

"I'll take two hot dogs and a jumbo bag of Skittles," Derek said.

"Ditto," Tony added.

"Screw you guys," Mary said. She turned on her heel and trudged up the stairs.

Scott went back to studying the group in the alumni section, ignoring the kick-off and his team's near-fumble of the return. Wykoff, standing again, talked animatedly, using his hands as he did so. He was shorter than everyone around him, but they gave him a wide-enough berth that he was practically spot-lit. Scott didn't know if he was imagining it, but it seemed as though everyone in the alumni section, even Renee, leaned toward him, like flowers tilting to the sun. Everyone except for the woman behind him, who was seated, studying her phone.

Without his noticing it, Genevieve Browning had appeared next to him. She touched his arm and smiled when he looked in her direction. "I'm surprised you came," she said. "I've never seen you at a football game before."

"You're a fan?"

She reddened. "I don't have a car, so I take what I can get on campus."

"You don't go home on the weekends?"

"My parents live in Michigan, so I'm stuck here."

"I usually supervise the concessions."

She smiled, the color of her cheeks returning to normal.

The Confluence quarterback threw an interception that North Tennessee returned for a touchdown, and the crowd groaned.

"Forget Dr. S's endowed chair," Tony said. "If Wykoff wants to make a difference around here, he'll start paying for some better players."

"Why, Mr. Hubble," Derek said, mocking their professor's use of their last names. "Are you suggesting we break the sacred student-athlete covenant? What would dear Pamela say about such a recommendation?"

"That chick just needs to get laid. I'm with Squire D."

"Excuse me," Genevieve said, making room for herself among the men. "There is a lady present."

"Where? I only see you," Tony said.

Derek remained silent, which made the moment doubly awkward. As far as Scott knew, he'd spent most of the weekend with Genevieve and should have defended her.

"Squire B." Scott couldn't help it.

Derek nodded. "Do you think Dr. S assigns this crap because he's, you know, *sexually frustrated?* I can't imagine Professor Calloway is that much fun in bed."

"Seriously," Tony added. "She's probably correcting his technique the whole time."

"I bet she gives him homework."

"'Go screw five coeds, then we'll see about a make-up fuck.'"

"Very nice," Genevieve said. "Even *my* mom didn't have sex with her professors, and she went to college in the 90s."

Scott couldn't help noticing that she said the 90s as though it was a long-lost decade.

Tony and Derek began to laugh, high-fiving the way Wykoff did with those around him, providing just the cover Scott needed to slip out of his seat and up the stairs. Even Mary's sullenness was better than listening to his roommates discuss their professors' sex lives. But he realized he had no idea where Mary had gone, so he walked against the flow of traffic, headed towards concessions and the restrooms, and went in search of the Sutherlands. He knew Dr. S wouldn't miss the game and hoped that if Katie was with him, he could get to her before Mary found them together.

Twenty

While she had no problem with sports in the abstract, Molly couldn't stand the crowds that lived and died with the players' every move. Didn't it embarrass these people, red-faced and screaming, to be so invested in the fortunes of a bunch of twenty-year-olds? Even the faculty that surrounded her, along with their families, the same faculty who complained during the week about the influence of athletics on the college, stood and cheered every time the team did something the least bit noteworthy. Except for Herman, who seemed to dislike the spectacle almost as much as she did. He sat on the far side of her husband, a book in hand, underlining passages and glaring every time he was jostled by one of the more enthusiastic crowd members.

In the past, she'd admired Rob's ability to seem at home in any circumstances. He went to one football game per year, but she'd never know it from his behavior. He knew the players by sight, understood the game with a level of detail that couldn't be feigned, and even managed to infect their children with his exuberance. It was the same whenever he took her to faculty recitals and art openings, or receptions for the school's latest crop of honors' students. To borrow a phrase her own father used in reference to Frank Sinatra, it was Rob's world; everyone else just lived in it. But now, with a pinprick of light at the end of this seemingly endless tunnel, she realized that Rob's ease was one of the things holding her back. He'd never leave Confluence.

Her phone chimed in her pocket, the sound loud enough to carry above the meager cheering around her, and she pulled it out, intending to silence it but changing her mind when she saw the Rocky Mount number. It was Nita Lewen, the Chair of the Philosophy department.

"Sorry to call you on the weekend," the woman said. "But Dean Whitmore implied that you weren't as enthusiastic about the job as we'd hoped. I wanted to see if there's anything I can do."

"On the contrary," Molly said. "I was in traffic, trapped among drivers who must have passed a correspondence drivers' ed course. Trust me, I'm very enthusiastic."

Rob had turned toward her at the sound of her voice. At *very enthusiastic*, his eyebrows went up, giving him the look of a silent-movie actor.

"That's a relief," Nita said. "But we'll still need a definitive answer soon, if we're to prepare for your arrival in January. Courses are being assigned almost as we speak."

"I have to check one more box on my end," she said. "And then I'll let you know. But it shouldn't be a problem." With that, they signed off, Rob still eyeing her.

They looked at each other, neither of them willing to give in and say something while, around them, people stood up to celebrate a rare Confluence touchdown. Finally, he leaned in, brushing his lips against her hair as he searched for her ear.

"That was them, wasn't it?"

She nodded. "They offered me the job."

"Just now?"

"Yesterday. I've been thinking about it."

He tried to seem casual. "Nice of you to tell me."

"Here we are," she said, not sure even she knew what that meant.

"Yes." He drew the word out. "You want to cut the suspense?"

"Unless you can come up with a better reason, I'm going to accept. I'll call the dean on Monday morning. They're anxious to move forward."

He nodded, tight-lipped. Everyone sat down and they did the same, keeping their proximity so that the conversation could be as private as possible.

"So that's that," he said.

"I guess so."

"It's no use. I mean, if you aren't swayed by what I've already said."

"It's not the end of the world."

"Just the end of the state."

She rolled her eyes at his lame quip. Why couldn't he see this as a positive development? Why couldn't he be supportive?

The crowd cheered when the football team left the field for halftime, the score tied 7-7, and the stands began to empty as people went in search of refreshment and relief. Robin, next to her father, had caught the football bug, her eyes glassy with excitement. Katie was typically the poised one of the two. Though Robin was an independent spirit when it came to her music, she was still more susceptible to her father's charms than her older sister who'd been anxiously looking around, presumably for that boy, Scott, ever since they'd arrived.

Once the crowd had thinned, Katie said. "I'll be back in a little while."

Molly frowned. She still hadn't decided if Katie should be punished for her night out, or if the better course was to let it slide, to build up Cool Mom cred. And she hadn't had a chance to discuss it with Rob, so she shook her head and then relented. "Take Robin with you."

"Seriously?"

"I want popcorn!" her sister said, bouncing on the balls of her feet.

Molly took a ten-dollar bill out of her purse. "No soda," she said.

"I need to go alone," Katie said, leaning closer.

"These are my terms. You want out of my sight? Take Robin." She pushed the two girls towards the stairs, before shifting back to her husband.

"I can't believe I let you talk me into this," she said.

"Doesn't it warm your heart, seeing so many people united in their school spirit?"

"A modern-day *Triumph of the Will*," Herman said without looking up.

"Not you, too," Rob said.

"I'm somewhat impressed," she said. "Based on his last exam, I didn't think Tucker Hart could tie his own shoes, but look at him out there, trying to concuss young men."

"He's failing my class, too," Herman said.

"Then I hope he's enjoying his last semester of eligibility," Rob said. His previously carefree attitude was gone, which she regretted, seeing how nervous he'd been all morning about Wykoff's impending big reveal.

"He can't be enjoying it as much as the fans cheering for him to draw blood," she said. "Why do they call him a *safety* when all he does is throw himself at people?"

"At least the girls are having fun."

"Robin likes anything you tell her to. As for Katie, she's on the look-out for that boy from last night."

"Scott? I hope not. His interests lie elsewhere."

"He's why she didn't come home last night."

From anger to confusion in five seconds flat. A new Rob Sutherland record. He leaned forward and called to Betsy Mullins, several rows away, "What time did the police break up the party last night?"

"For once, they didn't have to. No complaints!" Betsy gave him a thumbs-up, before turning back to Eleanor Pagliarulo and Annalise Granville, her co-conspirators.

"You're sure she was at Scott's?"

"That's what she told me."

"The little shit. I saw him this morning. He didn't say a word about it."

"Maybe he isn't as harmless as he seems."

"He's interested in Renee Dunhill." Rob shrugged. "The heart wants what it wants."

"What should we do?" She hated sounding as though she was deferring to her husband, but she was at a loss. It was in her best interest not to punish Katie, who she'd need as an ally now that the job had come through.

"Why don't we lock her in the car until the game's over? We can deal with it later."

"Don't forget to crack the window and give her plenty of water," Herman said without looking up from his book.

"Stay out of it, Herman," Rob said.

"Overreacting *always* works with teenagers."

"I forgot about your extensive experience."

"Look around. We deal with teenagers every day." Herman closed his book and studied both of them. "Katie's a good kid, one of the two best ones I've seen. You don't want to ruin that by jumping all over her the first time she slips up."

"He has a point," Molly said. If it came from Herman, maybe Rob would be more willing to accept it.

"It's none of my business, but it seems like she was just letting off a little steam."

"You should have heard Robin at the piano while you were gone," Rob said. "I thought she'd bring the house down around us."

"So we give Katie a pass?" she said, as guilty as she was relieved.

"What happens at Homecoming. . . ?" Rob said. "I don't know."

Before they could decide, Robin bounded down the stairs with an enormous bucket of popcorn cradled in her arms.

"Where's your sister," her parents said almost in unison.

"She ran into someone and told me to come back on my own." Robin crammed a fistful of popcorn into her mouth and watched the band march onto the field. "I hope this year's show is better than last year's. Disney soundtracks are so played out."

Molly looked over the girl's head at her husband, still struggling to process what she'd told him. They both counted on Katie's steadfastness to balance out her sister's eccentricities. In one night, that balance had been thrown off.

"I'll go find her," she decided.

SHE'D ONLY WANTED TO GET away from her parents for a few minutes. They were doing that thing where they pretended everything was fine in a way that was worse than out-right fighting. The politeness was driving her crazy. Her jaw hurt from grinding her teeth together, and without meaning to, she'd torn off a cuticle and opened a bloody wound on her right thumb.

She was standing by the concessions stand staunching the blood with a flimsy napkin when Mary suddenly appeared next to her. She smiled, and then looked over Mary's shoulder to see how long she had before Robin would make it through the line—two minutes, maximum.

"Hey, babe," Mary said. "Scott said you weren't here."

"I changed my mind."

"Obviously." Mary smiled. She furrowed her brow when Katie didn't smile back. "What's wrong?"

"Nothing," she said. "Crowds."

As though to prove her point, a hot-dog-brandishing family plowed past them, pushing them closer together. Mary put her hand on Katie's hip, smiling more broadly.

"We could always go somewhere else."

"I'm waiting for someone." She watched Mary try to control her reaction, to keep the smile on her face even as she seemed to be calculating a response to Katie's statement. "It's not a big deal," she added. "I can blow her off."

"Her?"

"A friend-of-a-friend. You know how it is."

At that moment, her sister appeared. "Look at this bucket," she said. "It's bigger than my head!" She pretended to bury her face in the popcorn, sending handfuls of it tumbling down to the ground around them.

Mary stepped back and studied Robin. "I know you," she said. "You're Dr. Sutherland's kid. You came to class."

"Yup." Robin continued chomping on her popcorn while Mary stared at her. "Are you ready to go back?" she said. "I don't want to miss the band."

"You two are together?"

"Duh," Robin said. "Want some popcorn?"

Mary looked from one of the sisters to the other and back again, like a spectator at a tennis match. In the end, her gaze stopped on Katie.

"Dr. Sutherland has two kids," Mary said.

Robin giggled. "Breathe, Katie. You're turning red." Then she mimed holding her breath and keeling over from lack of oxygen. "You're Katie *Sutherland*."

Robin swooned, pretending to fall on the ground, though she kept her popcorn bucket upright. She gasped for breath, then gave one of her manic laughs. Katie leaned down and whispered, "Go back to Mom and Dad. You don't want to miss the band, right?"

"They won't like it if you don't come, too."

"I'll be five minutes." She hoped she'd need the entire time, assuming Mary didn't just walk out on her right then.

She tried to keep her expression neutral. The crowd had thinned around them, but Mary remained close, so close Katie feared she might take a swing at her. Instead, Mary said, "You and Scott must have had a good laugh about this."

"It's not like we planned for anything to happen. I just needed to get away from my fucked-up family for a little while. He was nice enough to take me with him."

"Did you take notes for your parents, give them a full report this morning?"

"*Right.*" She couldn't help the sarcasm. The thought was too ridiculous to contemplate. "They told me to stay out all night and hook-up with one of their best students just so I could tell them what everyone said about them."

"Oh my God. You're still in high school, aren't you?"

"I'm a senior."

"You're a minor!"

"It's not like I'm going to press charges. I seem to recall last night being fairly consensual."

"Who else knows?"

"Nobody, I swear." Katie reached for Mary, but she stepped back. "And nobody will."

"As soon as those guys figure out who you are, my life is over."

"It's not like I hang out on campus." She almost added, *that's why you didn't know who I am*, but feared it would sound like a taunt. It was the truth. Though her sister enjoyed being Dr. Sutherland's Daughter, she preferred staying as far away from Confluence as possible.

"They're going to figure it out," Mary said, still glaring at her.

"You've all been here three years without knowing who I am. What's a couple more months?" She took Mary's hand, relieved when she didn't immediately let go. "After today, you won't have to see me again."

Mary groaned. "That's not what I want."

"Really?"

"Shit, shit, shit. I can't be seen with a high schooler. This isn't a Woody Allen movie!"

"Who are you trying to convince?"

"Don't get cute." Mary looked over her shoulder. "This is just great," she said.

Before Katie could respond, her mother stopped next to her. She didn't wait for a break in the conversation; she barged right in. "You left your sister."

"She's thirteen. She can walk back to her seat alone."

"Not my point." She turned and said, "Hello, Mary. Fancy running into you here."

Mary let go of Katie's hand. "Nice to see you, Professor Calloway," she said.

"I hope you looked after my daughter last night."

It was Katie's turn to groan. She didn't need her mother acting like the Cool Parent, the one who didn't care that her underage daughter had spent the night with a college student.

"Yes, *ma'am*," Mary said. Katie had never heard anyone but a cashier call her mother ma'am.

"I'm here now," her mother said. "You may stand down."

With that, Katie felt that her life was officially over. Having her father embarrass her at school was one thing. Her mother was practically leading her away from Mary by the ear.

Katie looked over her shoulder as she walked next to her mother. Mary stood frozen, a stunned expression on her face.

"You should play harder to get," her mother said as she put her arm around her and guided her towards the stairs. "You're worth it."

The third quarter had begun by the time they made it back to the stands, and as they weaved through the crowd and headed towards their seats, Katie kept thinking about her last look at Mary. The girl had seemed so small, not like she'd been the night before, when she'd been full of pithy one-liners and intelligent conversation. Faced with Katie's true identity, and her mother's performance, she'd deflated. She knew her mother had that effect on students—one of the guys at the party had referred to her as a "ball-shriveller"—but she hadn't expected it from Mary.

She'd seemed so confident, so far above the juvenile behavior surrounding them, that Katie couldn't help being attracted to her. It was as though Mary had pointed to her and said, "I choose you," leaving Katie no option but to accept the verdict.

Back at their seats, Katie studied her sister for signs of distress. The girl had eaten half the tub of popcorn. She bounced on the balls of her feet and cheered with the crowd. As soon as she noticed her sister's return, she said, "Can you believe they did Blood, Sweat & Tears for halftime? What is this, 1980?"

"What?" Katie was used to playing catch up with her sister, but this time she barely had the energy.

"The horns are awesome, but their 'God Bless the Child' can't compare to Billie's."

"Yeah."

Their mother was in quiet consultation with their father, which meant that a scene was about to begin. Neither of them had the least bit of tact when it came to moments like this.

Her father turned to her and said, "You were with Mary Lynn *Carlisle* last night?"

"God, no. Give me some credit."

"Mary Wardell," her mother said.

"That's a relief."

"*Rob.*"

"At least the girl's got taste."

"That isn't the point."

"You mean like you encouraging Scott to go after that Renee chick?" A low blow, to be sure, but this was Katie's sole trump card.

Her mother laughed. "You told that kid he had a chance with Renee Dunhill?"

"I may have offered him advice. But the idea was his."

For a moment, Katie thought her ploy had worked, but her mother quickly refocused her energy. "None of that changes what happened last night."

"So she spent the night with Mary? I can think of, say, fifteen-hundred undergrads I'd be more concerned about her being with."

"We give her a pass because she was with a woman?"

"The worst that could have happened was that the girl gave her a reading list."

Katie looked at Dr. Delacroix, on the far side of her father, who sat engrossed in a book. He underlined text with the flick of his pen, putting checkmarks in the margin, along with various scribbles that Katie couldn't make out. She needed help, but knew it wouldn't come from him. Dr. Delacroix could be counted on for a quiet word in her father's ear—like his support for her decision to go to fashion school—but he had too much tact to interrupt a full-blown argument. Next, she looked at her sister, seated again, swinging her legs while she continued to eat popcorn by the handful.

"She was with one of your students," her mother said. "Surely that bothers you."

"You think that gives her some kind of unfair advantage? The last thing Mary Wardell needs is bonus points."

"Did you hear me," she said. "Mary didn't use me. If anybody's getting used, it's Scott. Dad wants him to nail Renee because he doesn't have the courage to do it himself."

"Katherine," her mother said.

"I don't hear him denying it."

"Because it's preposterous," her father said. "If you hadn't noticed, I'm on your side regarding this Mary Wardell debacle."

"*Debacle?*"

"How else should I refer to your staying out all night doing God-knows-what with a house full of college students?"

"I believe it's called *spooning*."

"If you hadn't noticed," her father said. "We're surrounded by my colleagues and their families. Maybe now isn't the time to go into this."

"What's spooning?" Robin said between bites of popcorn.

"I'll tell you later."

"You'll do no such thing," her mother said.

"She's thirteen. She'll figure it out on her own."

Her father looked grim. "*Much* later is fine with me," he said.

She didn't understand why her mother was so upset. Like many faculty, she had a rainbow sticker affixed to her office door, a sign that she'd been through the LGBTQ training and was therefore designated a Safe Zone for Students of Difference. Faced with her own daughter's sexuality, however, she seemed to be freaking out. Katie had hoped they'd covered her transgressions from the night before already, so why the need to drag them back to the forefront?

Robin tugged on her sleeve. "I don't feel so good," the girl said. "Unhhhh." Her sister leaned against her. "Think I ate—" Too late. The girl heaved up everything she'd consumed in the last two hours. It hit the concrete with a splat and splashed up on all of their shoes. Their father scooped Robin up in his long arms and charged up the stairs.

"We're leaving," their mother said, practically dragging her past Dr. Delacroix, who was busy going over his shoes with a monogrammed handkerchief.

He paused long enough to make eye contact with Katie. He gave the slightest of nods, the first friendly gesture she'd seen since leaving Mary's side. At any other time, it would have come as a relief. Today, it felt like too little too late.

Twenty-One

He was about to give up and rejoin his friends when Mary appeared beside him, out of thin air. She dragged him away from the concourse and onto the ramp leading towards the stadium exit.

"How long did you know about her?"

"Excuse me?" He stepped back, instinctively, until he was more than an arm's length away. He couldn't imagine Mary was the violent type, but considering how grim she looked, he wouldn't put taking a swing at him past her.

"I just got ambushed by Professor Calloway. I'd like to know if you were in on this from the start, or if you figured it out later and didn't tell me."

"She made me promise not to say anything."

"We've known each other for four years."

"I know. It's just. . . . You should have seen how screwed up things were at the Sutherlands'. I mean, her father was drunk off his ass, her sister was in trouble for dressing up as Jackie

Kennedy, post-Oswald, and her mother showed up in some sports car none of them had seen before."

"You saw all of that?" The promise of gossip outweighed Mary's anger. The young woman was typically on the outside looking in, and though Scott was certain that this wasn't always the conscious choice she made it out to be, she seemed to be relishing a glimpse at the inside.

"It was truly fucked up." He would have felt guilty spilling so many secrets if he wasn't sure that they would remain locked in Mary's steel-trap of a brain.

"Did you know she was gay?"

"I didn't know *you* were gay."

"I'm not asexual, no matter what Tony says."

"Clearly." He was relieved. Mary couldn't keep the corners of her mouth from turning up into the thinnest of smiles. It was a start.

"Dammit," she said. "I haven't liked anyone since Gretchen Prine graduated last spring. Why did it have to be Sutherland's teenage daughter?"

"I know."

"You have no idea," she said. "But at least I'm not that idiot Burkas. If Sutherland finds out he dressed up like him, it's going to be rough until graduation."

They stood, silent, while the crowd noise swelled.

"God, I hate football," Mary said, finally.

Scott smiled. "Me, too."

"Then why are we still here?"

Before he could answer, he saw the entire Sutherland family exit the ramp a floor below them. The parents had the younger girl, Robin, braced between them while Katie trailed behind. Scott didn't know if he should point them out to Mary. But she noticed them as well. She studied them silently, staring intently. He too studied his professor's family as they raced toward the exit. Surely their haste wasn't a result of finding out about Katie and Mary. The Sutherlands had to be cooler than that.

Scott couldn't help smiling when he thought about the youngest Sutherland. She'd had such manic energy the night before, dressed in her Halloween costume. It made what happened afterward even sadder, the way that woman had practically dragged her up the driveway, the girl crying all the way. What was wrong with Sutherland and Professor Calloway? Why didn't they immediately race to her side to soothe those tears?

"You think they're okay?" Mary said.

"I don't know." He couldn't think of anything more to say. He felt like he'd been up for days, so much had happened already. While Mary watched them progress towards the parking lot, he said, "Dr. S says you're going to grad school. For rhetoric and comp?"

"That's the plan."

"I didn't know you were into that stuff."

"It's where the jobs are. Dr. Sessions says people like Sutherland are relics. The last of a dying breed. If I'm going to spend all that time in school, I want to get a j-o-b."

The Sutherlands turned the corner and disappeared into the quad. They must have been headed for Kreider, not their car, so whatever had happened, it couldn't be that bad, he figured.

"What about you?" Mary said. "What're you going to do?"

"I wish I knew."

"You better figure out something soon. Graduation is six months away."

He didn't know whether he should admit what had happened, but seeing how vulnerable Mary had been, he figured she wouldn't make fun of him too badly. "I talked to Dr. Delacroix about grad school, but he shot me down."

"No way."

"He compared lit professors to the Japanese holdouts after World War Two."

"If it's what you really want to do."

"I don't know any more. Maybe I'll suck up to Wykoff and beg him for a job."

"No need to get desperate," she said.

"Tell that to my parents. They're still mad I'm not an accounting major."

"Mine wanted me to go into *nursing*."

Mary W, a nurse? No way he could imagine that. "At least you can't outsource it."

"That's what they said!"

They were both silent, standing shoulder to shoulder, looking down on the empty area outside the stadium. Soon, President Vessey, Provost Blankenship, Evan Wykoff, and his female shadow appeared beneath them. They strode across the quad in the same direction as the Sutherlands. With all that had happened, Scott had forgotten about Wykoff's big announcement. Dr. Sutherland might have been a relic, but he was going to be one lucky relic once Wykoff made him an endowed chair.

Twenty-Two

Robin must have been feeling better. She was singing "I Gotta Right to Sing the Blues" in between sips of water.

Rob paced the floor of his office, still littered with all the books he'd removed from the shelves that morning. Robin kicked her feet, seated in his desk chair, which she spun slowly, bracing it with a hand against the window sill. Molly sat on the edge of the desk, creasing the stack of papers he hadn't graded yet. And Katie sat in one of the student chairs on the far side of the desk, her head cocked to read the titles on the spines of the closest books. Out the window, workers were putting the finishing touches on the platform they'd erected for Evan's big speech. Based on the time, Rob figured the game would end any minute, at which point campus security would funnel people into the quad for the announcement.

He'd never taken the possibility of an endowed chair seriously, not until that moment. The College already had several of them and though he didn't know the particulars, he knew they came with enormous salary bumps, a reduced teaching load, and an increased research and travel budget. For all he knew, his wife wouldn't have to work any longer, let alone move across the state for a meager visiting appointment. And fashion design school would no longer seem like such a ridiculous expense. He hated that it would all be on account of video-game money, but if he put it to good use, no one could begrudge him the source of the gift.

Robin reached for a high note, which she sustained with a crescendo.

"That's enough," Molly said. "At least sing something happy for a change."

"I just *threw up*. I can't help it if I've got the blues. The Low Down, Barfed Up Blues."

Unlike his friends who'd gotten jobs at research universities, Rob's lifestyle hadn't changed much once he'd gotten the position at Confluence. For starters, his salary had to feed three mouths, as Molly was still at home with Katie. They'd bought their house with the least money down possible, which came in the form of loans from their parents, and waited years to upgrade any of the furniture from their grad school townhouse. They rarely took vacations. They had almost nothing in savings, beyond the college funds they'd started, too late, for both girls. He couldn't help it if the grandiose vision of an endowed chair took up residence in his brain.

Robin sang about being called to oblivion, courtesy of the ocean.

"It's calling *me* right now," Katie said.

Before he could settle his daughters down, his cell phone buzzed. A group text from Betsy Mullins. *Evan has requested that we all stand up front for his speech. The moment is upon us!* He looked out the window. The first phalanx had arrived in the quad, mingling a respectful distance from the scaffolding. Maybe he could ask for a new office, something grander, or at least one that didn't reek of mildew most of the year.

"I have to go," he said. "Duty calls."

Molly ignored him, doting on Robin, who had warmed to all the attention. She'd moved on to "Between the Devil and the Deep Blue Sea."

He patted the girl's head. "Anyone want to come with me?"

"Pass," Katie said.

"We'll listen from here," Molly said. "Wouldn't want to be in the way."

He ignored her tone and headed out the door. Nothing was going to ruin this moment.

Outside, the wind had picked up again. More people had gathered on the quad, including all of the English department. He made his way through the crowd, nodding and smiling to familiar faces as he did so, and ended up next to Herman and Leah Sessions, at the far end of the row of faculty. Betsy paced in front of them, smiling maniacally. Even Tom Strelzik, who Rob had never seen anywhere near the football stadium, was dressed in Confluence blue and white.

Evan soon took the stage, flanked by President Vessey and Provost Blankenship, looking not unlike toughs who'd been hired to make sure he went through with his pledge. The young man's hair had thinned, wisps fluttering in the breeze that assaulted him on the platform. First- and second-year, before he'd remade himself into a campus politician, he'd worn it long, almost to his shoulders, its wavy curls the envy of the female population. Back then, he'd dressed in flannel shirts, jeans, and hiking boots, before the transition to the preppy style he still favored. He had on a black suit and white shirt, open at the collar, his trademark. He never wore a tie, not even on the night he was a guest for the State of the Union.

President Vessey moved to the microphone, leaning into it with practiced ease. "I know we're all disappointed by the way the football game turned out—" the crowd groaned "—but I appreciate everyone's willingness to suspend their merry-making for a few more minutes. This year, we've welcomed back the largest group of alums in our school's illustrious history, a testament to all of you and to our guest of honor. Without further ado, I'd like to welcome the president of the class of 2004 and co-founder and CEO of EvRo Productions to the stage. Evan Wykoff!"

The crowd whooped and clapped as the young man walked to the podium. But Rob paid little attention, focused instead on the young woman who stood at the bottom of the stairs. Dressed for a board meeting, she stuck out among the sweatshirted and tennis-shoe-wearing crowd around her. She was tall, a few inches under six feet, with shoulder-length hair that blew across her face. Magenta-colored hair, as though the typical color palate wasn't enough for her. She didn't bother moving it out of her way, the elements of no concern to her, instead remaining focused on Wykoff. It was all Rob could do to refocus his energy in time to watch his former student remove the microphone from the stand and begin stalking the stage.

"Thank you, President Vessey," he said, offering Provost Blankenship a nod as well. "It's great to be back at Confluence!" More cheering. "I haven't been back here as often as I would have liked, but the welcome I've received over the last twenty-four hours has been so wonderful that I can assure you I won't be a stranger. It's been great catching up with old friends and classmates and to see that so many have gone on to do impressive things with the tools they received here at Confluence. Michelle Nyburg's work for the Southern Poverty Law Center is familiar to many of us, I'm sure, but it's been wonderful hearing about Corey Diski's Habitat for Humanity projects and Carla Vanderhoff's prison outreach program. You put me and my humble enterprise to shame!"

The crowd laughed at his self-deprecation. Even Rob knew that EvRo had quickly grown into an almost billion-dollar-a-year leader in its industry. They focused on quality rather than quantity and were experts at merchandising. Even Katie, who played that silly game about presidential assassinations with a passion she demonstrated for virtually nothing else, owned any number of related items, from logoed t-shirts to concise histories of the presidents and their downfalls. Now that Evan had transitioned into film production, Rob figured it wouldn't be long before he had an Academy Award.

He'd seen a number of students who took Confluence by storm the way Evan had. But most of them settled into lives of quiet mediocrity post-graduation. He'd seen student body presidents turn into tubby machine-tool salesmen, stars of the college stage become regional commercial actors, and intellectual heavyweights settle for office jobs. He wouldn't have predicted the same fate for Evan—even as a student he was different, if only in the degree of his campus domination—but wouldn't have been surprised, either, if he'd returned for his ten-year reunion a quieter, humbled person, not the titan of industry he saw before him on the stage.

Rob remembered the day he'd finally lost his patience with Evan's egotism, his Shakespearean grandstanding. He'd been up late the night before arguing with Molly, who'd taken to printing job ads she thought he should apply for and affixing them to the refrigerator. He'd just submitted his materials for tenure and, though not superstitious, viewed applying for another job simultaneously as tempting fate. Molly would hear none of it. "I've been waiting five years," she'd said. "For you to get off your ass. If you don't apply for these jobs, I'm going to do it for you."

"Do you really think life will be that much better in Tampa or Bowling Green? We can't run away from all of this." He waved his hand over the living room, a mess of Robin's toddler toys and Katie's school books.

"At least those places have some civilization," she said. "And administrations that might take you seriously when you tell them we can't survive on one professor's salary."

Rob had tried, just that fall, for the second time, to convince Provost Blankenship to hire Molly full-time, or to at least make her position less tenuous. He'd been met by a blank stare that turned confused, then irritated. Not that Molly gave him any credit for the attempt. She seemed to think that the desired result was out there, that Rob had failed from lack of courage, not because the college purse strings were tied tauter than the clothesline they'd been forced to hang in the backyard when their dryer stopped working.

The disagreement had gone around and around, into the *wee small hours of the morning*, as Robin might croon, with no more results than any of their other fights. The sense of camaraderie with which they'd faced their early days in Elgin vanished when Molly began teaching at Confluence, right after Robin was born. Faced with apathetic students and pay that was beneath her level, she'd grown bitter, recalcitrant. She still did research and wrote articles, but without satisfaction. She attacked publication as though doing so would punish Confluence for their penny-pinching. To Rob's knowledge, no one other than her department chair, Dave Trillo, had any idea she was even conversant with the latest research into logic and analytical philosophy.

Rob kept all of this to himself, simply listened as Molly vented her frustrations, but when he didn't respond sympathetically enough, she changed the focus of her attack. "You actually like the way things are, don't you? You couldn't stand that I was the star when we were students, that you were Molly Calloway's Boyfriend."

"If that were the case, why would I have married you?"

"Because you knocked me up?"

"I forgot that I was the one who forced you to drop out of school and stay home with Katie. Then, as part of my plot, I waited *four years* to knock you up again, just so I could keep you barefoot and pregnant, once per presidential term."

"Make your jokes. You know I'm right."

Not only was Molly wrong, he was sure, but her attitude showed a surprising lack of insight into his life, as well as her own. Ever since Robin had been born, they'd drifted apart this way, no longer sharing the bond that had characterized their early years in Elgin, nor the unified front they'd presented to their families, who'd complained about how far away they lived, how rarely they were treated to visits. Instead, Molly had taken to concocting conspiracy theories that showcased him in the role of villainous mastermind.

In those years, before Herman, he'd had no one to talk to about such difficulties. He was the youngest member of the department by a decade, the only one whose children weren't at least in junior high, the lone member of the department who hadn't planted his flag permanently. If he'd mentioned to Betsy or Annalise or Tom that he was considering looking for another job, they would have been bewildered.

So he internalized it, as he always did, until Evan went on about Shakespeare for the umpteenth time in History of the Novel, bringing up *Coriolanus*, the one of the Bard's plays that Rob had performed in college. Like Evan, Rob had once fancied himself a budding Shakespearean, though contrary to the young man, he'd been self-aware enough to realize the folly in attempting such a specialization. Rob quickly realized that he had nothing new to say about the great playwright's work and shifted his focus to his second love, the early novel. Experiencing the clash between these subjects every Tuesday and Thursday for seventy-five minutes, in the form of that arrogant little prick, grew to be too much for him.

He didn't cry himself to exhaustion like Leah Sessions. Instead, he wore himself out trying to find new, decisive ways to shift the conversation back to Defoe, Richardson, and Sterne. But the kid just wouldn't get it. Everyone else, even Trent Fulton, that year's dimmest bulb, realized that Evan was driving their professor crazy.

"I've been rereading *Coriolanus*," Evan said. "And even though it isn't a major work by Shakespeare's standards, it's a lot better than this." He waved his copy of *Humphry Clinker* before him like a geisha with a fan. Rob cut him off. "I appreciate your love of Shakespeare. I wish more people shared it. But oranges are not the only fruit." He could tell that Evan was undeterred, that he intended to launch into another pseudo-lecture, so Rob did the only thing he could think of under the circumstances. He dredged up Coriolanus's only soliloquy from the deep storage of his memory and prayed that he'd get it right. The more he recited, the more excited he grew, though he worked hard to remain even-tempered, bored-sounding, even, as he made his way to the end. "I'll enter: if he slay me, He does fair justice; if he give me way, I'll do his country service." He mimed a yawn, and then shifted back to one of Matthew Bramble's letters to Dr. Lewis without bothering to look at young Wykoff. He knew he finally had him cowed. There was no need to gloat.

From that point on, Evan was a quieter, though no less enthusiastic, student.

He'd missed much of Evan's speech, but tuned in just in time. "Today, I'd like to talk about the future of Confluence College, this great institution we are all so proud to call alma mater," Evan said, still pacing the stage. "It's no longer enough to offer a premiere education. As those of you who've spent any time re-exploring campus know, Confluence, like many schools, has entered the so-called student services *arms race*. We have climbing walls and skate parks, luxurious suite-style living accommodations and gourmet-caliber food in three cafeterias. While all of this is wonderful—and makes me truly envious of the current student population—when I began to discuss my gift with President Vessey, I knew that it would focus on academics. What this college needs to put it over the top is a bold vision that transcends what students do in their off hours."

Rob had to admit that, so far, Evan's speech was living up to its billing as *the* event of the weekend. The crowd was transfixed. No one uttered a word or shifted from foot to foot, even as the temperature seemed to be dropping, the wind picking up. Herman and Leah to his left, Betsy and Eleanor to his right, everyone around him looked up at the stage where Evan continued discussing what he called The Future of Academe.

"I understand the need for increased attention to career preparedness. I've talked to many graduates, just today, who wished they'd spent more time thinking about what their degrees would be worth on the open market. But at the same time, if I hadn't been exposed to the variety of classes and ways of thinking that I was—let's face it—*required* to take at Confluence, I never would have been able to take the leap of faith I did when my interest in graduate school waned." He paused to look around, making eye contact with some of his professors, fellow alums, and other interested parties. "Today, I stand before you to announce the addition of another piece to the Confluence Experience."

Rob was nervous for the first time in he couldn't remember how long. He'd grown so comfortable at Confluence that the nerves that tingled through his body came as a surprise. He spent his days confident in the knowledge that life at Confluence held no surprises for him. He taught, he prepared for class, he graded, he served on numerous faculty committees. Every day was pretty much the same. Today, finally, would bring a change.

"But in order for this to work," Evan said, coming to a halt at the very edge of the stage, "I'm going to need your help. Beginning right now." He looked around once again. "I'd like to ask one of Confluence's illustrious faculty members to join me on stage. This person is, to my mind, an example of the direction this school needs to head in."

Whether consciously or not, Betsy had grasped Rob's arm, holding on with a surprisingly powerful grip for such a petite woman. Eleanor, to her right, leaned forward to smile at him. His life was about to change. He wished his family was with him. Even jaded Molly would have to admit that Confluence was finally rewarding them, *both* of them, for their years of service.

"Ladies and gentlemen, alums and current students, faculty and staff, please help me welcome Professor Leah Sessions to the stage."

Betsy clung to Rob even more tightly. The smile froze on Eleanor's face. To his left, Herman tilted his head to the sky in what Rob could only hope was surprise. While the crowd around them applauded, Rob did his best to remain calm, not shouting, *What the hell is going on?* Leah was in her second year. Evan couldn't be giving her his endowed chair.

"Dr. Sessions came to my attention several years ago, when she was still a graduate student. Though I've been out of academe for years now, I still keep up with relevant research in the fields that interest me, and Leah's dissertation—*The Rise of Twitterature: Remaking the World 140 Characters at a Time*—was one of the most impressive pieces of scholarship I've ever seen."

Rob waited for Herman to stop contemplating the cloud-filled sky and look his way. When Herman finally did so, Rob said, "Did you know about this?" The man's blank look was enough of an answer.

To his right, Betsy had let go of his arm. Eleanor had stopped grinning. Evan needed to stop milking it and get to the fucking point already.

"Since my years at Confluence, the college has made great strides in developing their engineering, nursing, and business programs in response to student and parent demand for hands-on training. But the time has come to stop reacting to what's going on around us and begin *leading*. For that reason, today I'd like to announce the creation of Confluence College's Evan Wykoff Center for Technology and Culture, a new venture that will provide an interdisciplinary approach to the study of the defining innovations of our era."

A roar went up among the crowd. All around him, people were cheering and clapping and stomping their feet, while the row of English faculty continued to stare at the stage.

"I want all of you to join me in recognizing Professor Sessions as the Center's first executive director!"

Rob wasn't positive, but he thought he heard Betsy groan at the news. Herman slid his hands into the pockets of his overcoat and whistled a single, low note. At the far end, Tom Strelzik said, loudly enough that everyone around them could hear, "This is a joke, right?"

WITHOUT MEANING TO, MOLLY LET out a sigh and said, "Oh, Robert." Unlike her husband, she'd never trusted that the convergence of Confluence College and Evan Wykoff would mean anything good for their family. No matter what Wykoff insisted in his various reminiscences, Rob had spent four years hounding the young man, who, to his credit, had refused to let his professor's animosity grind him down. But that didn't mean she'd anticipated this. Technology was the bane of her husband's existence.

Now, here stood Wykoff, introducing his ideas for the new center: courses in video-game history and design, film and television production, the intersection of popular culture and any number of academic disciplines. Molly realized, as she looked down on her husband, that she had no idea of the depth of his disappointment.

"What's wrong?" Robin had stopped fidgeting in her father's desk chair and leaned her head against her mother's thigh.

With the window open, they'd all been able to hear Wykoff's amplified words, but Robin, unlike her sister and mother, had no idea what they actually meant.

"Dad just got screwed," Katie said.

Molly shook her head. "It's a good lesson for all of us." She hated being this way.

"Spare us the *don't count your chickens* speech."

She was surprised by her older daughter's vehemence. "Try this on for size: don't assume the world owes you anything."

"Does that apply to all of us?"

"I'm so confused," Robin said. Molly could feel the girl's jaw working on the ice chips Rob had retrieved for her through the fabric of her slacks. She had yet to lift her head from her mother's leg.

"Dad thought he was getting a big promotion. But he's really getting nothing."

"Is he losing his job?"

"No."

"Then what's the big deal?"

Molly ran a hand through her daughter's hair. "Your father had his hopes up. We should all be extra supportive when he comes back up here."

Katie snorted, but thankfully, Robin, who was usually attuned to the slightest emotional changes in a room, let it go without comment.

Molly closed the window as Evan continued to drone on about his plans for the new center. She couldn't believe how many people had remained after the game to listen to the man. The quad was full.

She looked down on the stage once more, at Leah Sessions, frozen in place by the mic stand, at Evan Wykoff. Without sound, it looked like bad undergraduate theater, a mismatched pairing of an attractive but awkward ingenue with a scene-stealing, overly confident leading man.

She turned away, noting the stacks of books on Rob's floor and desk, the dusty, empty shelves on his bookcase. Had he finally taken her advice and begun the great reorganization? She picked up a book at random, noted the name of one of his graduate school mentors on the flyleaf. Rob had been his department's equivalent of Evan Wykoff in graduate school, the student from whom everyone expected great things. She remembered the many reading and critique groups that used to meet at their townhouse, the way everyone clamored for his approval. The young women envied her her position as the great Rob Sutherland's girlfriend, while the men offered their grudging respect. His professors were much the same. How many nights had she tagged along to dinner parties where they were the only graduate students or, worse, the only guests. Under the latter circumstances, she would spend hours listening to Rob and the host debate whatever point had come up in class that week, whatever book from one of his reading lists he was aggressively consuming at the time, while she was left to fend for herself.

When they'd first moved to Elgin, Rob had hosted similar dinners for his students and various faculty but had given up the tradition once he'd realized that the former had little in the way of intellectual conversation to offer and the latter were happier avoiding their fellow faculty members in their off-hours. Wykoff's class must have been one of the last to darken the door of their home, though she couldn't remember any specifics.

Instead, what she remembered was the summer day, a year after graduation, when the young man had appeared in search of advice. She'd been outside with the girls when he'd pulled up in a rented sedan, but she'd paid little attention, focused instead on refereeing the latest tussle between seven-year-old Katie and her just-turned-three little sister. Robin, enraged by some grievance Molly couldn't remember, had a Wiffle-ball bat that she was using to fend off her sister.

Evan had sat in his car long enough that she'd forgotten he was there, assumed he was lost or, worse, one of the census-takers who'd been going door-to-door of late. But as soon as he emerged from the car, she remembered who he was. "Evan Wykoff," she said as he made his way up the driveway. "Aren't you supposed to be living the grad student life?"

"It's summer break."

"Did they close the library?" She'd meant it as a joke but could tell immediately that it had fallen flat. She tried again. "Grad school must be agreeing with you. You've got that pasty, washed-out look that only spending weeks in the bowels of some archive can achieve."

"I turned in my last paper ten days ago," he said.

"That's it," she said, turning her attention to the girls, rolling around on the grass. "You're twice as big as her. Let your sister win once in a while."

She looked at Evan, who seemed to be on the verge of fleeing for his rental car. "I don't want to know your romantic situation, but whatever it is, make sure your preferred form of birth control is reliable."

"Okay," he said.

"Seeing how you're so far from home, I assume this isn't merely a social visit."

"I was hoping to speak with Dr. Sutherland for a minute."

"You came all this way for a minute of the sage's time? Too bad. He's running errands. If I don't keep him busy in the summer, he drives me crazy wandering around the house *sighing* all the time." Without turning away, she yelled, "Inside, both of you. You're about to crack your heads."

"Crack, crack," Robin said. "I'm a duck!"

"Katie, take your sister inside and get cleaned up for lunch."

The girls trudged off, and she turned her attention back to Wykoff. "I'd invite you in, but experiencing a meal with those two isn't for the faint of heart."

"My sister has a two-year-old. She calls my parents once a week to apologize for whatever she could have done as a toddler to deserve retribution."

"I know why you're here," she said. "Don't worry. The first year fucks up everybody."

"So I'm told."

"Rob was ahead of me, so I didn't experience this first-hand, but he got thrown out of the library for giving a dramatic reading of 'The Rape of the Lock.' When I asked him about it, he told me he was so sleep-deprived he thought the voice was in his head."

The kid was dying, standing before her in the already-hot June air. She could tell he needed a life preserver, so she did her best.

"We can all find things to get us through one class, one day, one bad week. But until you figure out the big thing—the goal, belief, philosophy, whatever you want to call it—that does it for you, you'll still be white-knuckling it."

"And you figured that out?"

"I'm not the best example, seeing how I don't have those three little letters after my name."

"Would it be rude if I asked?"

"Early in my second year, I had this hellish course load. Three classes, each demanding we read two to three books a week with written responses to all of them. I was going out of my mind, spending my mornings on Schopenhauer and Feuerbach, then switching to logical positivism—practically a negation of what I'd just read—after lunch. Total mindfuck. Meanwhile, Rob's in the other room reading *novels* for his exams. So one day, I threw down the books and went for a walk. I walked for five hours, all over town, letting my mind wander wherever it wanted, so long as it had nothing to do with any of my classes. I missed a seminar, got docked a letter grade for failing to turn in one of those precious response papers, but who cares? What I decided was that just because I went to grad school didn't mean I had to finish. A high school education is a given. College is becoming virtually the same way. But if you go on, you're there because you *want* to be there. *You* make a conscious choice to apply, to decide where to go, to get up every morning and go to class. *You* are in control. So if you're miserable or you have doubts, *you* have the choice—the right—to leave."

"That's it? I mean, it doesn't sound like much."

She shrugged. "After that day, I woke up every morning with purpose. I *chose* to do the work, to go to all the classes and put up with my pretentious cohort. I made that same decision every day until I couldn't any more, when life got too complicated." She paused to look back toward the house. The windows were open, and she thought she heard Robin scream from inside, but the longer she waited, the more she was convinced that she'd imagined it. "My advice to you? Make the choice early. If you don't like grad school, fuck it. Find something you want to do. If you decide to make yourself like it, clear everything else out of your way and dive in."

Evan had been silent so long after her speech that she'd expected him to turn tail and flee. Finally, when she was about to excuse herself to check on the girls—that time, she really *had* heard a scream—he said, "That sounds better than anything my counselor said all semester."

She waved away the compliment. "Guess I should have charged you. Now, if you'll excuse me, I need to get inside before they destroy the kitchen."

He was still standing in the driveway when she made it to the front door, so she smiled and said, "Would you like to wait? I can put you in the study until lunch is over and the girls are projectile-free."

Evan stared at the roof above them, his prominent Adam's apple bobbing up and down. Finally, he said, "I guess not. I don't want to be in the way."

"Not at all," she said, feeling guilty all of a sudden. "You're welcome."

"No," he sighed more than said. "I should be going."

She knew Rob would have given Wykoff a more uplifting pep talk, something that might have at least gotten him through his master's degree, but she was just as certain that his words would have rung hollow. He didn't like the young man, had come close to celebrating when he'd assigned him that fateful C, but he enjoyed doling out advice. He would have taken him onto the back porch, offered him a beer, and spent the afternoon reminiscing about the good-old-days. Some of them had been good, especially in comparison to fighting with a three-year-old who had no interest in potty training, but that would have served Rob better than Evan. No, she'd done the right thing, not that she'd gotten any credit for it. She'd read and heard plenty of interviews with Wykoff, many of which made a big deal out of the adversity he'd faced, as though getting one C and enduring a year of grad school were akin to going off to war, but she'd never seen him say anything approaching, "You know who really set me straight? This harried philosophy adjunct at dear old Confluence. She made it okay for me to quit school and become a raging success."

She didn't need the pat on the back, not the way Rob seemed to enjoy the attention Wykoff's TED talk had attracted for him, but a simple Thank You would have sufficed.

"Hey, Mom," Robin said. "Are you listening?"

"Of course," she lied. When neither of the girls responded, she added, "What was the question?"

"When do we get to meet that guy?"

"I thought you didn't like video games."

"I don't," Robin said. "But he's *famous*."

Outside, the speech was over, the crowd dispersing, but Wykoff and Leah Sessions remained on stage, having their picture taken with President Vessey and Provost Blankenship. Sessions seemed more comfortable now that she wasn't on display before the multitude. She smiled for the camera, pinned between the administrators and their beaming faces. As far as Molly was concerned, one of the girls would have a chance to meet the famous alum as Rob's plus-one. She had little interest in attending the evening's cocktail party, even less after Wykoff's announcement. She and Rob may not have been seeing eye-to-eye, but that didn't mean she'd enjoy spending time with the man who'd obliterated her husband's hopes, no matter how much of a long-shot they'd been. And she highly doubted that he would complain when she bowed out.

Twenty-Three

She'd overdressed, but her parents had called it a cocktail party, so why wouldn't she wear a cocktail dress? She'd chosen a knee-length, form-fitting black number that plunged as far as her parents would allow in the front. She'd made it herself, out of silk her mother had bought with what she now realized were casino winnings. She'd accessorized simply, to match the minimalist approach of the dress, opting for a plain silver necklace, with a matching bracelet and small hoop earrings, avoiding the clichéd string of pearls that her mother had offered her. She had on low heels, her feet still sore from tramping around town the previous night.

The party was at President Vessey's residence, on campus, a two-story colonial, with almost as many caterers as there were guests. Every time she tried to move, she found herself bumping into a waiter. She hated to think what Robin would have been like in such tight quarters; she wasn't called Hurricane Robin for nothing. Not that this would have made her feel any better about being passed over when their father came looking for a date. "Looks like we'll be seeing more of Evan," their father had told Robin. "You'll have plenty of opportunity to bask in his glow."

Katie couldn't figure out why they were there. According to her mother, everyone on campus had assumed that her father would be the beneficiary of Wykoff's largesse. This had to be embarrassing. If it had been her, she would have hidden away in her room until everyone had a chance to forget. But hiding wasn't her father's strong-suit. He worked the room—*spreading his personality around*, her mother called it—shaking hands with the various alums and board members, patting fellow professors on the back. He behaved as though he was the host of the party, which came in handy when he steered her toward Evan Wykoff.

"Professor S!" the young man called. "I've been looking everywhere for you."

"And here I am." Her father had his hand on her back, almost pushing her before him. "I'd like to reintroduce you to my daughter. A lot changes in ten years."

Wykoff smiled, genuinely, it seemed. "Katie Sutherland," he said. "My spies tell me you and I have something to discuss."

Of course he knew, she realized. Though she played *The Service* under a pseudonym, she'd had to register with her real name and email address.

"In that case," her father said. "I'll excuse myself. I'm parched!" He headed for the bar.

"I can explain," she said once he was out of earshot.

"Please do."

She hadn't expected that, had assumed Wykoff wanted to lecture her, to threaten her with expulsion from the game. Instead, he stood, hands in pockets, a bemused look on his face.

"I've played the game a lot," she said.

"I know. I've seen your stats."

"I wanted to see if it was even possible."

"Everyone knows it is, thanks to that hate group in Kentucky.

They've put more holes in Martin Luther King than James Earl Ray ever could have."

This wasn't going to be easy. He seemed to have a nose for bullshit. "I was bored, okay? And the people I was playing with took it *so* seriously. I wanted to shake them up."

"How did it feel?"

"I thought it would be fun—exciting, at least—but the other players freaked out, like I'd actually killed the president. So I panicked."

"You haven't logged on since."

"I don't think I'm going to."

He nodded. Up close, he wasn't as handsome as he was in the videos she'd seen on YouTube. But she did realize something she hadn't known before: he was wearing makeup. Not enough that it was noticeable from a distance. Just a little bit of foundation.

"You're brave enough to kill JFK but not to see the fuss you've created?"

"It's that bad?"

He frowned. "In a way, it's actually been very good. The numbers have been up ever since word spread. Everyone's on alert for copycats."

"Are you upset?"

"I never thought it would take seven years for someone to do it."

"So you knew all along?"

"I designed the game, didn't I? But I figured it would be McKinley or Garfield who got it first. People are less invested in them."

"I can't play it anymore. No offense."

He nodded, as though what she'd said held no interest for him. "I'm going to send you a new game. Are you familiar with Hannibal's crossing of the Alps? It doesn't matter. You'll figure it out." He handed her a card. "Here's my email. Once you've played it for a while, I'd like to know your thoughts. It's still in beta."

"You want me to *test* it?"

"If you're anything like your parents, you have high standards. Which is what I'm looking for." Without turning away, he said, "I see someone I need to speak with, if you'll excuse me."

She watched him stride across the room. He had almost as much confidence as her father, who continued to glad-hand his way through the crowd as though he actually had received the endowment. She couldn't figure him out. He'd barely uttered complete sentences when he came back to his office, but now that they were surrounded by a hundred or so people, he was the life of the party. The more she'd learned about her father the last day or so, the more she had the feeling he saved his best self for others, leaving his family to settle for the scraps.

If her father seemed unperturbed, the same couldn't be said for the other English faculty. They huddled in groups of twos and threes, whispering among themselves, even when no one was nearby. All except for Dr. Sessions, who was being dragged around the room by President Vessey, and Dr. Herman, who did a much less manic version of the circulating her father was doing. It took her a while, but she finally realized he was shadowing her father, playing the chaperone, which left her free to wander into the dining room.

Like the rest of the first floor, the dining room had a vaulted ceiling and a row of windows even taller than her. Warming pans and platters had been arranged on the table, everything from crab croquettes to Chinese dumplings to bruschetta, a United Nations of pretentious food options. Nevertheless, she was so busy filling her plate that she made it all the way around the table before she noticed Scott at the bar in the corner. He had on the boxy tuxedo once again and stood talking to a striking woman dressed in a navy pin-striped skirt and a matching cardigan. Katie was about to slip out of the room and rejoin the party when Scott looked up and saw her.

"I didn't want to interrupt," she said when he raised his eyebrows.

"Not at all," the woman said. "Oh my. Katie *Sutherland?* You've grown! I'm Renee Dunhill. I used to babysit you and your sister."

"Wow." Her father had been right about Renee. She *had* blossomed late. Katie had trouble keeping the parade of babysitters straight in her mind, seeing how they had rotated through with the changing of each academic year, but she did remember Renee. She'd been one of the nice ones, one who'd played endless rounds of Candy Land and Chutes and Ladders, enduring Katie's Byzantine rules, designed on the fly to ensure that she won each time, and never complained about changing Robin's diaper. Katie developed a crush on most of them, though she wouldn't have called it that at the time. But now, Renee was downright hot. Even with the granny glasses.

"Do you know Scott?" Renee said. "Of course you do. He's one of the current stars of the department, isn't he?"

"I'm hardly a star," he said, with a broad smile on his face.

"Scott and I go way back," she said. "We've known each other at least twenty-four hours."

Renee offered something close to a smirk. "Homecoming makes for strange friendships. I'll leave you two alone, brave the lion's den for a bit."

"Don't leave on my account," Katie said. "Not if you're in the middle of something."

"I think I've monopolized Scott's attention long enough."

When they were alone, Katie said, "You really are working her, aren't you?"

"No," he sputtered. "Maybe a little."

"Good for you." She liked thinking about him being more assertive than he'd been among his classmates the night before. "I thought you had the weekend off?"

"Somebody called in hungover. So my boss asked me to fill in. The money's good."

"Good enough for you to buy a new tux?"

He laughed. Like Renee and her father, he was in high spirits. Was everyone at this reception drunk? "This is company-issued. Even I'm not clueless enough to think it looks good."

"That's a relief."

"You, on the other hand, look great."

"Thanks." She blushed. Compliments were never her strong suit, maybe because her parents rarely bothered with them. Not that she minded. It allowed her to remain so under the radar that when she asked Scott for a vodka tonic, she knew her father would never notice.

"I could get fired."

"Which would give you more time with Renee."

"A *small* one," he said. "Heavy on the tonic."

"Yes, Dad."

She drained half of it in one swallow, looked around, then finished the rest and handed the glass back to Scott. Just a small pick-me-up, she figured.

"Hope I didn't get you into too much trouble with Mary," she said.

"I'm the one who should be apologizing. I tried to keep her occupied."

"Easy come, easy go, I guess."

"I don't think she's like that."

"After this weekend, I won't be seeing the light of day for a while, so she'll have to be patient."

"That bad?"

"If my parents weren't so busy punishing each other, I'd be in lockdown already."

"Instead you're at the president's house getting tipsy." He passed her a fresh glass. He really was a good bartender; she'd never noticed him mixing the drink.

"Bottom's up," she said.

"Here's hoping."

"Scott!"

"Sorry. Bad joke."

"You'll need better material than that with Renee. That woman is *hot*."

She felt relaxed, almost dangerously so. She'd have to be careful. Her father may not have been watching, but nothing got by Dr. Delacroix. "What's your game plan?"

"I've got a lit mag in my car with a bunch of her poems in it. I figure I'll read them, if I ever have the chance, and slip a few compliments into the conversation." He noticed the look on her face and added, "You don't think it'll work?"

"Seems a little cheesy."

"What would you do?"

"Something unexpected, in-the-moment."

"In-the-moment isn't my strong suit. I do better with preparation."

"Then you need to loosen up."

"That's what people keep telling me."

"Try this. When the party dies down, grab a couple of bottles of that fancy champagne and let the bubbly do the talking."

"You think it'll work?"

"No offense, but it's a long shot any way you try. What if she has a boyfriend?"

"She doesn't."

"She told you that? Maybe you've got a better chance than I thought."

TRY AS HE MIGHT, ROB couldn't help watching Wykoff's girlfriend. She circulated, always near the man of the hour, smoothly, as though she'd known the donors and Board members for years. They were all buzzing about the gift—rumored to be in the $25 million range—while the carefully curated group of alums who had been included at Wykoff's behest sought another chance to reminisce. Meanwhile, Rob shifted positions to keep Wykoff's date in his line of vision. But his fellow English faculty interrupted him, wanting to eulogize the department.

Betsy Mullins grasped Rob's arm and pulled him into her colloquy with Eleanor Pagliarulo and Annalise Granville.

"This is the beginning of the end for us," Betsy said. "In another ten years, we'll be teaching nothing but First-Year Comp."

"It's not really that bad, is it?" Eleanor said. "Communications has been teaching New Media courses for years, and we haven't lost that many students."

Betsy shook her head. "This is completely different. A shiny new building, money for new hires, plus the imprimatur of the great Evan Wykoff? All those students who would rather write about television shows and video games are going to flock to his new center."

"What do you think, Rob?" The trio turned to him in unison. Typically, none of them cared the least for his opinion, but now they looked as though he was their last chance at a life preserver.

"Maybe this is an opportunity for us to show how our classes are still relevant in today's world. We've all seen the statistics about humanities majors and the job market."

"So we give in to the trade school-ification of the University?" Betsy said.

"On the contrary. We need to make it clear that English stands apart from the various trends, like Wykoff's new center, that everyone else is tilting towards."

"How can you be so optimistic?" Eleanor said.

"I don't know." The truth was, he was lying. If he weren't a full professor already, he would have skipped the party to update his CV. "Honestly, it's our own fault. How many of us teach films because they're an easier sell than books, or pick a shorter text? We've grown complacent."

Evan Wykoff interrupted the group. He'd been so quiet on his shiny leather shoes that no one had heard him approaching. "No one's going to major in playing video games, Dr. S., though the students will have plenty of opportunities to *design* games, which is a whole other story. I hoped you'd embrace this challenge. Video games, like the novels we read in your class, are merely the latest innovation in storytelling. And that's not all this center will be good for. Students will have opportunities to look at technology in all of its myriad forms."

The three women nodded, none of them willing to disagree with their star pupil to his face, so Rob stepped into the fray. "That's all well and good, but why spend a semester studying the uses of status updates on Facebook when something new will come along to replace it?"

"I seem to recall friending *you* on Facebook, Dr. S."

"Not everything I do in my off-hours is worthy of academic study."

Wykoff smiled. "Social media is here to stay, in one form or another. Part of my center's goal is to help students reflect on how and why they use it. Thoughtful use of Facebook—"

"That's where we part company, Evan. I don't believe our students need any help crafting Tumblr posts or pithy tweets. They've been doing that since they were children."

Wykoff's smile broadened. Rob couldn't tell if he was being condescended to or if the expression was the younger man's attempt at masking frustration. Regardless, Wykoff patted Rob's arm and said, "I'm afraid I need to circulate. But I'll be happy to discuss all of this at a later date. Maybe I could Skype into one of your department meetings and allay everyone's fears. Why would I want to kill the English department? You're the people who made me what I am!"

Once Wykoff had left the group, Eleanor said, "He has a funny way of showing his gratitude."

"I hope you hadn't made any plans for that chairmanship," Annalise said.

"I never really believed in it," he lied.

"You deserved it," Betsy said, the first time in recorded history that she'd offered him a compliment.

"At least you've been here long enough to learn your way around campus," Eleanor added. "Now I know why Provost Blankenship pushed so hard for us to hire Leah."

Betsy blanched. "At least it'll get her out of the classroom."

"You know about that?"

"I've had a steady stream of students coming through my office complaining about her. Where there's that much smoke, there tends to be fire."

"None of us were brilliant from the get-go," Eleanor said.

No one wanted to argue the point. Rob finally extricated himself from Betsy's grasp and headed for the bar, where Scott Kenney stood talking to his daughter.

"So this is where you're hiding."

"I went looking for a friendly face."

He handed his empty glass to Scott. "Whiskey. Hold the ice and water. Hell, hold the glass. Just give me the bottle."

"That's just what you need," Katie said.

He ignored the comment and turned to Scott. "Do I need to liberate you, once again, from the ranks of the service industry?"

"I'm just filling in."

"Isn't there a party somewhere you could be attending?"

"Everyone's pretty much paired off tonight."

"And you've been left standing once the music's stopped. Speaking of which," he leaned in. "How go things on the Dunhill front?"

"I don't know."

"Be bold, young man. If you fail, fail exuberantly." He had no idea what that meant, only that he wished he could do the same with Wykoff's girlfriend.

"Thanks for the advice."

"I can't believe you're coaching him," his daughter said. "Doesn't that strike you as unprofessional?"

"I'm a full professor. That still means something around here." Once again, his own words put him at a loss. The college had clearly splurged on the good stuff.

"When are we leaving?"

"I still have a few more people to speak with. And you haven't had your talk with the man of the hour yet."

"If you'd hung around a little longer, you'd know that I had a nice, long chat with him."

"Was he all you'd hoped he would be?"

"He didn't disappoint."

"Good for him. And you."

He left them to puzzle over his words and wandered back into the living room, where the entire English faculty remained in conversation. He ignored Betsy's imploring look, and Herman's more bemused one, and went in search of the bathroom. His first wrong turn led him to the kitchen, where a staff of eight bustled around, placing miniature desserts on silver trays. In the hallway, he walked into the person he most wanted to see, Wykoff's girlfriend.

"Excuse me," he said. "I was looking for the restroom."

"And I was looking for a break. It's pretty intense in there."

"So it is."

She was taller than he'd thought, taller than Wykoff, with shoulder length hair, whose waves he wanted to run his hands along. Its magenta coloring was so thorough that it almost looked natural. It cascaded down onto the collarbones that stood out beneath her cream-colored silk blouse. He couldn't help staring. The woman was perfect. He was drunk, he now realized, and no longer confident in his words. The woman stared at him, openly curious, and he leaned against the table, his fingers inches from her hip.

"You're the famous Dr. Sutherland, aren't you? I saw you talking to Evan earlier."

"I don't know about famous. Call me Rob."

"Willa."

He clasped her extended hand in both of his, lingering a moment longer than was necessary before releasing the slender fingers. She had a small tattoo on the inside of her forearm, something delicate and tasteful, though he didn't have time to decipher it. "You must find this hopelessly dull, compared to the parties Evan normally takes you to."

"Hobnobbing with tech geeks isn't all it's cracked up to be."

"Really?" His smile verged on a leer, and he dialed it back, pursing his lips in the process.

"But this is for a good cause, no?"

"I suppose," he said.

"You aren't convinced?"

"Neither are my colleagues."

"Innovation is often met with retrenchment." She stood up straight, resting her hand on the table, even closer to his than her hip had been. He could feel his palm growing damp, feared that he'd leave a tell-tale smudge on the antique wood finish.

"Tell me, doesn't it all seem a bit much to you. The new ... *center* ... the stage, his own airplane? The man designs video games for a living."

"It took me a while to adjust. But he's merely a supplier. The market dictates the return."

"Spoken like a true MBA."

"A JD, actually. From Stanford."

"How did you end up with Evan?"

"Is that really what you want to know?"

Was it just him, or were they standing even closer together? The slightest tilt of his head and they'd make contact.

"I saw you looking at me," she said.

"And?"

"I like the way you wear that suit. Tweed is so clichéd, but you've got this disdainful attitude, as though you know all about the stereotype and don't care one way or the other."

He ran a hand through his mustache, doing his best to keep from fiddling with it the way Katie had nagged him not to. Katie. What would she think if she saw him standing so close to this strange woman?

"I don't know what to say," he admitted, finally.

"I could help you figure out something," she said. "If you'd like to go somewhere more private."

"And your boyfriend? What'll he think?"

"He's in Palo Alto. He'll never know."

"He's in the other room."

"Why would he be here?"

"Correct me if I'm wrong, but didn't he just announce a multi-million-dollar gift?"

She cocked her head to the side, squinting at him. "Evan's my boss, not my boyfriend."

"Boss?"

"I'm his P.A." She stood up straighter. Smiling, she said, "You thought we're dating? Do I sense a revenge fuck somewhere in the back of that academic mind of yours?"

"No," he said. *Get your hand out of your mustache*, he thought as he went for it, reflexively. "You can't blame. . . ."

"Don't try that." She crossed her arms over her chest and squared her shoulders, standing almost eye-to-eye with him. "You were far more interesting before you tried blaming *me* for your dirty thoughts. Not that you have it in you to go through with it."

"I. . . . My daughter's in the other room."

"So now it's her fault? You need to try taking responsibility for yourself. By the way, if you truly want revenge, go after Leah. She's the one who's behind this whole thing."

"What do you mean?"

"She sold Evan on the whole Technology and Culture angle. Originally, he was going to donate the money for scholarships and a laptop initiative. She got him thinking bigger."

"That snake in the grass."

"If we don't look out for ourselves—" Her phone, on the end table next to them, buzzed before she could finish her statement. She picked it up without looking. "Evan needs me in the other room." She sighed. "A pity. I was looking forward to continuing our *tête-à-tête*. Another time?" She straightened her skirt, which had looked fine to him, and gave her hair a quick toss. "Are we good?" she said.

"Excuse me?"

"I don't want you walking around mooning at me anymore."

"Don't worry."

She shrugged, then strode down the hallway. "Give me a couple of minutes. We don't want to let anyone's imagination run wild."

Alone in the hallway, he realized he felt exhausted from the day he'd had. He wanted to go home. He wanted to jerk-off in the trash can beneath the side table, and then set it on fire. He wanted the night to be over.

WHEN HIS BOSS CAME TO relieve him at the end of the party, Scott took Katie's advice and slipped two bottles of champagne inside his overcoat. Then he went in search of Renee, hoping she hadn't left early. To his surprise, most of the guests were still in the living room. But before he could find Renee, Katie grabbed him by the arm.

"Have you seen my father?" she said. She was glassy-eyed from the two vodka tonics, her pupils threatening to swallow up the blue of her irises.

"Not recently."

"Then can I have a ride? I think he left without me."

"Would he do that?"

"He's been acting weirder than usual. I wouldn't put anything past him."

He sighed, shifting the weight beneath his overcoat. The bottles clinked together when he did so, and Katie reached down to feel the lump he'd been doing his best to conceal.

"You're going for it!" she said. "Forget about the ride. I'll find my own way home."

"I can drop you off, if you really think he ditched you."

"He's probably passed out in the bathroom or something."

Scott didn't know what to do. Abandoning Katie seemed rude, though he'd already rescued her once. That should count for something, he reasoned. While he was debating, he saw Renee putting on her coat in the foyer. He had to make a decision. "Maybe you could call your mother," he said. "I mean, your house is only a couple of minutes away."

"I'm not a child. I can figure it out for myself." When he made no attempt to leave on his own, she added, "*Go*. Before I change my mind."

He caught up to Renee on the front stoop. She was with the group of alums he'd seen her with all weekend, but when she saw him trying to catch up to her, she told them to go on without her.

"I looked for you on my way out," she said.

"I was on a top-secret mission."

"Do tell."

He opened the coat and showed her the two bottles nestled against the wool fabric, feeling as illicit as a flasher. He'd chosen the less expensive of the two brands on offer. Unlike many of the students he worked with, he never smuggled food or downed leftover booze, so he felt entitled to this one theft.

"I didn't know you had it in you," she said. "Be careful. Supplying alcohol to a minor is a serious offense."

"Excuse me?"

"If Dr. S finds out you're getting his daughter drunk, you'll really be in for it."

"They aren't for Katie."

"I thought the two of you. . . . My mistake."

"I was hoping to share them with *you*." He hadn't meant to be so forward, but now that the words were out, he felt surprisingly confident in their effect.

"Champagne gives me a terrible hangover," she said. She looked around, smiled at the trustees who weaved past them and down the front walk.

"It's Homecoming," he said, doing his best to look and sound charming.

"Where do you propose we take these?"

He hadn't thought of that. He couldn't take her back to his house. And he wasn't about to suggest going back to Renee's hotel room, at least not yet. "How about the cemetery?" he said, finally.

Her eyes, her whole face, brightened. "How did you know? We used to drink there before we were old enough for the bars in Asheville!" She pulled him by the arm. "You drive. I'll show you where to park so no one notices us."

He led her to his car, which he'd left on the street behind the president's house. He couldn't think of anything to say now that his plan—Katie's plan—had worked, so he merely asked her if she'd enjoyed the party.

"I think I've made enough small talk for one weekend," she said, and then remained silent the rest of the way to the car.

When he opened the door for her, he remembered Dr. Sutherland's copy of *The Paris Review*, still sitting on the passenger's seat, where it had remained, unread, since he'd liberated it from his professor's office. Renee noticed it right away. She picked it up and said, "No offense, but you don't strike me as a great reader of our nation's literary journals."

"I borrowed it from Dr. Sutherland," he admitted.

"What did you think?"

"I haven't had time to read them yet."

"The story of my life." She tossed the journal in the back seat. "You'll have to wait for another opportunity. No way you're reading them in front of me."

He followed Campus Drive out to High Street, and then turned left and headed for the cemetery. Renee instructed him to forego the main entrance, having him turn at the access road instead. They bumped down the rutted, potholed path and ended up at the utility shed, where there was just enough room for his car between the brick building and the fence separating the back of the cemetery from a cow pasture.

"How do we get out?" he said, trying not to sound apprehensive.

"Like this," she said, then demonstrated what she had in mind. She rolled down the window, shimmied through it, and dropped quietly to the ground between the car and the fence. "Hand me the bottles. It'd be a shame if we made it this far and they broke while you were climbing out."

Outside, Renee led him to the series of mausoleums that skirted the back of the cemetery. She stopped at the second to last one. "We should have come better prepared. The ground's a little wet, I'm afraid."

"I don't mind if you don't."

"This is a new dress," she said. "Screw it. Let's drink!"

He spread his tuxedo jacket on the ground for her to sit on and popped the corks on both bottles of champagne. Once Renee was situated, he passed her one of the bottles before sitting down and taking a swig from the other one. Now that they were finally alone, his nerves were threatening to ruin the evening. He hoped that one bottle of champagne would be enough to drown out the pessimistic voices in his head.

They sat with their backs against the cold stone of the mausoleum, staring out at the empty field before them. To their left, car lights traveled up and down High Street. Now that they were alone, Scott had no idea what to say. Everything he thought of sounded trite or embarrassing.

Finally, Renee broke the ice. "Some weekend," she said.

"Yeah."

"I was sitting at breakfast this morning thinking, *why did I go to all the trouble to come back here?* Ten years is a long time to be away from these people."

He remained silent, next to her, staring into the distance. He feared that if he turned, tried to make eye contact, or said anything, she'd stop talking, and they'd be right back where they started.

"I think I like following everyone's life online better. The more time I've spent with them, faculty included, the more I'm remembering how relieved I was when graduation came."

"Something drew you back here."

"Faulkner was wrong. Sometimes the past *is* dead. And nothing signifies that better than Evan's big announcement." She stopped to take a sip from her bottle, and then continued. "He's revised his life—our lives—on campus to fit into this narrative he's crafted about himself. *The great man in training.*"

"But the new center, isn't it about education?"

"It's a way to churn out more Evan Wykoffs. I wouldn't be surprised if, instead of scholarships, they give out development deals. *Design the next EvRo hit game!*"

"I like *The Service*," he admitted.

"Did you need a college course to figure it out? I'm not an elitist. I teach at a community college, for God's sake. But all he's doing is saying forget studying literature, history, philosophy, whatever. What you really need to get ahead is one good video game or series of viral posts."

"It's what the students want."

"No offense, but college students are too young to know. I see this all the time. The eighteen-year-olds in my classes are clueless. They drift along, doing the bare minimum, and about half of them come back the next semester. Give me the older students any day. Even the twenty-five-year-olds have enough life experience to realize that what we offer them has value. They see the big picture. Even if they never read another line of Elizabeth Bishop, they know that going through this makes them better people. Now, substitute a course in video games for a literature survey. Tell me how that makes them more empathic or deepens their understanding of human nature."

The bottle was cold in his hands, beaded liquid dripping on his tuxedo pants. This wasn't what he'd had in mind when he'd asked Renee to join him. He hadn't imagined they'd just fall on top of each other, but he hadn't expected a lecture either. Even so, she had a point.

"I know you didn't come here to listen to me drone on," Renee said. "But I find it troubling that Evan decided that this was the missing piece, that the best thing he could do with all his money was to create an entire apparatus that glorifies people like him. What's worse, the administration went along with him. President Vessey and Provost Blankenship looked like kids on Christmas morning. They walked around the cocktail party with these blissed-out looks on their faces, as though they couldn't believe their good fortune. The school can't afford to keep the Philosophy department open, but now they're going to create an entirely new discipline just because Evan wants to airlift in a bunch of money."

He hadn't thought of it that way. If Wykoff had given the money to the English department, his name would still be all over it. But that wouldn't change the content of the classes. They wouldn't all of a sudden start sitting around discussing how great Evan Wykoff was. But he'd be Exhibit A in the new Center for Technology and Culture.

"Let's talk about something else," Renee said. "What about you? Glean any insights from seeing where all of us have ended up?"

"I'm so confused," he blurted out. "I mean . . . I don't know *what* I mean."

She turned to him. Her eyes were bright from the champagne, but even so, he could see the concern they expressed. "Try," she said.

"I don't want to come back here in ten years and discover that all the blowhards and the slackers are winning."

She laughed. The sound echoed off the stone around them, and the longer and harder she laughed, the more he feared someone would discover them. Finally, she wiped her eyes and said, "What a positively *Wykoffian* way to put it. He's impressive,

I'll give you that. His own plane, a personal assistant shadowing him at all times, but that doesn't mean he's *winning*."

He thought about the Sutherlands. About the drab house, his professor's decade-old car, the argument he'd witnessed. Winning might be difficult to pinpoint. "I think Dr. Sutherland's having a nervous breakdown," he said.

"Because he's been drunk all weekend?"

"Not just that." He explained what he'd seen, gave her a sanitized version of their various conversations, and threw in Katie's behavior for good measure. "If that's not grounds for a nervous breakdown, I don't know what is."

"You might be surprised by how resilient he is. I used to babysit for them, so I've seen some of what you're talking about. But here they are, ten years later. . . . It might not be as bad as you think it is."

"That's even more depressing. If this is normal for them, they're really fucked."

"How many long-term relationships have you had?"

"None."

"I've learned it's best not to judge from the outside."

He hadn't meant for the conversation to go in such a depressing direction, and now that it had, he wasn't sure how to steer it back onto happier terrain. The champagne was muddling his thoughts, what thoughts weren't focused on Renee's thigh and shoulder, pressed against his own.

"What about you?" he said. "How many long-term relationships have you had?"

"Enough to know I need a break from them."

"You don't strike me as being anti-romantic."

"Too much the opposite," she said. "My armor needs time to build back up."

"Will you recite one of your poems for me?"

"No way!"

"Come on."

"I'm not going to sit here and read my poems while you go all moony-eyed on me."

"I'm not moony-eyed."

"Give me some credit. I can see a crush when it's right in front of me."

"A crush?"

"You really think a night with me is going to solve whatever you're going through?"

"Am I that obvious?"

"It's sweet," she said, patting his leg. "Though I'm not sure I'm the best one to help you solve your problems. If you want direction in life, Michelle Nyburg is the one to go for. I'm just as confused as you are."

"You don't seem confused."

"I give up writing once a year, only to go back a month later when being away from it drives me out of my mind. But as long as I'm writing, I'm not *just* a community college instructor."

"At least it's a job."

"You'll figure something out," she said, shifting the focus back to him. "If you really want to go to grad school, ignore Dr. Delacroix and go. His isn't the only opinion out there."

He thought about Dr. Sutherland, who'd all but pushed him to apply that very morning. Renee was right. He could get plenty of letters of recommendation without Dr. Delacroix, even if none of them would have the cache of the great scholar. He should at least see what would happen.

"I think it's time we got out of here," she said. "I'm freezing, and we're out of booze."

He hadn't realized they'd been there long enough to finish both bottles, but they had. When he stood up, his eyes seemed to swim in their sockets. Renee's hotel was on the way to his house, a route he'd driven enough times that he figured he could do it blindfolded, let alone drunk. He held out a hand and helped her up. Standing toe-to-toe, they were almost the same height. He wanted to reach out, to at least make a gesture, but before he could convince his limbs to do what he wanted, she wrapped her arms around his neck and gave him a hug.

"Don't get any ideas," she said. "You just look like you could use a little affection."

Twenty-Four

The party was breaking up: people headed toward the coat room, making plans for where they were headed next, and the first few handed tickets to the valets outside, but try as she might, she couldn't find her father. Finally, about to give up and begin walking, she came across Dr. Delacroix, waiting for his car.

"I haven't seen him," Dr. Delacroix said in response to her question. "But if his car is still here, he must be around."

"I don't want to be the last person inside."

"I'll give you a ride."

She hesitated. It wasn't Dr. Delacroix's offer, but the destination. Arriving home without her father would give her mother new ammunition. She'd hardly seen her parents together this weekend, but that hadn't kept them from talking, endlessly, about each other and their faults. She wasn't about to add fuel to this dysfunctional bonfire.

"Where do the seniors live?" she said once she'd come up with another destination.

Dr. Delacroix raised an eyebrow. He said, "It depends. Some of them live in the suites. Others are still in the dorms."

"What about Mary Wardell?"

"I don't know for sure, but I'd bet money she's in Winsor Hall. It's all singles." Before she could turn away, the professor handed her a roll of breath mints. "Unless you want to smell like the inside of a cocktail shaker, I'd pop a few of these."

"I couldn't resist."

"I was a teenager once, too. But you could have gotten Scott fired."

"It seemed worth it."

He handed his ticket to the valet, and then pulled her off to the side. "It's none of my business," he said. "But wouldn't it be better if I took you home?"

"I need time to think first."

"Understood." She could tell he had more on his mind, so she remained silent and waited for him to decide how to proceed. "I'll buy you a coffee if you like. Won't even sit with you if you need space. I'm not sure that hanging out with Mary Wardell is what you need right now."

She hugged him, burying her cheek in his wool overcoat. She'd never touched him before, but she held on tightly until he reciprocated, patting her on the back with an open palm. She stepped back after a few seconds and said, "I'm okay. But thanks for being concerned." She didn't wait for a response.

The president's house was on the outskirts of campus, so it took her almost fifteen minutes to wind her way through the empty quads and find Winsor Hall. She'd never been to the residential side of campus. In the growing darkness, she had to walk up to each building in order to see its name. Finally, when only two buildings remained, she found Winsor Hall. It was a narrow, three-story building with an ID reader at the front door that she didn't have a card for. She knocked on the glass and waited for the bored front desk attendant to walk over and open the door.

"I forgot my card," she lied.

Katie couldn't believe it was that easy to get in. She knew from the previous night that she could pass for a college student, but she'd expected some hassle before she'd be allowed entrance to the building. But the young woman was back behind the desk, watching television, before Katie had even crossed the lobby. She followed the illuminated EXIT sign around the bend in the hallway, where it led to a set of stairs that she climbed to the top floor. She ended up at the far end of the hallway, and as she walked down the corridor she heard music coming from most of the rooms.

She scanned doors until she ended up in front of 301, the door with Mary's name on it, and listened for noise behind the door but heard nothing. She wasn't sure why she'd chosen Mary's room as her preferred destination. After the scene at the football stadium, she didn't know if Mary would even want to see her again. It was worth the risk, however. And not just because she didn't want to go home. She found that she actually missed the feel of Mary's body pressed against her own. If it wouldn't have sounded pathetic, she would have begged the woman for a few minutes of cuddling, nothing more.

Silence greeted her knock, followed by the sound of someone shuffling across the floor. Finally, when she was about to knock again, the door opened. Mary stood before her, blocking the entrance like a sentry. The woman's face went from annoyance to surprise and back to annoyance so quickly Katie wasn't sure that she hadn't imagined the changes.

"I was in the neighborhood and thought I'd stop by," she said.

"You've been drinking."

"You're still mad."

"Dogs get mad. People get angry."

"Don't you ever switch off?"

"Now you really do sound like a college student." She walked back into the room, the door swinging closed of its own accord, until Katie stopped it with her foot. She followed Mary inside, letting it slam after her.

The walls were covered in reproductions of paintings by Georgia O'Keefe and creepy photographic portraits that must have been done by Diane Arbus, though she only knew the woman by reputation. There were so many of them that they often overlapped, creating a strange effect whereby O'Keefe's *Pineapple Bud* bled into a black-and-white photo of a man in curlers, with a lit cigarette in one hand. If Katie had to live in this tiny room, she feared she'd go crazy from all the stimuli.

"This place is tiny."

"It beats having a roommate."

It was warm. Hot air blew from the radiator beneath the small window. If it weren't for the walls, Katie would have felt like she was in a prison cell. She took off her coat and hung it from the back of the door knob.

"Don't you ever wear normal clothes?"

Katie had forgotten about her outfit. If she'd been over-dressed at the cocktail party, she was even more so here. Mary had on jeans, a green flannel shirt, slippers so worn that her big toes poked through, and she had on glasses for the first time since Katie had known her. She looked like she was on the verge of going to bed, no Homecoming party for her.

"I was my father's plus-one at the president's reception."

"How was it?"

"I would rather have been here."

Mary sat down on the edge of the bed and picked up the book she'd left spine-up on the bedspread. She turned down the corner of the page she was on and tossed it on the desk.

"Any good?"

"If you've read *Jane Eyre*. It doesn't make much sense otherwise."

"I like *Wuthering Heights* better."

"Me, too."

"So we're both into doomed love affairs."

"Why didn't your mom go to the reception?"

"They offered me one last reprieve before I'm permanently grounded."

"Because of last night?"

"It was worth it," she said. She sat down on the far end of the bed, leaving as much room between them as possible, though what she wanted was to curl up next to Mary, head in her lap. "Speaking of reprieves."

Mary got up and walked to her desk, where she straightened a stack of books that sat next to her laptop. Finally, without looking up, she said, "You look good."

Katie crossed her legs. She would have shown up at Mary's door even if she'd been in sweats and a t-shirt, she wanted to see her badly enough, but she knew the advantage she had, dressed as she was. Her mother rarely let her wear the dress, convinced it was too form-fitting, too mature, for someone her age. But when she'd put it on that night, her mother had merely shrugged, told her to have a good time, and then gone back to the board game she'd been playing with Robin at the kitchen table.

"Come sit by me," she said.

"I don't think I should."

"I'll be eighteen next month."

"So come back then."

"You want me to leave?"

"I didn't say that."

"You want me to stay?"

Mary went back to straightening the papers. She stood up and went to her. Mary didn't look up as she approached, kept her back to her, so Katie stopped when she was directly behind her, even though she wanted to wrap her arms around Mary. Let her make the first move, she decided.

"You're not making this easy."

"Sure, I am. All you have to do is tell me to leave, and I'll go."

Mary turned around. Face-to-face, Katie was at least a

couple of inches taller, thanks in part to her heels. She loomed over Mary, looking down, into her eyes, swaying slightly from nerves and anticipation and alcohol. Mary's hands were on the desk chair behind her. She leaned back to put as much distance between them as possible. Katie leaned forward, bridging the gap.

"I'm not asking to be your girlfriend," she said. "I just want to be with you."

"What's the point?"

"It could be fun?"

Mary bit the corner of her mouth, a flash of white incisor poking past her full, pale lips. Her eyes seemed unfocused. "You can't spend the night," she said. "I don't want your parents to completely hate me."

Katie stepped forward, pressing herself to Mary, whose hands finally reached out for her. They rested against her hips, offering the slightest resistance.

"I'm serious," Mary said. "I still have to pass your father's class."

Though she was taller, Katie did her best to fit herself to Mary's body, burrowing her nose into the other woman's neck, wrapping her hands around her, pressing a thigh into the space between her legs. Mary still held onto her hips, but now she was running her hands up and down them, making the material crackle with static. Katie could feel Mary's exhalations on her bare shoulder, the way the woman tried to keep her breathing under control even as she became more frantic in her movements. Finally, Katie raised her head and found Mary's waiting lips with her own.

They shed clothes on their way to the bed, Katie's dress tossed in the corner, Mary's flannel shirt and jeans in a heap on the desk chair. Slipping beneath the sheets, in their underwear, they continued groping for each other's mouths. She found the clasp at the back of the older woman's bra, releasing her heavy breasts, and struggled to do the same with her own. She longed for the feel of skin on skin, the brush of her nipples against any part of Mary's body. Without knowing who had initiated it, she found her panties tangled around her feet, could feel the heat from Mary's pelvis grinding against her. It was like something out of a dream; she had only to think of something and it happened.

The grinding stopped, replaced by fingers that explored and caressed, knuckles bumping against knuckles in their desire. Closer and closer, Katie's fingers began to twitch and jump, which only excited Mary more, causing greater sensations for both of them. They climaxed almost simultaneously, Katie first, Mary right after, the two of them shuddering so violently Katie feared the bed would break apart. Spent, they lay against each other, their limbs heavy, breathing in great gasps of air.

"Shit," Mary said. "This is so wrong."

"Can't you just relax and *enjoy* it?"

"Am I lying naked next to you, or is that someone else?"

"I don't want to argue."

They lay silent until their breathing slowed. Katie felt like vaulting off the bed and running naked around the dorm, announcing what had happened at regular intervals to make sure that everyone knew. This went so far beyond the previous night, beyond her previous, abbreviated encounters. What Mary had done to her, what they'd done to each other, was so fantastic that if she'd had the energy, she would have done it all over again.

"Fuck, that was good," Mary said.

Katie hummed into the woman's hair, practically purring her agreement. She longed to tell Mary how she felt but feared admitting this was her first time. Mary was too erratic, too prone to guilt; if Katie told her the truth, she'd probably freak out and push her off the bed.

"Better than *Wide Sargasso Sea?*"

"If I hadn't been sitting here reading, would you be in this position now?"

"I would have gone door-to-door. Surely somebody in this building is horny."

"Not likely. Sometimes I think everyone left their libidos at home."

"Didn't seem that way last night."

"The great Halloween party is an excuse to let off steam. Come Monday, everyone will go back to their repressed selves."

"How sad."

"Maybe not *every*one." Mary shifted and pressed herself against Katie's shoulder. "How'd you know how to find me, anyway?"

"Dr. Delacroix told me where you lived."

"You asked *him* about me?"

"Don't be mad."

"I don't have the energy to right now, but I reserve the right to change my mind later. I can't believe you asked Confluence College's finest scholar where your booty-call lived."

"He was right, wasn't he?"

"That must have been some reception to get you this worked up."

Katie told her about losing track of her father. "I hope he's going crazy looking for me right now, but more than likely, he's forgotten I even went with him."

"Your Dad went from thinking he was getting an endowed chair to being obsolete in the space of a twenty-minute speech."

"Really?"

"No one I know, except for Scott, would major in English with this new option."

Lying pressed up against Mary suddenly felt claustrophobic. She looked around the room, at the paintings and photographs, the bulletin board covered with postcards, and felt the walls closing in on her. Not an original insight, she knew, but no less true for its triteness. What if *she'd* abandoned her father, and not vice versa?

"I have to go," she said.

"You can't just fuck and run."

"My Dad—I have to find him."

"A bit dramatic, isn't it?"

She ignored Mary's words, and her arch tone, got out of bed, and went in search of her dress, stockings, and shoes. She put them on without giving a second thought to her appearance, didn't even stop to fix her hair or give herself a once-over in the mirror behind the door. She looked back once, to make sure Mary was still paying attention to her. She was. Katie waved goodbye and swung open the door and took off, striding down the hallway so quickly she'd taken a dozen steps before she realized she was heading in the wrong direction.

Twenty-Five

Molly watched her daughter roll the dice and then move the metal thimble five spaces to Baltic Avenue. The girl had asked three times to be excused to play the piano, but Molly had realized she'd been letting the instrument babysit her youngest in much the way other parents used television. It was time for her daughter to receive some direct, human contact.

"You passed GO. You get $200."

"Yay."

She'd hoped Robin would be excited that her mother had decided to stay home, but she feared the girl would have preferred having Katie around. She had no idea what they did together, having so little in common, though she knew the same could be said about her and Rob.

"When will they be home?"

"Any time now," she said. Though if she knew her husband, he'd be the last one there, shaking hands and patting backs as though he were the host.

That wasn't fair, she knew, but it had been a long day. Her sympathy for her husband had waned as the evening wore on. She knew she had to find a way to get it back, that he was wounded by what he was bound to take as a rejection, even if he'd never admit it. She also knew that if he'd received the endowed chair, it would have been both easier and more difficult for her to leave: easier in light of the college's—of Wykoff's—largesse, which would have left him in a position to take care of the family while she was gone. But more difficult for the same reason. More money would have made her own position unnecessary, superfluous, and she could have remained, teaching a reduced load, safe in the knowledge that her husband could provide for them.

But she also knew that she would have resented Rob's success. An endowed chair would have been more evidence that she was merely Mrs. Rob Sutherland. It was better this way, she decided. Let him have a small taste of what life was like for her.

It had been Robin's turn for two minutes, but she had yet to roll the dice. She sat slumped over the table, a hand propping her bored head. When Molly had been her age, game night had been exciting, a rare chance to play with the adults. Now, it was punishment.

"I'll make you a deal," she said. "You can play the piano as long as I get to choose the repertoire. I'm tired of all that moody jazz."

"No Tchaikovsky," Robin said, perking up. "Too Romantic."

"I couldn't agree more."

They retired to the study, as Rob had probably retired, scotch in hand, to an anteroom at President Vessey's house with Herman and some of their circle. She hated being so bitter but couldn't come up with a happier emotion when she thought of her husband, even amid this latest setback. He had a way of landing on his feet that would have been admirable if it weren't so damned annoying.

While Robin sat with her back to her at the piano, working through a Bach fantasia, she settled into the easy chair in the corner. Half a section's worth of ungraded problem sets lay next to her, soon to be joined by another week's output. She considered picking them up. Robin was beyond the point where she required undivided attention to her playing at all times, but she couldn't make herself do it. She'd never been a procrastinator, but the last few weeks, as her anxiety over the visiting position grew, she'd found it difficult to make herself do the work at hand.

Robin moved on to an Invention, Molly couldn't remember which one. She knew her daughter preferred the even ones, had a thing for easily divisible numbers, but to her ears, many of them sounded the same. Robin played it straight for once, adding none of her own embellishments to Bach's work, though she swung from side to side as though she were playing the jauntiest boogie-woogie. She figured Rob and Katie would be home soon, putting an end to the peaceful evening. Katie would turn on the TV—even when she played Robin's albums, she did it at a volume that made thought or conversation difficult—and fire up the sewing machine. Rob would want to rehash what had happened, listing everyone he'd talked to, what had been said, particularly if it was critical of Wykoff and his gift, and what the caterers had prepared.

Robin's tempo picked up as she began another Invention, and she attacked the keys with vigor, even more so after one of her rare mistakes, which she seemed to atone for with increased dedication. When Robin was younger, Molly had caught her smacking herself in the head when she made an error, a habit Molly had broken her of only by remaining in the room for her entire practice sessions.

"I've started on *The Art of the Fugue*," Robin said without turning away from the keyboard. "When I was little, I thought it sounded boring, but I'm starting to get it." She played what sounded like the opening of one of the Fugues, a slow passage with her right hand, soon joined by the left in counterpoint. "They're all in D-minor," she said. "Which is the real challenge. How do you vary the mood without key changes or preludes or *anything?*"

"I don't know."

"It's all in the rhythm. For once, I'm following the notations *exactly.*"

"That's a big shift."

"If you can't trust Bach...."

The counterpoint increased, staccato notes passing from one clef to the other. Molly couldn't remember hearing her daughter play this before, but she often chose times when no one was around to try out new pieces.

Molly could see what she meant about the rhythms. The tempo of each Fugue varied dramatically, and though she couldn't say that she enjoyed them as much as the Inventions, she was coming to appreciate the challenge her daughter had placed before herself. What could have been monotonous came off as deft, subtle.

She looked out the window, at their neighbors' yard, raked free of leaves that now lined the roadside, where the town would send around a truck to suck them up. She and Rob waited until every leaf had fallen, until the end of the semester, to spend a miserable weekend raking and bagging. Even with the girls' help, it took twelve hours; but they couldn't afford to hire a company to do it, and had no interest in doing it piecemeal, like their neighbors. With a little luck, Molly might not have to do it the following year, holed up in an apartment beyond Raleigh.

Twenty-Six

R ob could hear the party breaking up, but he had no interest in leaving the hallway, stuck as he was at the sight of his humiliation. He was no better than his male students, being led around by their dicks. At forty-four, he thought he was beyond this, but evidence pointed to the contrary. His first reaction to the setback he'd suffered wasn't to work harder or to buffer himself from the hurt by surrounding himself with his family or to take solace in his friendship with Herman who had a knack for putting life in perspective. No, his impulse was to envision fucking away the problem.

It was time to grow up and face the enemy head on.

When he rejoined the party, he discovered that more people remained than he'd expected. The living room and foyer were still half-full. Rob passed the bar, where someone he didn't know was packing up, and broke through the circle of people that took up most of the living room. At the center, he saw President Vessey and the man of the hour.

As he entered the ring, he saw Willa, off to the side, holding a tablet computer in one hand while the fingers of the other typed furiously.

"I want the college community to feel a sense of ownership over the new center," Evan said. "So I'm offering matching funds for all who feel called to contribute as well."

Rob spoke up. "But it'll still be your name on the building, no?"

President Vessey looked his way, frowning. "Evan's name provides an element of cachet. Having his name on the center will only enhance its reputation."

"You don't have to defend me, Dr. Vessey. I'll cop to the charge of vanity, but I *am* the one donating the lion's share of the money. Aren't naming rights how these things are usually done?"

"Of course." Rob felt tired all of a sudden.

"You sound troubled, Dr. S."

He yawned. "Forgive me," he said. "But isn't this whole thing just one big ego trip?"

"I'll remind you, Dr. Sutherland, that you're in the presence of the largest single benefactor this school has ever had."

"I don't need reminding. It's written all over that scale model in the foyer."

"You don't approve of my gift."

"It seems to me that we have enough problems—budgetary problems, no less, as President Vessey never fails to remind us—that a shiny new program is the least of our concerns."

"Evan's gift will be a boon for us, I assure you. We've studied it from all perspectives, and it's sure to increase our visibility, thus adding to enrollment and providing the cutting-edge program we need to stay ahead of the competition."

"You make it sound like we're manufacturing cars."

"Not a bad analogy," the President said. "You can get by with a cheap one, or a used model, but the higher-priced options come with their own advantages."

"So Evan's gift is akin to power locks?"

"Don't be so glib, professor."

He nodded. "My apologies," he said. "Forgive my skepticism."

"Now," President Vessey said, turning his attention back to his guests. "Once the land has been cleared, we'll organize a ground-breaking ceremony for you and the other upper-tier donors."

"Pardon me again." Rob couldn't help himself. "Where do you intend to put this glass-and-steel monstrosity?"

"The center will replace Breen-Higginbottom."

"You're going to replace the old library with Video Game Studies?"

"As you know, BH has been vacant for two years. I can't think of a better use for the space than as the home of the new Center for Technology and Culture."

"That's another thing," Rob said, trying to catch Willa's eye. The woman was clearly listening to the debate, though she was occupied with the tablet before her. "What kind of culture are we left with when everything has been replaced with technology?"

Evan smiled at President Vessey and raised a hand to silence the older man before he could respond. "Aren't you the one who taught me about the role the printing press played in the growing popularity of novel writing? Today's technology is no different. It may seem like a threat, but the advances it offers will be equally influential for coming generations."

"Better graphics hardly compare to the printing of great works of literature."

"You should come out to California, let me give you a tour," Evan said. "You might be surprised by what we're doing. Bring your daughter. I gather she doesn't share your qualms."

"Much to my dismay."

"You'll feel differently once the center is up and running. Leah has some wonderful plans for faculty involvement. Who knows, she might be able to sway you better than I can."

"I don't know that I'll be around that long," he said.

"Forgive me if I'm taking you too literally, Dr. Sutherland, but are you implying that you'll be leaving us?" President Vessey leaned forward.

"I don't know that I can work at a school that thinks this is the answer to its academic prayers."

"We've all been drinking, Robert, so I'm not going to give that statement too much credence. Still, I hope you come around sooner rather than later. It's a buyer's market out there."

"Is that a threat?"

"Merely a word of warning, from one colleague to another."

Vessey had ascended the ranks from Provost to President during Rob's early years at Confluence. The man had introduced himself to Rob, anew, each time they'd encountered one another until Rob received tenure, hardly what he would consider collegial behavior.

"On a personal note," the President said. "I'm not sure where the rumor about the endowed chair came from."

"You think this is about a wounded ego? I've been here longer than either of you," he said. "Longer than most of the people around us." He paused to take in the crowd, wondering briefly where his daughter, his English department colleagues, and Scott had disappeared to. "I may not have made the same financial contributions as some in this room, but I've given more hours, more of my life to this institution than you can imagine. And I'm here to tell you, this is a bad idea."

"Do tell, professor."

He looked from face to face, savoring his moment in the spotlight, but found no friendly faces. Still, he pressed on. "I may not know as much about this field as some in this room, but isn't most of the designing and coding of video games already farmed out to Southeast Asia? What good is it going to do to teach people how to code, how to design, when there won't be any more jobs left for them than there would have been if you'd actually taken responsibility for your education and finished your PhD?"

Wykoff's smirk was gone, replaced by a flat affect. "You mean like your wife, professor?"

Even Willa looked up at this remark.

"You say you're going to attract students, train the next generation. I have no doubt that you believe that, but how many Evan Wykoffs do we need, with their private jets and personal assistants with finer pedigrees than their employers? Why don't you grow up, use the knowledge you gained here, and do something useful with your life? That's what we *trained* you for."

Vessey stepped between the two men. "You are completely out of line, Robert."

Wykoff waved a hand at the president, who tellingly silenced his rebuke at the motion. Rob knew who was truly in charge of the College from here on. The president, a scholar of the Boer Wars, had ceded control to a mere adolescent, masquerading as an adult.

"This is the future, professor. Either embrace it, or wither on the vine."

"Perhaps I am a pessimist," he said. "But if we give this much ground to this *possible* future, we'll be giving up everything that makes this school great. And, as I said before, many of us, myself included, are not going to stand for it." He looked around for allies but realized that none of the faculty remained. With that, he too headed toward the foyer. He was about to leave the house when a hand grasped his shoulder. Willa. She slipped through the door and let it swing shut on its own, without relinquishing her grip.

"Committing career suicide isn't the way to impress a woman," she said. "You should see the writing on the wall. This *is* the future."

"I've heard enough about the future for one night. As I said, I've given sixteen years to this school—which is nothing compared to how long some have been here—and now, just because some jerk-off wants to donate a ton of cash, he gets to dictate the direction of the college."

"Money talks. If you haven't figured that out by now, you're awfully naive."

"What are you doing out here? Why do you care what happens to me?"

She reached out for his shoulder again, but he stepped backward and slipped away from her touch. "I've been listening to Evan talk about you, and his other professors, for months. Obviously, you mean something to him. I don't want to see you flush it all away out of hubris."

"You think this is about my *pride?*"

"What else could it be?"

"How about professional standards, personal integrity?"

His phone buzzed in his pocket. He studied the screen, letting his eyes adjust. He'd had too much to drink. It was from Katie. *Need to talk. Where r u?* He left without another word.

Outside, he found Katie waiting for him behind the President's residence. The weather had turned cool as the sun had set, and she was shivering in her thin dress without a coat. He slipped out of his own and draped it over her shoulders. She was swimming in it, but at least she'd be warm.

"Thanks," she said. "I misplaced my coat."

He reached out and smoothed her hair. "I don't think I want to know where."

Rob led his daughter to a bench at the far side of the quad, wiped off the pine needles that had collected on it, and sat down. He was tired, too tired for a serious conversation, but that had never stopped him before, so he prepared to listen to whatever his daughter had to offer. Instead, he was met with more silence. The pair sat shoulder to shoulder without looking at each other. Finally, he said, "I'm sorry I abandoned you after the party. I ended up talking to President Vessey and Wykoff, and time slipped away from me."

"I don't care about that."

"You seem upset."

"I am, but not because you left me."

"Do I have to drag it out of you, then?" Her mother was the same way. At least with his daughter he had enough stature that he could make her talk.

"Why didn't Evan give you the endowed chair?"

"That's what you're concerned about? It was never in the cards. Just one of those rumors that passes for truth on a small campus like this." He frowned. He'd never mentioned the possibility himself, he was sure of it. Not out of superstition but out of the same need to keep expectations low that had kept him from announcing any of his plans when he was a kid. "How'd you find out about that?" he said.

"Mom. Mary Wardell. Everybody."

"And when did you see Mary?" She didn't respond, merely brushed something off the lapel of his coat. "So the two of you are. . . ."

"We're not dating, if that's what you mean. I just like hanging out with her."

"You could have told us," he said.

"I didn't want to make it a thing."

"'A thing?'"

"Something we needed to discuss, at length. You and Mom would tie yourselves into knots showing me how *open* and *supportive* you are, and after it was all over I'd end up with a reading list to help me understand my *lifestyle*."

"Are we that bad?"

"Sometimes."

"For the record, I don't see it as a lifestyle. Nevertheless, she's four years older than you. I know you're infatuated—"

"It might be more than that."

He sighed. "She'll be gone in six months. Then what? I don't want you getting your heart broken."

She leaned against him, and it was all he could do to keep from wrapping his arms around her. He didn't deserve such affection, but he was so relieved when it presented itself.

"Mary says Evan's announcement makes you obsolete."

"She said that?"

"Verbatim."

"She's awfully smart, that one." He'd meant to sound flip.

"So it's true?"

"It might be." He didn't know how to continue the conversation without admitting that he'd all but handed in his resignation. He doubted President Vessey would hold him to his words, but how was he supposed to stay at Confluence once he'd told the President and his largest donor that they were ruining the school?

"Just this once," Katie said, "could you not treat me like a child. I'm worried about you."

"I don't want to burden you," he said.

"Even Mom told me she's basically moving to the other side of the state."

"She did?" No wonder Katie was jumping into Mary Wardell's arms.

"So what do we do now?"

"Right now? Or down the line?"

"Take your pick."

He pictured telling Molly any of what had happened. He wasn't sure which news she'd take worse, their daughter's escapade or his announcement to President Vessey. Was he wrong to think that none of it would have happened if she'd been there? Katie would have been home with Robin, he wouldn't have had the opportunity to pursue Willa, and, therefore, wouldn't have ended up confronting Evan and Vessey. But though he was tired and drunk, he knew not to blame the evening on Molly.

A group of students filed past them, belatedly dressed as ghouls and vampires, several of them nodding shyly in his direction. If he went through with his threat, this was the part he'd miss, his relationship with the students. He remembered what Scott had been like as a first-year, so unsure of himself that he behaved as though even his answers to personal questions might be wrong. He'd matured over the course of these four years, now asserted his ideas in class and felt confident enough to chase Renee Dunhill, who'd gone through much the same transformation. The first time she'd shared a poem with him, junior year, her hands had shaken so badly he'd immediately rejected the impulse to have her read it aloud. He'd taken the quivering paper from her, soon amazed by the confidence of her voice on the page. He still had a copy of the campus literary magazine it had appeared in somewhere in his office.

"Remember Fluffy?" his daughter said, bringing him back to the present.

"You loved that dog." They'd gotten her when Katie had been in first grade, in one of Molly's rare moments of weakness. The dog had been pampered by all of them, until she turned nasty, suffering from pancreatitis, and had to be put down.

"At the end, the vet made a crack about more treatments being like rearranging deck chairs on the Titanic," she said, avoiding his eyes. "I feel like that's what this weekend has been."

"For all of us?"

"Maybe."

He wrapped an arm around her shoulder, no longer fearing a rebuff. He considered placating her with empty promises. Instead, he remained silent, hugging his daughter with all the strength she'd allow.

Twenty-Seven

She lay quietly in bed, listening to the gentle murmur of her husband's snoring. He'd come home distracted, not wanting to talk. Try as he might to deny it, he was a regular snorer, though this rarely bothered Molly. He wasn't overly loud or obnoxious, and she liked knowing that he, at least, was sleeping on the nights when she lay awake. Being the only one awake in the house gave her the same thrill it had when she was young, living with her parents, and in the throes of insomnia. She listened for a few more minutes before slipping out of bed and heading downstairs to her study.

On nights like this, she often took refuge in one of the authors whose books she knew well, but she didn't feel much like reading. The day had been interminable, the only relief coming when Rob went to bed early instead of staying up to discuss all that had transpired. She wouldn't have begrudged him the need to talk. He'd been through even more than she had. But she needed to process all that had happened. She wanted to take the Mustang for a spin, craved the by-now-deserted roads outside of town, but knew that she couldn't. Leaving the house might wake her family. Instead, she sat down at her desk and turned on her computer.

Once she'd logged on, she studied the icons on the screen for something that would help her mind relax. She'd never been much for computer solitaire, or any of the other games that came preprogrammed on the machine, most of which she'd never even opened, so she passed by these mindless offerings and stopped, instead, on *The Service*. Katie had loaded the game onto the computer the week it had come out. Molly had never been interested in it, but after Wykoff's announcement, she was curious to find out what all the fuss was about.

She opened the program and waited for the menu to load. Instead of a log-in page, it opened with what she assumed were her daughter's last actions in the game. A chat function took over the screen, and she read through her daughter's last game out of curiosity.

RedSoxSux: What the frack?

Ernie_from_Erie: True that. NC?

MajorTom: We're waiting. . . .

nowhere_NC: There's activity in the crowd. I see at least three of them!

RedSoxSux: What's going on?

MajorTom: You see anything, Ernie?

nowhere_NC: The girl disliked living in their small town almost as much as Molly did and planned elaborate escapes, post–high school, to New York or Chicago or L.A. If only she and Rob could afford to send her to one of those places.

She clicked the Replay button at the bottom right of the screen and watched as President Kennedy's motorcade made its way through downtown Dallas on that fateful day. Nothing seemed out of the ordinary at first. The President and Mrs. Kennedy waved to the crowds, the Secret Service officers surrounding them, but then the protector directly behind the vehicle moved closer, on Kennedy's side, and drew a pistol from inside his suit jacket. Even with the volume off, Molly flinched when the gun went off. Her daughter had shot the president. It only got worse, as she watched her daughter's avatar shoot every one of her teammates. She did it carefully, distracting them at first, with comments about suspicious activity, only to chase down the last two openly. It was well-planned. It was disturbing.

Why had her daughter done such a thing? She considered watching the footage again, but the game was realistic enough that she preferred not to watch the killings a second time. She couldn't watch it again, which left her to replay the image in her mind. Even doing that offered no clues. Was it a cry for help? If so, why had she logged off so quickly? Was she sadistic? She rejected this idea quickly. No one who looked after her little sister as lovingly as Katie did could possibly take such actions for the sheer pleasure of them. A thrill-seeker? That was more like it. Molly could understand that impulse. She, herself, longed to feel the Mustang's engine revving and humming as she took curves at twice the legal limit. Perhaps Katie was the same way. Perhaps killing the president and her team, as bizarre an action as that was, was her way of feeling reckless and safe at the same time. It was only a game after all.

She swung her feet up on the desk and leaned back in the chair. Outside the window, the streetlight bathed their yard in its halogen glow. She remembered their early days in the house, when it had seemed like an expansive refuge. They'd spent the first summer painting all of the rooms, covering the drab white with eggshell, lilac, and canary yellow. They'd saved the kitchen for last, choosing a bright red that accented the black counters and appliances. Rob's father had spent a week planing and staining boards for the bookcases he'd installed in her study. Then she'd reveled in the time it took her to unpack all of the boxes and place the books on the new shelves. Once she'd had them all arranged on the beautiful pine shelves, she sat at the desk admiring their spines. Then she'd decided to remove their dust jackets, preferring the near-uniformity of the bare books to their more colorful coverings. She rarely took the time to sit and enjoy her collection any longer. If she remained seated in her study for too long, Robin would appear with an offer to serenade her at the piano, or Rob would interrupt her thoughts with a question about dinner or what had become of his favorite shirt, the white one with the blue checks?

She wondered what would happen to her collection if she took the job at Rocky Mount. Would Rob, in a fit of anger, toss the books? Would Katie help him? Or would life go on as before, just without her presence? The girls were old enough that they would adapt to her absence. Life would continue without her, she was sure. She knew plenty of academics who lived hours, hundreds of miles, away from their families, and only saw them on the occasional weekend and at holidays. She wouldn't let Katie's guilt trip and Rob's anger dissuade her from pursuing the opportunity.

Still, something was bothering her.

She thought about Robin's performance earlier, her explanation of Bach's Fugues. Boredom had been the bane of the girl's existence since she'd learned the word, her life a constant battle against the feeling. Molly was impressed that she'd overcome that attitude and given the Fugues a try. She realized, sitting in the dark, that she would be gone before her daughter had learned the rest of them. She imagined their debut, Robin at the piano in an outfit her sister crafted expressly for the occasion, looking serious, poised. Later, she and Katie would convene to debrief, her older sister the only critic whose opinion mattered. Rob would be supportive, excessive in his attempt to cover up his dislike of classical music, but Robin would see through his good cheer. The girls had both inherited their mother's finely attuned bullshit detector, something Rob thought he had as well, though he'd allowed the rumor mill at Confluence to convince him of the most ludicrous of unsubstantiated gossip.

Thinking about the future recital, Molly felt her first pang of guilt at leaving her family. Robin could play the pieces over Skype—she'd insist on it—but even this would pale in comparison to the excitement of a debut. She'd miss hearing her daughter's playing, miss Katie's anxious bustling as she prepared for the main event, even Rob's humorous attempts at keeping his attention from wandering during recitals that could stretch beyond an hour. The computer screen went to sleep, leaving the room in total darkness. Molly stood up, leaving the computer on, and headed for the kitchen. Perhaps a glass or two of water would help her get to sleep. If she didn't go to bed soon, Sunday would feel even longer than usual.

Twenty-Eight

The air was crisp and cool, and Rob sat on the patio with his hands wrapped around a warm mug of coffee for comfort. Though he was cold, he wasn't ready to go inside yet. For once, he'd awoken before his wife, and the thought of facing her now that she was milling around in the kitchen was too much for him to bear. It wasn't the hangover, at least not entirely, that was bothering him. He felt like an idiot, a fool, for all that had happened over the course of the weekend.

He heard the neighbors leave their house and pile into their minivan for church. The families had never been close, the twin girls between Katie and Robin's ages, the parents suspicious of outsiders like Rob and Molly, people who hadn't grown up and gone to school there. That morning, he felt more isolated than usual. Even after all these years, his neighbors were just acquaintances, his friends at Confluence not much closer. Even Herman.

As though the thought had conjured the man, Molly opened the sliding glass door and let Herman pass by her onto the patio.

She closed the door again, without acknowledging her husband. Herman, looking fresh in his Sunday finest, strode across the concrete slab, whipped out a handkerchief, and brushed off a chair before seating himself opposite Rob. He folded the linen back into a square, then slipped it inside his suit coat. He smiled at Rob, seeming to enjoy the shock on his colleague's face.

"Imagine my surprise when Dr. Vessey grabbed me on my way in to church this morning. He usually sits up front so he can absorb the Gospel directly. But not today. Today, he kept me outside so long we missed the processional. All because of some harebrained ideas one of his professors was spouting off after the party last night."

"Do tell."

"It seems one of Confluence's finest decided to let off some steam. You know how literal Dr. Vessey is. If someone threatens to quit, he believes it."

Rob had spent so much time feeling remorseful for his encounter with Willa that he'd forgotten what he'd said to President Vessey after the fact. He *had* threatened to quit. But the reality of that announcement didn't leave him nearly as panicked or depressed as almost cheating on Molly had.

"Sounds like someone has the integrity to say how he feels."

"Sounds foolish, if you ask me."

"I'd have thought you, of all people, would applaud the act."

"Don't flatter yourself into thinking you're taking a stand against the evils of the Vesseys and Wykoffs of the world. That's what I thought I was doing when I came here, but has anything changed? Do schools use fewer adjuncts, pay them better, offer them benefits? All I did was set my career back a decade."

"If more people did what you did, maybe things would change."

"Or maybe there would be a whole lot of unemployed, middle-aged academics. The job market isn't what it was even when I came here. And no offense to Confluence, but it's not like this was my first choice when I was on the market. What kind of offers do you think you're going to get now? Who wants to pay for a tenured professor when they can save thousands going with some kid fresh out of grad school?"

"Being a professor isn't the *sine qua non*. I have other skills."

"Such as?"

It took him far longer to respond than he would have liked. "I could be an editor. Surely all those papers I've graded over the years have taught me a few things about good prose."

"Read the news lately? Good editors are becoming as rare as good professors."

"So I don't have everything figured out. Maybe it's time to leap before I look."

"Maybe you need to go into Vessey's office first thing tomorrow morning and put on the charm offensive of your life. The man practically has a job ad written for your position already."

"He works fast."

"With the budget as it is, he's probably thrilled to get a full professor off the books."

"You don't have a problem with Wykoff's gift?"

"Did I say that? The last thing we need is to give students an incentive to stick within their comfort zones. We'll be known as the school where you can major in Instagram or Applied Video Gaming, whatever the hell that is. Do you know how hard my predecessors had to work to make *African-American* literature recognized as a serious discipline? It would have been so much easier if we'd just gotten somebody to write a big check."

"You sure you don't want to join me?" If his decision was doomed, why did he feel so at peace with it? It was beyond mere acceptance. He actually felt relief at the prospect of being free of Confluence. Talking to Herman merely reinforced this feeling. He knew problems would arise, but at the same time, he imagined a happier existence, a life that wasn't dictated by the whims of the administration, the demands of his increasingly needy students. Not that this made explaining how he felt any easier; he feared that Herman, still trapped in the maze of academia, would criticize him for romanticizing his decision. Instead of trying to explain this, he remained silent.

"You're being awfully smug about this whole thing," Herman said.

"I have no idea what you're talking about."

"Look, I didn't want to come here, but if I didn't, Vessey would send Betsy after you, and we both know how that would go. I don't expect you to change your mind on the spot, but at least think about this a little. Have you even told Molly? She's a logician."

"So I'm being irrational?"

"Your ego took a serious bruising. No matter how cool you were about it, I know you were counting on that endowed chair. Don't cut off your nose—dammit, you've got me spouting clichés at you!"

"You talk like no one has ever quit before. It's not the mafia."

"If it was, I'd have put a bullet in your head long ago."

"Why are you taking this so personally?"

It was Herman's turn to remain silent. He looked past Rob, into the back yard. "You think it's easy here for me? With you gone, it's going to be *bleak*."

"I'd feel the same way if you left," he admitted.

"You have no idea."

"So it's a race thing?"

"It doesn't help."

"I can't stay just to make you feel better."

Herman frowned, leaned forward, hands resting on the table. He had bags beneath his eyes. Rob knew he'd rather be anywhere else, that a conversation this direct wasn't one of his preferred pastimes.

"You look tired," Rob said.

"You're not the only one who's had a rough weekend. I planned on spending today holed up at home, not sitting in the cold with you."

"What about the recital?"

"I've had enough festivities for one weekend."

"Robin will miss you."

"Damn," he said. "I forgot. What's she playing?"

"Beethoven. The Tempest Sonata, I believe."

"Sounds about right."

Rob would miss these conversations, Herman's forthrightness, which brought out the same quality in him. "So you'll come?"

He brushed off his hands and stood up. "For her, not you. I want to see her dazzle everyone. Hell, maybe she can save your job for you."

Twenty-Nine

The weekend had been a total bust. Scott found himself alone on Sunday morning, the only one awake in English House. None of his professors—none except Dr. Delacroix—had assigned any reading that weekend, so he didn't even have homework to distract him. Renee would be leaving for the airport soon, but as much as he wanted to see her again, he refrained from driving the two miles to the hotel.

Instead, he filled a cup with coffee and retreated to his room where, with the door closed, he took out his binder full of notes for the literature GRE. Renee was right; he had to stop worrying about what other people told him and start doing what he thought was best. So Dr. Delacroix wouldn't write him a letter of recommendation? He'd had half a dozen other English professors who might be more charitable in their view of graduate education. He already knew he could count on Dr. Sutherland. But before he could begin, he heard someone fumbling with the lock for the front door. It was a constant source of annoyance, the way it stuck, and the sound of metal grating against metal irritated him. No wonder Tony and Derek had been so willing to give him the large front bedroom. Even with the door closed, he could hear everything. He walked out of his room and encountered Genevieve Browning, barefoot in jeans and an oversized flannel shirt, attempting to unlock the door.

"You have to push the door closed while you turn the dead-bolt," he said.

She flinched, her hands scrabbling more desperately at the door knob. When she looked over her shoulder and saw that it was only him, she relaxed. "Thanks," she said.

He followed her onto the porch, squinting at the bright sun. While he leaned against the railing, trying to think of something to say, Genevieve slipped her feet into the ballet flats she'd had tucked under her arm. Even disheveled as she was, she still reminded him of Audrey Hepburn.

"I thought you were Derek," she said. "I just wanted to have a little fun, but he won't leave me alone. He wrote me *poems*."

"He's enthusiastic."

"Too enthusiastic."

They sat at opposite ends of the front steps, leaving enough room between them for Derek and his ego. Traffic was heavy on the road facing them, families on their way to church, others heading to one of the breakfast places along High Street. Yet another reason Scott disliked having the front bedroom. He hadn't slept past 7:30 on a Sunday all year.

"I only came on Friday because I knew you'd be here," she said. "My roommate is in Dr. Sutherland's class, and she's always going on about how smart you are. But then you spent all night with Mary and Dr. S's daughter."

"You knew about Katie?"

"I babysat her little sister a couple of times freshman year. Thought it would help me get an A in 101. That man is a tough grader."

"You didn't say anything."

"I can't stand Randy. I hope she told Dr. S all about his stupid impersonation."

"Still."

"She looked like she was having so much fun. Why ruin it? Besides, it was kind of cool, being in on it." Genevieve looked down, studying the cracks in the concrete steps. "Are you together?"

"Just doing her a favor."

"That's cool," she said.

"What about you and Derek?"

"He's fun in a group, but one-on-one, he spends too much time checking himself out."

"So we're both available," he said.

Minivans full of families late for church raced down High Street while the neighbor's cat waited for a gap in traffic to get across the road. Scott watched the cat edge forward, then backward, several times before she finally made it to the other side where she lunged for a blue jay that flew to safety in the upper branches of a tree.

"That was close," Genevieve said.

"Blue jays are mean. I had a deaf cat as a kid, and all the jays in the neighborhood used to dive bomb him from behind."

He thought about the GRE binder. Then he thought about Genevieve, who he could have sworn had inched closer to him. The GRE was weeks away. He was hungry now. "Listen," he said. "Do you want to do something?"

"The recital?"

Seeing the Sutherlands was out of the question. As much as he'd like to see what Robin would play, he needed a break before he saw the professor again on Monday morning.

"Want to get breakfast in town?"

She stood up and looked down at him. "I thought you'd never ask," she said.

Thirty

S he was almost caught up on her grading when Herman came back into the house alone. She'd never gotten along that well with him. He seemed too fussy, always picking at loose threads or inspecting his surroundings for imperfections, though she appreciated his relationship with Rob. For as expansive as her husband could be, he didn't have many friends, most of the ones he did have dating back to graduate school, friendships that he maintained largely via email. At least he had one person to talk to, face-to-face, whenever he had a problem. And from the look on Herman's face, there most definitely was a problem.

Herman stopped by the television and cleaned his glasses with a cloth he produced from inside his suit coat. He frowned at the glasses then put them back on. "I'm all out of ideas," he said.

"It's that bad?" She had no idea what Herman was referring to so aimed for a general statement that wouldn't announce her cluelessness.

"His mind is set. But that doesn't mean it's correct."

"He can be stubborn."

"Tell me about it." He seemed to weigh the possibility of sitting down opposite her on the couch in his mind, finally coming to the conclusion that standing was preferable. "I still maintain that one should spend more than a day contemplating career suicide before taking the plunge."

"You know what he's like."

"This is different. He seems positively calm about the whole thing. I can't decide if he's achieved Enlightenment or gone out of his damn mind."

Robin struck a chord on the piano that, while not ominous on its own, sounded portentous, to say the least. She must have been holding down the sustain pedal, because it reverberated through the house for close to half a minute. Finally, just before the chord died out completely, she added a rapid fire run up and down the keyboard, something angular and dissonant, the kind of passage that, a year ago, Molly would have assumed she'd played incorrectly.

"I don't want to intrude any more on your Sunday morning," Herman said. "But I'm worried. See if you can't knock some sense into him before tomorrow."

"I'll do what I can," she said. Just what she needed: another chore. The house was a wreck, and she had work to grade. Now she was on Rob duty, too.

Herman let himself out, and she went back to the final problem set for her 10 AM class. Thankfully, she'd saved the best for last, so she was able to grade it and wonder about Rob's *career suicide* at the same time. Surely it wasn't as bad as Herman had said. Her husband was impulsive, but he was also responsible. At least he'd been that way in the past. She had to admit that the week had been a trying one. Their arguments had escalated in frequency and severity, and they'd never fought so much that someone had actually left the house before. She should have told him about the job at Rocky Mount sooner.

She wouldn't apologize for buying the car, but here again, she could have found a more graceful way of going about it. So they could both be impulsive. Looking back on it, she should have paid for the thing and left it sitting where it was for another few days, and then introduced it to the family, though for the life of her, she couldn't think of a less dramatic way of bringing it up. *By the way, I dropped thousands of dollars you didn't know I had on a classic sports car. Want to see it?*

The final homework assignment graded, she curled her legs beneath her and listened to Robin attack the piano in the other room. The girl seemed more intent, more furious, than usual, and Molly said as much to Katie when she left the room and began heading up the stairs. "Is she okay in there?" Katie shrugged.

Katie seemed to relish the opportunity to be mysterious and defiant in the face of her mother's curiosity, reminding Molly that if she and Rob were having problems, she was still on thin ice with at least one other member of the family as well.

She poked her head in the study but received no answer. Her younger daughter was so focused on the keyboard that she doubted the girl even realized she'd been addressed. Her posture was suffering from the hours she spent at the piano, but at least she was doing something productive, not playing video games or texting. It amazed Molly how the girl could block out everything and focus on the sound coming out of the piano. The rest of the time, she was so easily distracted, so unfocused; it was as though she saved all of her energies for the piano, with nothing left over for the other twenty hours in the day.

Upstairs, Molly lingered in the kitchen doorway and watched Katie stirring batter for waffles, one of her specialties. Like her younger sister, she refused to look up, though Molly was certain this was a conscious choice, not a compulsion.

"Did your father say anything last night?"

"He said lots of things."

"Anything . . . distressing?"

"You mean something that would lead Dr. Herman to interrupt his Sunday morning to make an unannounced visit?"

"For the sake of argument."

"Nope."

"Thanks for your help."

"Any time."

She thought carefully about what she planned to say next. She didn't want to sound overly dramatic, but at the same time, she was tired of Katie's aggressive knowingness. The girl had something on her mind, something more than just another rendezvous with Mary Wardell.

"I think your father is in trouble," she said.

Katie paused in her stirring, grimaced. "You're paying better attention than I thought," she said.

Molly swallowed what she wanted to say, the kind of *watch it, young lady* comment her own parents would have made in the face of such open hostility. She knew it would get her nowhere with her daughter, would only reinforce the antagonism between them. Instead, she let her silence make the point for her. Finally, she said, "I'm trying my best, you know."

"God, I hope that's not true."

"Meaning?"

"If your best is ignoring Dad while you plan your escape, then we're all in big trouble."

"Aren't you the one who wants to move to New York after you graduate?"

"I'm seventeen. I'm supposed to want to do that."

She wished she'd never stopped in the kitchen. She could be in the bedroom with the door closed, minding her own business. She thought they'd moved beyond this, that their exchange of secrets—her trips to the casino, Katie's night with Mary Wardell—had put them back on an even footing. Now, out of the blue, the girl was back to behaving as she had in the car the day before, when Molly had first told her about her plans.

"At what age is it okay to be trapped?" she said. "I've done plenty to try to make things work here."

Katie poured batter into the hissing waffle iron. Once she closed the lid, steam poured out of the vent as the batter spread out. Then she moved to the sink, where strawberries and blueberries were draining in a colander. She sliced the strawberries into quarters, shook the remaining water from the blueberries. Anything to avoid answering her mother's question.

Molly said, "Life would be a lot simpler if it was as clear-cut as you make it out to be. Believe it or not, I think doing this will be good for all of us."

"You know best," her daughter said, still avoiding her eyes. She dumped the berries into bowls. By the time she was finished, the first waffle was ready, so she emptied it onto a tray, refilled the iron, and slipped the tray in the warm oven.

"I just want you to see my side of the situation," she said.

"Mission accomplished."

She left the kitchen without another word. She wasn't going to get through to her daughter, though she still had no idea why she'd taken such a sudden turn in her attitude. From the hallway, she noticed Robin in her room, trying on outfits for the recital on campus. Now that Molly thought about it, she couldn't remember the last time she'd heard Robin play the Beethoven Sonata. Maybe she was just being superstitious, saving it for the big event.

In the bedroom, she closed the door and lay down on the bed. She'd been up for six hours already, beginning yoga a little after five, and though she feared she'd fall asleep, anything was better than rehashing what she'd just gone through with Katie. A few hours without any more drama, that's all she wanted.

Thirty-One

The Talley Recital Hall was practically full by the time the Sutherlands arrived, but Professor Faulkenstein, who Robin had painted as a villain just two days earlier, had reserved three seats for them directly in front of his own, in the center-middle of the auditorium. While Molly and Katie headed for those seats, Rob roamed the aisles, saying hello to various alums he hadn't seen previously, nodding to the occasional colleague. He'd made it all the way to the first row and was about to head back when he felt a hand on his back.

Willa had on another pencil-skirt-and-blouse combination. She was shorter than Molly, he realized, now that she didn't have three-inch heels on, and was standing entirely too close to him for comfort. He felt aroused. He felt ashamed.

"Hey, stranger," Willa said.

He smiled. For once, he had no idea what to say.

She ran her hand along his arm, the corduroy of his jacket humming with her touch. "Is your wife here?" She looked around, feigning concern.

"I just . . . can't." He didn't know how to explain, within earshot of the front row of audience members, that everything from the previous night had been a mistake.

Before Willa could respond, Evan Wykoff appeared. "Dr. Sutherland," he said, sounding as though the words were a benediction.

"Mr. Wykoff. I'm surprised to see you here. This isn't a multi-media spectacle. Just plain old human-operated instruments."

"Let's not," he said, as though he were the older, better man. "We were both keyed up last night. Bygones and such."

"If you insist." He didn't realize until Evan looked down that Willa still had her hand on his arm. He couldn't help but look past Evan's short frame and toward the middle of the hall. Molly was staring at him as though he was a recalcitrant student. Worse, she stared at him as though he was her awful, no-good husband, which, in fact, matched exactly how he felt.

"I have to go," he murmured, breaking free and heading back up the main aisle. Along the way, he heard the main doors close behind Mary Wardell, Katie's odd choice for her first girlfriend. Not odd, exactly; Mary was as smart as anyone he'd taught, and though he'd never have accused his daughter of being superficial, he'd expected someone a little more *polished*. She was coming down the aisle toward him, and they met at the row where his family sat.

"I hope you don't mind," Mary said. "I know I'm late, but I thought Katie and I could. . . ." She waved a hand toward the back of the hall, where a standing-room-only crowd had begun to form.

"Why not," he said. "I'm sure she doesn't want to be stuck with the old fogeys." He looked to his wife, but she had her eyes trained on the stage.

Once Katie had climbed over her mother and fled with Mary, he took her vacated seat, reached out to grasp his wife's hand, an act he hadn't attempted in he didn't know how long. But she pulled away, squaring her shoulders to look at him finally.

"Who was your friend?"

"Her? That's Willa, Wykoff's assistant. It seems that, in my dejected, alcoholic state last night, I may have said some inopportune things to Evan and Dr. Vessey."

"So Herman implied. But *that* was about something else."

He'd hoped that a self-deprecating fall on his own sword would appease her, but he should have known better. "You really want to do this here?"

"Depends. Do you really want to come back home afterwards?"

"I was drunk. And angry. And I might have made a pass at her, all right. But it didn't come to anything," he said.

"I'm not surprised."

Faulkenstein chose that moment to sit down behind them. "Now comes the magic," he said in his thick German accent.

"Is Robin ready?" Rob only wanted something to say that would break the uncomfortable spell he was under.

"She enjoys an audience even more than you, professor." Faulkenstein winked.

The lights dimmed. Molly turned to him and said, "This isn't over."

Even without being able to see her clearly, he knew she meant it.

KATIE WOULD HAVE PREFERRED HER seat in the middle of the auditorium, where she was in the acoustic sweet-spot, but being with Mary made up for this disappointment, not to mention the disappointment of the first few performers. Several older alums had joined together as a string trio that was badly in need of tuning, and then a few current piano students had each stumbled their way through pieces by Chopin, Mozart, and Debussy. The only thing that distracted her was Mary's hand in her own, squeezing tightly at every obvious mistake. They looked at each other in the dim light and smiled in relief once the performance was over.

In between acts, Mary whispered into Katie's ear, "What's going on with your parents?"

"Whatever it is, it's worse than usual. Mom was gripping her seat like she was on a plane going down over the Pacific."

"Your dad really did it this time."

"What makes you think he's at fault?"

Mary stared at her, silently, until the next performer took the stage.

A young trumpeter played a rousing "Carnival of Venice" to piano accompaniment, and though Katie didn't know the tune, besides the explanation in the program, she could tell he was good. Decent, at least. His was the last name before her sister's, so she figured he was the beginning of the grand finale.

When he finished, he waved to his pianist, who came out from behind the keyboard and bowed with him. As they did so, Katie found herself growing nervous. She hoped her hand wasn't sweating but couldn't be sure.

She waited for the emcee, the chairwoman of the Music department, to announce her sister. "We have a special guest this afternoon," the woman said. "Our final performer happens to also be our youngest. Robin Sutherland—note that last name!—comes to us from Dr. Faulkenstein's studio and is said to be quite the prodigy. She is an eighth-grader at Elgin Middle School and will be performing Beethoven's Seventeenth Sonata, aptly referred to as 'The Tempest' Sonata."

Her sister took the stage, but in place of the navy-blue dress Katie had helped her pick out at Bernice's Thrift Shop, Robin was dressed all in white. She had on white tennis shoes, white cargo pants, a white sweatshirt, and a white ski cap. She looked like a cartoonist's sketch. She walked not to the piano but to the emcee, who seemed as taken-aback as everyone in the audience.

Robin spoke to the woman, who responded off-mic, with a series of hand gestures and a string of inaudible sentences. Robin, as calm as she ever looked, responded briefly, and the woman shrugged her shoulders and lifted the mic back to her mouth.

"It seems there has been a change to the program," she said. "Instead of 'The Tempest,' Miss Sutherland intends to play an original composition entitled. . . ." she conferred with Robin again before completing her sentence with, "Improvisation #3."

"What the hell?" Katie said into the air around her.

"WHAT THE HELL?" HER HUSBAND whispered into her ear. She almost recoiled at the touch of his lips.

She couldn't believe that he'd been so stupid. One of the things she'd appreciated about Rob was that he never got his head turned by pretty coeds. Back when the Philosophy department had existed, when she'd had actual colleagues, she often came across Dr. Trillo and Dr. Ignatius comparing notes on which students were most attractive. As though either of them had been a prize. But not Rob. He'd been faithful ever since they'd begun dating. She'd been the reluctant one, the one who'd insisted on seeing other people for the better part of a semester before committing. She knew for a fact that he hadn't taken her up on this freedom, that only she had actually *seen other people*. But that had been twenty years earlier when they were in grad school, before they were married and had children. In other words, it had been at a time when commitment hadn't mattered. And she'd been open about her decision, her wants. She hadn't snuck around behind Rob's back.

Robin sat at the piano and removed a pair of thick, black-rimmed glasses from her pocket. Molly had never seen these before; Robin didn't wear glasses. Nevertheless, she slid them into place, wedging them beneath the ski cap that she'd tucked all of her hair into. She had no sheet music before her.

She had no idea what was about to happen and had to fight the urge to turn around and look at Katie, who almost always knew what her little sister was up to. When they'd left the house, Robin was dressed in a rather mature-looking navy dress that flowed to mid-calf, with her book of Beethoven Sonatas sticking out of her tote bag. Had the bag been bulging enough to contain this second outfit? To her shame, Molly realized she'd been so absorbed in her own issues that she hadn't given it a second glance.

Robin sat at the piano, tested a few keys individually, and then launched into a loud, dissonant opening. Her left hand thumped minor chords low in the bass register while her right hand, at the extreme opposite end of her reach, tinkled at the high end of the keyboard. She continued striking the chords, letting them alternately ring out or dampening them almost immediately with one of the pedals. Finally, her left and right hands stopped warring with each other and coalesced into the melody of "Caravan," a piece Molly actually recognized. She had no idea how she made the transition so deftly, but suddenly, all of the crazy noodling she'd been doing made sense. It was as though she'd broken up the tune's phrasing, playing every third or fourth note, mixing in embellishments of her own creation. Now, she attacked the piece with a vigor she couldn't remember hearing from her, the tempo quicker than usual, the chords heavier, the right-hand runs even more impressive.

As quickly as "Caravan" had come to the fore, it disappeared again, this time for good. Robin played even more fleetly than before, hands racing up and down the keyboard, away from each other, and then meeting back in the middle again, so fast they came close to blurring into the keys. Molly couldn't make sense of most of the sounds ringing throughout the hall, sounds that never stopped long enough for her to catch her breath.

Robin's grunts were audible above the jagged lines she was playing, and somewhere in what seemed like the middle of the piece, she began playing the strings in the open top of the grand piano, plucking and dampening them with her right hand while her left continued its onslaught against the keys. Molly could hear Faulkenstein behind her rustling his program, and she imagined him squeezing it between his hands the way he'd probably like to squeeze Robin's neck. He rarely let her play anything from the twentieth-century, finding most of the repertoire too modern for his taste. Nevertheless, he was forced to sit there while his star pupil attacked the piano.

She thumped her foot in time with the music, adding her own percussion, returning her right hand to the keys, which she banged with renewed vigor. Her hands rose higher than her teacher ever would have allowed, but she always came back down onto the exact key she was aiming for. The piece had no discernible melody to it, but that didn't stop Robin from continuing for what seemed like twenty minutes, the same length as the Sonata.

The longer it went on, the more proud of her daughter Molly grew. The girl wasn't giving Faulkenstein, her parents, and the audience the middle finger, as she feared the old teacher assumed. No, she was planting her flag in the most public venue she had, declaring her independence from everyone within earshot. It might still have been a *Fuck You*, but it was so much more than that, too.

He had no idea what was going on and worried that his daughter had cracked under the pressure of a full auditorium, that she had had the same kind of break everyone accused him of undergoing. It was as though her hands were fighting with each other, the right disagreeing with everything the left played, and vice versa. From the sound of it, they might have been having different arguments entirely. Still, Rob found himself mesmerized by his daughter's focus, her attention to the task at hand. Her eyes never strayed from the keyboard. Her back was curved over the keys, shoulders hunched. She scowled at the keys, letting out more grunts. She'd always been intense at the piano, but this was different. He didn't notice any of the joy that typically accompanied her performances; in its place was work, work, and more work.

She lunged at the keys, pounced on chords, and even made small hops on the bench at the most percussive-sounding passages.

He wondered if Molly had known she was going to do this. He knew he was Robin's favorite, but he also knew that he took that for granted, that he wasn't as tuned-in to her life as he should be. No, he came home from work, tussled with her on the couch, and cheered her on at the piano, but making arrangements, organizing lessons and therapy appointments, soothing the occasional bruised ego, those were all Molly's terrain. That would have to change if she took the job at Rocky Mount. He'd have to be a better parent, more involved. He would do it, he pledged.

As best as he could tell, Robin was reaching the end of her piece. She slowed almost imperceptibly, though even Rob could tell this was a deliberate choice. More chords chimed, some of them even in major keys. She went back to plucking the strings inside the piano once again, though for a briefer period this time. He feared she'd do damage to the piano, that the Music department would expect him to pay to replace it, but he also found himself enjoying the piece, to his surprise.

When he relaxed, it began to make sense. Yes, it was dissonant and discordant, and no, it had no melody, or even a clear harmony, but he began to sense the occasional syncopation, the stride-piano stylings she played when she was in a good mood, and even some of the angularity he'd come to expect in the embellishments on Bach's Inventions that drove Faulkenstein crazy. By the final run of "Improvisation #3," he found himself missing the music. He'd ask her to play it again, he was certain, perhaps even offer to record it.

The piece ended with a thumping bass line, both hands well below middle-C. She stomped her foot, the grunts she'd been making all along beginning to mirror the tones coming out of the piano. Finally, after three quick stomps, her hands crashed down onto the keys, almost on top of each other, and she fired off one last run to the top of the keyboard. She was finished.

The audience didn't know what to do, didn't trust its own judgment, didn't know whether to clap or flee, until finally, off to his right, Rob heard a single pair of hands clapping. A second joined in, and then others, tentative at first but building in enthusiasm. The lights were still low, but when Rob looked to the source of that first clap, he saw Herman—his lone friend, he had to admit to himself—rapt in his attention toward the stage, clapping almost as quickly as Robin's hands had moved on the keys. A whistle went up from the back of the recital hall: Katie, he knew. And then another, which he presumed came from her—girlfriend?

Rob stood up, almost without planning it, and clapped with his hands above his head. His wife pulled at his coat, but when she realized he wasn't going to yield, she gave up.

Robin stood at the edge of the stage, smiling out into the darkness. Rob could see the sweat that had collected along the band of her ski cap. She smiled. She bowed. She bowed again, though the applause was dying down.

No matter. Rob kept clapping, stretching his arms up as though reaching for the ceiling, as though he was about to execute one of his wife's yogic contortions. She'd said that after her first year of doing yoga, she'd been a quarter-inch taller on account of the extra space between her joints, and he'd never believed her. But now, standing in the middle of the recital hall, he longed to make himself even taller, to raise himself to the level of the music he'd just heard.

Robin stood in the spotlight, her smile growing wider even as the audience began rising to leave. Only Rob, Molly, Herman, and the two young women in the back were clapping as the lights came up. Robin removed her glasses and her cap, letting her hair fall to her shoulders. She threw the hat into the audience, and though it didn't make it past the third row, Rob still reached out, as though if he tried hard enough, he might catch it.

Acknowledgements

Thank you to everyone at SFK Press, especially Steve McCondichie and April Ford for taking on this manuscript; Eleanor Burden for a wonderful, perceptive first reading; Cade Leebron for her thorough, incisive editorial remarks; and Grant Miller for his careful eye for detail.

Thank you to the wonderful teachers I've learned from over the years: the late Barry Hannah, to whom I owe more than I was ever able to express; Julie Schumacher, Valerie Miner, and Charles Baxter at the University of Minnesota; Margaret Lazarus Dean and Allen Wier at the University of Tennessee; and Fred Leebron at Tinker Mountain Writers' Workshop.

Of all of my teachers, I'd like to single out two for special thanks: Steve Yarbrough believed in me long before I deserved such faith, and Steve Polansky taught me so much, not least what it means to dedicate oneself to the writer's life. Thank you both.

Thank you to Dave Massey for listening to me agonize over this book and for a timely kick in the ass, as well.

Thank you to Amy Shearn for always answering my questions, no matter how far afield or out-of-the-blue.

Thank you to two good friends, Hannah Allford and Mariah Richardson, who helped get me through the final push. I don't know how I would have stayed on track without their regular writing sessions. Thank you, also, to my colleagues at Gardner-Webb University for supporting me along the way.

Thank you to my entire family, none of whom asked, "Are you ever going to finish that book?" Their love and encouragement has helped sustain me.

Thank you, most of all, to Cheryl and Isabel. I was only able to write this book because Cheryl was willing to accept the burden of providing financially for our family while I worked part-time. Without her belief in me, not to mention so many, many readings of everything I've written over the past twenty years, I never would have made it. Thank you to Isabel, who, though this book took up much of her first four years, never complained when I went out on Saturday morning to write or returned distracted after a bad writing session. Whatever good I've accomplished with this book would have been impossible without both of you.

About the Author

As the director of the Gardner-Webb University writing center in Shelby, North Carolina, Matthew Duffus is dedicated to writing transformative fiction. Strongly influenced by the late Barry Hannah, he crafts character-driven cathartic stories that he believes "need to be told," exploring the tensions and challenges of the varying communities we all inhabit. A loving husband and father, Matthew is also the author of the forthcoming story collection *Dunbar's Folly and Other Stories*.

Share Your Thoughts

Want to help make *Swapping Purples for Yellows* a bestselling novel? Consider leaving an honest review on Goodreads, your personal author website or blog, and anywhere else readers go for recommendations. It's our priority at SFK Press to publish books for readers to enjoy, and our authors appreciate and value your feedback.

Our Southern Fried Guarantee

If you wouldn't enthusiastically recommend one of our books with a 4- or 5-star rating to a friend, then the next story is on us. We believe that much in the stories we're telling. Simply email us at pr@sfkmultimedia.com.

Do You Know About Our Bi-Monthly Zine?

Would you like your unpublished prose, poetry, or visual art featured in *The New Southern Fugitives*? A bi-monthly zine that's free to readers and subscribers *and* pays contributors:

$100 for book reviews, essays, short stories
$40 for micro & flash fiction
$40 for poetry
$40 for photography & visual art

Visit **NewSouthernFugitives.com/Submit** for more information.

Also by SFK Press

A Body's Just as Dead, Cathy Adams

Not All Migrate, Krystyna Byers

The Banshee of Machrae, Sonja Condit

Amidst This Fading Light, Rebecca Davis

American Judas, Mickey Dubrow

A Curious Matter of Men with Wings, F. Rutledge Hammes

The Skin Artist, George Hovis

Lying for a Living, Steve McCondichie

The Parlor Girl's Guide, Steve McCondichie

Hardscrabble Road, George Weinstein

Aftermath, George Weinstein

The Five Destinies of Carlos Moreno, George Weinstein

The Caretaker, George Weinstein

RIPPLES, Evan Williams

9 781970 137972